UNTIL IT SHIMMERS

A novel by

Alec Scott

Praise for *Until It Shimmers:*

"London at the height of the AIDS crisis, the dynamics and history of an Ontario family, and the nuances of a loving mother-son relationship – all are rendered in evocative, gorgeous detail. An atmospheric and immersive debut."

– Marjan Kamali, *The Stationery Store*

"Wry, diamond-hard, vigorously alert, *Until It Shimmers* is a moving coming-of-age story, at once heartbreaking and wickedly sly. Alec Scott's writing is so precisely observed, it's easy to fall into its rhythms, to submit to the book as if it's a lost memory, one you want desperately to hold onto, protect and live by."

– Heidi Sopinka, *The Dictionary of Animal Languages*

"Readers of any sexual orientation will find Ned's voyage of discovery a vibrant reminder of life's multicolored bounty. A potent, vigorous coming-of-age tale."

– *Kirkus Reviews*

"*Until It Shimmers* holds the reader right to the end with grace and quiet empathy."

– Eibhear Walshe, *The Last Day at Bowen's Court*

"*Until It Shimmers* is a compelling and transporting contribution to the literature documenting the AIDS era. I enjoyed discovering London alongside Ned, our affable hero, as he wrestled with love, sex and friendships, and tries to make sense of his complicated relationship with his family. This is a rich and satisfying debut."

– Christopher Castellani, *Leading Men*

"Contemplative in its approach and incisive in its characterizations, *Until It Shimmers* is an involving novel about finding one's place in the world."

– Ho Lin, *Foreword Reviews*

AOS Publishing, 2022
AOS Fiction, 2022

ISBN: 978-1-7775139-9-3

Cover Design: Lara Chauvin

Visit AOS Publishing's website:
www.aospublishing.com

Dedicated to my parents

Lynne Kenny Scott

&

Simon Scott

and to

David Bruckmann

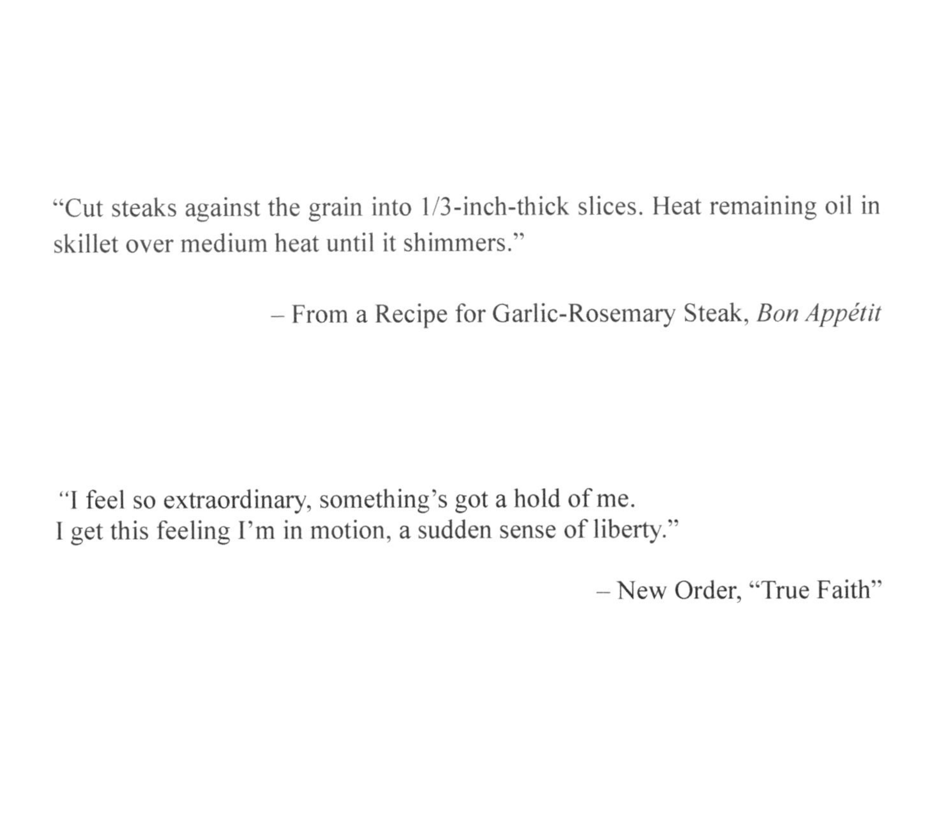

"Cut steaks against the grain into 1/3-inch-thick slices. Heat remaining oil in skillet over medium heat until it shimmers."

– From a Recipe for Garlic-Rosemary Steak, *Bon Appétit*

"I feel so extraordinary, something's got a hold of me.
I get this feeling I'm in motion, a sudden sense of liberty."

– New Order, "True Faith"

Chapter 1:
Courage, My Love

Ned and Daniel planned to mark the end of their time at Trinity with a fancy dinner to celebrate what was to be celebrated and mourn what wasn't. But shortly before the meal, Ned's best friend from high school, Cameron, phoned. He would be in Toronto, visiting from Vancouver that evening. Ned should have said he was busy, but he didn't, instead proposing Cameron join them at what they were silly enough to call their Last Supper. Daniel wasn't happy about it, but Ned insisted he couldn't disinvite Cameron.

When the evening came upon him, Ned found he regretted doing so. His friends had little in common, and he had presented them with such different versions of himself. Who would he be this evening?

He stood in his briefs in front of his open closet, leafing through the few remaining clean clothes hung there. He assessed himself in the mirror attached to the open closet door. He was tall and slender, that was how his grandmother spoke of him, those were the somehow affirming adjectives she chose. When he looked at himself, he saw scrawny, skinny. He cupped his cock and balls—there could have been more there. But there could have been less, too. Anyway, at least it looked a lot on him, thin as he was. It was vulgar, grabbing yourself—and felt the more sexy to Ned for its being a departure from his careful training.

He turned back to his room. What a mess. Exams had been done for a few days, but he hadn't yet knuckled down to a big tidy. His narrow bed was unmade, laundry mounded in one corner, piles of books on his desk and all around, an overflowing ashtray on the windowsill and more spent ashes spilling out of the stone fireplace onto the floor.

He thought about wearing his old school uniform, the blue blazer, grey flannels and striped, double-blue tie that both he and Cameron had worn every day at Appleby. But that would seem sort of pathetic, like Ned had not grown at all since then.

His Trinity friend Daniel would certainly go for a louche look. Where Appleby's uniform and general approach had been Spartan, Trinity's ethos was more, well, Athenian. Whenever they went for dim sum in Chinatown, Daniel insisted on stopping in to his favorite vintage shop, *Courage, My Love*, in nearby Kensington Market, picking up maybe a top hat, a dressing gown worthy of Noel Coward, or an opera coat with shiny silk lapels.

Ned navigated between these two approaches to dressing, wearing a charcoal grey suit and a white shirt (Sparta) with a floral, Liberty-print tie (Athens—Socrates would have liked the tie), a charcoal-grey wool coat over top (Sparta, again). He inspected himself in the mirror over the dresser, and didn't like what he saw. His cheeks were too pink, his lips too thin, his hairline too high, his head too oval, his eyes too full of uncertainty. He stuck out his tongue at himself. Only his nose, his grandmother's long, straight, Roman nose, was a credit to him. He straightened his tie. It would have to do; he would have to do.

He mounted the stairs up to Daniel's room, at the top of what was called a house, but was merely one section of the quad. The college was built from stone, and had several copper cupolas on top, weathered green, a square tower over one gate. His friend's door was ajar. Daniel was sitting before his fireplace, a book on his lap, opera playing, a cigarette on the go beside him.

"God," Ned said, "What a pretentious tableau."

"I thought you'd like it. Anyway, you don't get to criticize someone else for being pretentious if you're using the word 'tableau.'"

He offered Ned an espresso from his machine, the first one in the college.

"No, I'm quite jumpy enough," Ned said.

Daniel had on a purple velvet suit, something Ned had helped him pick up, with a black bowtie and a mauve shirt.

"This is not a dress-up party," Ned said. "This is a… smart restaurant."

"God," Daniel said. "Would you listen to yourself? I don't care how intelligent the restaurant is, this evening is not about it, but about us."

Daniel got up, not to change clothes, as Ned had hoped, but to open his small fridge, topped with a small oriental rug. He took out two little clear plastic containers, each with white lily-of-the-valley over some greenery. "One for you, one for me."

"Cameron won't understand that the flowers are a joke."

"Ah well, then he won't. And anyway, are they a joke?"

Daniel pinned one boutonniere on Ned's lapel then asked Ned to put one on his. On their way out of the room, Daniel grabbed a present, a book from the looks of it, wrapped in violet paper.

"To match my suit," he said, holding it up next to his outfit. Worse and worse.

"I didn't know we were exchanging gifts."

"It's a book," he said. "No big deal. Read this in remembrance of me."

"I wish I'd never told you… about the liturgy running in my head."

"But you did, more fool you."

Ned had grown up singing in a boy's choir in their church, St. Jude's, and, at Appleby, each day began with chapel. And so, he'd internalized the many prayers, the call-and-response, of the Anglican service. He told Daniel that often his mind responded to the passing show by pulling up some passage from the missal that seemed to it, on point. When he saw a mountain in the distance, and he was feeling down, the psalm about lifting one's eyes up onto the hills, seeking help there—that came to him. When a green field with a stream next to it presented itself, he thought of the Lord leading him through pastures green, the quiet waters by.

The son of Armenian immigrants to Canada, Daniel hadn't grown up with the same prayer book, but he sang in Trinity's choir, so had learned much of the Church of England liturgy.

They passed through the quad, waved to the white-haired porter at the desk—"Don't wait up," Daniel said—and walked along the tree-lined path, Philosopher's Walk, that passed by one side of the College.

"I always feel like I should be saying something philosophical here," Daniel said. "Something deep. Deeper than the Mariana Trench. But I never do."

There was still enough light to see the large maples, as they sent down twirling seed-pods, investing energy in the hopes of seeding a next generation. When they reached Bloor, one of Toronto's main arterials, East-West, running parallel to the lake's shore, a few miles north, the streetlights started flickering on. Night was falling down on them.

"I've never been to this restaurant," Ned said. "My parents brought home an ashtray from it. One of their few evenings off from the hard work of bringing us up. My mother said it was far and away the best meal she'd had in Toronto."

Three Small Rooms opened in the year Ned's younger brother Henry was born, in Canada's Centennial year, 1967. It was a big deal. Everyone said its opening marked the dawn of a new culinary era for this provincial city on Lake Ontario's north shore. Each of the three rooms in the basement of a little hotel had a different style, different culinary offerings, from the casual Grill, where they were going, to the more traditional Wine Cellar, to the formal Restaurant. They passed a church Ned sometimes attended, the Church of the Redeemer, that had ensured its survival by selling off its grounds, and a high-rise condominium now wrapped around the Gothic Revival building. They deked onto a side street, and walked down some steps to the subterranean entrance. The font on the sign above them was the same as on the ashtray, the words all in lower-case. The Grill had bold, geometrical Op-Art on the walls, and spare Scandinavian furniture.

The maitre d' took them towards their table. Cameron was there already, and had left the two seats on the wall for them, a gentleman giving the others the better view. He got up—he'd grown a bit taller and his freckles were almost gone. He was in a navy suit and had chosen to wear their old school tie. They hugged, and Ned caught his friend's scent: he was still using the sandalwood soap his father used to send him.

When they separated, Cameron pointed to the boutonniere. "Might have crushed your wee flowers a bit." His parents were both Scottish, and their words and accent sometimes crept into Cam's mouth.

"Just a bit of a lark," Ned said, blushing.

"A flowered tie, too," he said.

"Celebrating the coming of spring," Daniel said.

His friends shook hands, and Cameron's hand dwarfed Daniel's. Daniel's had a dusting of hair on its back; Cameron's had none.

"You're looking well," Cameron said to Ned. "Still haven't put on any weight, I see. You eat, I've seen you, so I don't know where you put it."

"You haven't gone all hefty either," Ned said.

"Still jogging," he said. "My body wants to get chunky, but I won't let it."

Ned turned to Daniel, "We used to get up early most mornings and run through the campus."

"And cross-country ski through it in the winter," Cameron added.

"Whose high school has a campus?" Daniel said.

They sat down, and Cameron asked after Ned's parents.

"They're the same," Ned said. "Helena and Oliver never seem to change."

"Lucky you," Cameron said. "Your folks are great."

"They have their moments," Ned said.

How Ned's mother Helena had fussed over Cameron, as, in his quieter way, had Oliver. At Cameron's graduation, she'd said, "You're like another son to me,"—in part because it was a nice thing to say, and in part because Cameron's own mother had decided, at the last minute, not to show up for the event. How abandoned Ned felt in his final year of high school with Cameron gone, the older boy's deep voice no longer booming out during the singing of "Jerusalem" in the morning chapel—"Bring me my bow of burning gold, bring me my arrows of desire."

"I'd say I've heard so much about you," Daniel said to Cameron. "But I haven't. Not one word."

"That's as it should be," Cameron said. "I wouldn't want to be the subject of idle gossip."

"There is only one thing in life worse than being talked about, and that is not being talked about," Daniel said.

“That's true,” Cameron said, chuckling politely. Did he think the line was Daniel's, not Oscar Wilde's? Probably he didn't care much either way.

Ned seldom spoke of Cameron, not because he didn't think of him, but because it seemed to violate something high to do so.

The waiter came their way, and they ordered cocktails—Daniel and Ned got G&Ts, Cameron, a Scotch on the rocks. How happy Ned was to be sitting down with him. Cameron asked after Ned's studies, his next year's plans.

“London, a couple of jobs, publishing, a law firm, trying to figure out what to do with my life.”

“I always knew you'd be going places.” He turned to Daniel. “I first saw this guy, this tall, skinny guy, new to the school. He was midway through a tennis match. Playing this bigger guy, a couple years older.” He gulped down his Scotch. “Not sure why I stopped to watch. Tennis is not really my thing, but there was something in him, some hunger to win. He and his opponent both end up near the net one rally, and Ned tries to float one over the other guy's head, but he didn't hit it hard enough. It sat there, mid-air, an easy put-away. The guy can hit it anywhere in the court, but he takes aim, smacks it right at Ned, hits him in the head, gives him a black eye. You should have seen how angry Ned was. After that he played like someone possessed. At the end, after Ned has destroyed him, the guy mumbles something, 'Sorry about hitting you.' and Ned looks him square. He says to him: 'You're sorry now. That's for sure.' I loved that.”

“I was just so happy to have found a sport I could do,” Ned says. “I couldn't do hockey, soccer, rugby, any of the team sports. And Henry was always a better skier than I was.”

“He always does that, doesn't he?” Cameron said to Daniel, “Runs away from a compliment.”

"Sprints away from it really," Daniel said. "He worries if it catches him, it'll infect him with something."

Cameron asked Daniel what he'd be doing after he graduated. "My family expects me to join their import-export business and to get married. Every time I go home, there's a new girl for me to meet. This total parade of Armenian Princesses."

"Nice. Send any you don't want my way, ok?" Cameron said. "And if that's not what you want, what is it you do want?"

"I am excited to go to law school. You look skeptical, but I'm passionate about jurisprudence."

It sounded like a joke, but Ned knew it wasn't. The summer after First Year, Daniel read through the many tomes that make up *Blackstone's Laws of England.*

"Where will you go?" Cameron asked.

"Harvard," Daniel said. "Or Yale."

Cameron whistled. "Suddenly I feel like the dumb one at the table. Correction: I don't just seem it, I am the dumb one at the table. In high school, Ned won just about every prize there was."

"That was high school," Ned said.

"He wrote half my essays."

"I edited your essays. I didn't write them."

"Sometimes that amounted to the same thing."

Ned asked Cameron how the business that had brought him to Toronto was going.

"Just lots of meetings with clients we mainly deal with over the phone. It makes a difference to meet people face-to-face. I mean, of course, it does. But it hasn't been challenging. And it turned out, I had last night free as well," he said. "Caught up with some of the other guys."

"So you were available for dinner last night, too," Daniel said. "This wasn't your only free night."

"No, why?" he asked.

Cameron then began naming a few people Ned had seldom thought of since graduating, rugby teammates of Cameron's, guys in the year above Ned. For Cameron's sake, some of them put up with Ned, this bookish, pencil-thin guy—and some of them didn't.

Daniel chatted through the items on the menu, wondering whether to ask what a *restigouche* of smoked salmon was and what the *oeufs filet* in the consommé would look like.

"The food is a bit fancier than we get out west," Cameron said. "Listen, I'm thinking of moving back east."

"For the fancy food?" Daniel said.

"There's this girl. She's coming out here for grad school. I don't know where we're going, she and I, but we're going nowhere for sure if I can't find a way to get here. Would your Uncle Max be willing to meet with me? His firm is in the same general line of things as the one I'm at. He takes our logs and makes them into paper."

Ned could see a dangerous expression coming on Daniel's face.

"Say," Daniel said, "here comes the waiter. Maybe we should order first, and… ask each other for favors later. Ned tells me he hasn't seen you, heard from you in many years. I guess you thought of him when you realized his uncle… was in your field."

"I thought of Ned lots," Cameron said. Now it was Cameron's turn to blush. "The other day in Stanley Park at the ocean's edge, I remembered how you and I, Ned, we stopped on one of our jogs, took a breather down by the lake." He turned to Daniel. "We were on this rocky beach. Ned says, 'The light makes the shore look mythic'—or some such thing. 'This seems like the sort of beach where Odysseus might have landed.'"

Cameron said the Greek hero's name tentatively.

"What drugs was I on that morning?" Ned said. "The infirmary must have given me something."

"He was always saying queer things like that."

"I like it," Daniel said. "Odysseus plying the wine-red waters of this freshwater sea, Lake Ontario, maybe mooring for the night at the Port Credit Yacht Club. Going to a Mississauga strip club where he gets enchanted by a pole dancer named Circe."

"On another morning, Ned showed me where the trilliums bloomed in the spring," Cameron said. "In the woods, in this glade by a creek running into the lake, this whole patch of them. Red ones."

"Burgundy," Ned said. "Some of them, they bloom burgundy, maroon, dark red. Also known as the wake robin, the stinking Benjamin. They're rare."

"An odd duck, right?" Cameron said to Daniel.

"Quack, quack," Ned said, elbows out, flapping them like wings.

"Rare," Daniel said. "A rare bird. *Rara avis.*"

They ordered, Daniel getting the *restigouche* of salmon out of curiosity, Ned taking the consommé for the same reason, to see how the eggs would be done. Cameron chose the house paté on toast points.

"I'm just not great at keeping in touch," Cameron said. "I wanted to see Ned, to see you, and then I thought of Uncle Max. But it's no problem, if it's too much."

"No," Ned said. "No, of course not. I'll call him tomorrow. He'll remember you, for sure. There may be nothing doing, nothing in that field, but he'll know what's what for sure. And I'm sure he'd be willing to do a sit-down."

"Somehow I pictured Trinity as very… WASP-y," Cameron said to Daniel.

"Not full of little brown fellows?" Daniel said. "The names on the walls, past scholars, student leaders—there are Ridouts and Chapmans, Connachers and Oslers—a whole slew of Baldwins." Here Daniel nodded at Ned. "There are not a lot of Derounians."

"Not yet," Ned said. "Daniel's name will be up there on several of the boards."

"That so?" Cameron said.

Ned bragged some about Daniel's accomplishments—that he was the Scribe of Trinity's invitation-only student society, Episkopon, the star of the student production of the *Misanthrope.* Ned realized neither of these things would mean much to Cameron. He thought about trying to build a bridge between his two friends by asking Daniel to speak about his family's escape from Turkey, about how a few of them, sensing the massacre that was in the offing, had hiked over a mountain into Iraq. Daniel could tell the story well. But Ned decided not to. The story would seem too "intense" to Cameron—"That was intense" was a phrase he used to push things away from him.

"Your parents," Ned said to Cameron, "Did they ever get… divorced?"

"They did at last," Cameron said. He explained the situation to Daniel: "My father sent me out here for school so I wouldn't get sucked into their drama. To protect me. And my mother didn't want me underfoot anyway, while she firmed up the thing she had going with… her fellow. But it took them years to get it all done, Mom sometimes going back to my Dad. All to say, I was so—I am so grateful that the Baldwins would have me for the holidays during term. One year for Christmas, too, when things were bad at home. You guys do Christmas up!"

"Lots of pageantry," Ned said. "Often a lot less warmth."

"There was plenty of both as far as I could see," Cameron said.

"Maybe back then." Ned sighed. This was not what Cameron wanted to hear, so Ned supplied what he did. "I told them I was meeting up with you, Mum and Dad, Helena and Oliver, and they said to say 'hello.'"

"I was so envious of him that he had these solid folks, while mine were complete fuck-ups. Sorry, but they were. They are."

Cameron started to speak of some other people they had in common.

Daniel got up, nodding towards the door to the washrooms. "If you'll excuse me."

Ned got up, too. "Sorry, I need to… also," he said. He could tell Daniel was angry at how the meal was going, and he wanted to placate him.

By the time Ned got to the men's room, Daniel had taken a cubicle, and Ned waited at the sinks in front of the mirror until Daniel emerged. Daniel fluffed up the boutonniere on his lapel, and Ned looked in the mirror at Daniel, scrunching up his face and slanting his head.

"It's a joke that," Daniel said. "You always do it. Distort your face. In front of a mirror." Daniel soaped and washed his small hands. "You know that unless you do that to your face, you're handsome."

"Thank you for noticing," Ned said.

"It wasn't a joke," he said. "Don't make it one."

"I don't really like how I look."

Daniel rearranged Ned's boutonniere, which Cameron had, indeed, crushed.

"So he's moving to Toronto, he thinks. Following a girl," Daniel said.

"*Cherchez la femme*," Ned said. "There's always a girl."

"Is there?" he said. "Is there always a girl?" He looked at Ned hard. "Ned, I know."

Ned swallowed. "What exactly do you think you know?"

"If I didn't know before, which I did," he said. "Well, now I do. Watching you swoon over this guy. How your face fell when he mentioned this girl."

"What… the fuck are you talking about?"

"It's okay, Ned," he said. "It doesn't matter."

"What doesn't matter?"

"Let's talk about it later. I shouldn't have… I just was a little mad. This fucking Cro-Magnon spoiling everything."

"Cro-Magnon" subbed in for Neanderthal in Trinity's jargon.

Daniel dried his hands and walked out. Ned went to sit in the cubicle, to collect himself. Then, after a few minutes more, he returned to the table, noting how fast his heart was beating as he walked, the rancid smell coming from his underarms.

"Everything okay?" Cameron said. "Thought we'd lost you."

Ned hardly noticed the rest of the dinner passing. He must have eaten some carefully selected entree. He must have participated in the conversation, must have consumed whatever wine they'd chosen upon advice. But he was not there, not really.

Once they got outside, Daniel lit up a cigarette, offering Ned one and lighting it. Cameron hailed a cab to take him to his downtown hotel, declining an offer to go to some friends' party in the college. "I've got an early start tomorrow," he said. "Let me know what I should do about Max, okay? So great to see you again. Let's not leave it so long the next time."

On the walk home, Ned went at Daniel. "I don't know what you were on about, but that was not the time. To float some, some idea about what is none of your business."

"I'm not wrong, though, am I?"

"You ruined it," Ned said. "Our Last Supper."

"No, Ned, you ruined it. Our entire last year. Why do you think I gave up on our weekly dim-sums? I was tired of giving you the chance to tell the truth. I asked you in so many different ways."

"Do I owe you that?"

"Yes," he said. "We're friends. I want to know what is going on with you. You've got this big thing on your mind, and you'll only talk about other things, the more trivial the better. What's the point of being friends then?"

"It wasn't—it isn't that. It's just… my parents. I always wanted to tell them first. They deserve that at least."

Ned examined Daniel's face for signs of distaste. Ned suspected that Daniel wanted to end their friendship anyway, given what he'd guessed, and that Ned's supposed dishonesty had given him the pretext he needed to do so. Never mind what Ned would have to risk to say that out loud and then to live it.

"It was a disaster," Ned said. "What must Cameron have thought, with the boutonnieres, the purple suit?"

"Did it matter at all what I must have thought of him? Anyway, the suit is aubergine."

This made Ned laugh a bit.

"What?" Daniel continued. "The suit is aubergine. It's darker than purple. And Cameron, well, he can think what he likes of my suit, of our boutonnieres. But maybe he thought the truth. If he didn't know it already, which I'm sure he did, maybe he figured out who you are. Would that be so very bad? Maybe he was jealous. Maybe he thought you and I were… an item."

"He wouldn't think that of you. Of us… God, what a disaster."

"It's okay," Daniel said. "To be that. It's not a big deal."

"It is a big deal," Ned said. "Are you like that, like me?"

"No," Daniel said. "I'm not. I'm straight."

"That's not why you're rejecting the Armenian princesses out of hand?"

"I just don't want to get married. Not yet. Certainly not to someone chosen by my parents."

"But your clothes. They're so—out there."

"I'm a dandy. Anyway, why do you ask what I am? Do you want me?" He struck a pose.

"Hardly," Ned said.

"What's wrong with me? What has Cameron got that I haven't?"

"It's not a joke, Daniel, all of this."

"I know, I know it's not. It's just, I do that. When things get crazy, I tell jokes. It's shitty, I know. I make light of heavy situations."

"I wake up and it's the first thing I think of, the last thing before I go to bed, that I'm this… faggot. That I'll always be this faggot."

"Don't use that word."

"When I look in the mirror, do you know why I make faces? I'm hoping I don't see the mark of Cain on me, this sign that the devil has marked me out as one of his own. I know it's crazy, but that's what I'm looking for there. The mark of the beast."

They passed the rest of the short walk in silence, the orange glow of their cigarette ends more noticeable once they got off bright Bloor back onto dark, tree-covered Philosophers' Walk.

"Did you miss us?" Daniel said to the porter.

"Terribly," the porter said.

In the quad, they could hear a song coming out a friend's open window—the Talk Talk song, "It's My Life", then everywhere. The chorus's declaration of independence—"It's my life, don't you forget"—spoke to Ned. He didn't want to go to the party, but his shoulders did—they started moving to the song's insistent beat. His body had its own agenda.

"Are you coming up?" Daniel said.

"I don't think so."

They stopped, looked at each other—would they even stay friends?

"I want to," Ned said. "But I'm tired. And my Dad and brother are coming in early tomorrow to help move me out. You going?"

"Of course. I need to be among my people. Thank Fritzie for the meal." Ned's grandmother had given him some money to treat his friends.

"I will thank her," Ned said, then mimicked his grandmother's voice. "'How is your little friend, the Armenian boy?'"

Fritzie had taken Ned and Daniel for lunch to the members' lounge at the Royal Ontario Museum, which sat just across Philosophers' Walk from Trinity. Daniel thrust the present into Ned's hands. "It didn't seem the sort of thing to give you in front of that lug."

"He's a good guy," Ned said. "A nice guy."

"You know, if he hadn't wanted that meeting with your uncle, you probably wouldn't have heard peep one from him. He likes you well enough, but you're from a time in his life, from a particular place. His past. You lobbed that comment about Odysseus at a guy who barely knows who that is. You took him to that flower patch, when he doesn't—he doesn't care. At least not as much as you do."

"That's probably true."

"True, yes," he said. "But cruel of me to say it. Especially when he clearly means… the world to you."

Ned dropped his cigarette, ground it out with his shoe, and started to unwrap the present, but Daniel said he should open it later. "I hate to watch. What if you're disappointed? But then again, I don't think you will be."

Daniel turned to go, but Ned laid a hand on his friend's arm to stop him. "I'm afraid, Daniel," Ned said. "What if they… my parents, they say no, not okay."

"I don't think they will. They seem like good people."

"And AIDS," Ned said.

"I know," Daniel said. "It's terrible. But you know what to do to be safe. You have been safe, right?"

Ned nodded yes—he'd never had sex at all, but didn't want to tell his friend that. "I thought maybe that was why you didn't want to go to lunch with me anymore. Because you knew what I was."

"No," Daniel said. "I'm sorry. I'm going to be honest, once I figured it out, it did give me pause. But my sister gave me a talking to. In the end, what was hard to take was it felt like you were hiding the essential thing from me."

"I wasn't ready to talk about it. It took me years even to write the word down in my diary. And when I did finally manage it, I tore the page out and burned it in my fireplace. And then I tore out the page behind it, with just the vague impression of that word on it, and burned that too."

Ned returned to his room, poured himself a shot of vodka from a nearly empty bottle on his mantle. He took a cigarette from a pack on his bedside table and unwrapped the present. It was a first edition of *Brideshead Revisited*—far and away, the nicest gift anyone had ever given him.

Ned and Daniel had watched the television version of Evelyn Waugh's book together in Trinity's common room. Ned was obsessed with the book—he didn't exactly like it, but he'd read it multiple times. In it, the handsome lordling Sebastian Flyte ends up in exile from his family's castle, Brideshead, living in a hovel in North Africa, a prey to his addictions, with a syphilitic German soldier for a companion. The man who loved Sebastian when he was young has married Sebastian's sister—a woman who resembles Sebastian to an uncanny degree. Sebastian is no longer attractive; he is a disappointment to himself and a caution to others. In the books with gay characters in them that Ned tracked down, there were few happy endings for his kind. He wanted something better for himself, but was that even possible?

He held up the book. His mother said certain people would belong to a certain time and place in his life, others—they would last. Which was Daniel? His thoughts turned to Cameron—this meeting meant little to his old friend. It was pleasant for him in the same way his reunions with the others were. Even knowing theirs was a lopsided relationship, it thrilled Ned to have seen Cameron again. Was it love, what he had for Cameron? Maybe, maybe it was. But what even did that mean, when you'd not ever… been with each other? When he'd never laid hands on Cameron—or had Cameron's hands on him.

His dorm room was still a pit. No elves had come to clean it up in his absence. He'd have to get it all packed up in the morning. He finished his vodka and flopped down on his bed. Daniel had dragged the disclosure out of him. Ned realized he'd not said it, "I am gay." He'd not claimed it for his own. The thought of telling his parents made him nauseous—he knew it would hurt them, but why? He wasn't doing it *to* them. He'd tried so hard to pluck it out of himself. It was time to stop that effort, to give in to it. It couldn't, it wouldn't be plucked out. The terrible dishonesty of his efforts with girls and women, the inadvertent damage done by those… A wave of retrospective embarrassment coursed through him.

Chapter 2:

The Nightingales Of North America

Ned woke up late the next day, a thick gluey tongue, a fierce headache. He went to the washroom on his hall, got himself into the shower, out of it. He nicked himself shaving, but otherwise made it through his ablutions.

Back in his room, in his bathrobe, he surveyed his small, disordered kingdom. He had only dress shirts and pants that were clean, so he put some on and got to work. First, he got rid of the empty bottles and dumped the cigarette butts from his ashtray in a garbage in the hall. From his closet, he got some duffel bags and his big knapsack down, and shoved all his undone laundry into them. He got his milk-crates full of albums into the hall, and packed his stereo away into the boxes its components had come in. The room had bookcases built into the walls around his fireplace, organized by subject matter. He'd had the foresight to get some liquor boxes from the government-controlled outlets—small enough that, even when filled with books, no one, he hoped, would break their backs moving them.

With just a few minutes to spare before his brother and father arrived, he got all the gay-themed books he'd gathered over the years, all of which were stored behind other, less incriminating books. Into one box went Yukio Mishima's *Forbidden Colors*, E.M. Forster's (one overtly gay book) *Maurice*, Radclyffe Hall's *Well of Loneliness*, Mary Renault's *The Charioteer*, James Baldwin's *Giovanni's Room*, some books about the trials of Oscar Wilde, as well as a couple of handbooks to coming out that he'd drummed up the courage to buy at Toronto's gay bookstore, Glad Day. Its name was cockney rhyming slang for Ned's condition. (As in, "You know 'is son's Glad Day, don't you? 'e's a right poofter.") Henry wouldn't necessarily know what it meant that Ned had amassed all these books, but Oliver certainly would. Once they were safely stowed away, he taped the box up and used a marker to label it "Q".

He heard a knocking at the door—it was Henry, a few minutes early, here while their father parked the car. They hugged. "Bit of a bender last night, I'm afraid," Ned said. "I'm not as ready as I should be."

Ned's younger brother, as Henry was mainly known, was shorter and broader than Ned, his hair darker and curlier, his cheeks more olive, with pits from the acne that had bedeviled him for years, but now showed signs of departing. Four years younger than Ned, he'd been slow to grow and seemed to both glory in, and resent, his status for years as the runt of the extended family. Their mother called him her Celt, where Ned was her Saxon, sometimes her flaxen Saxon a reference to a childhood game she'd played growing up in England, sort of a mix of Capture the Flag and Cowboys and Indians from the sounds of it. "Who goes there, Saxon or Celt?" she'd sometimes call out when one of them came in, and she wasn't sure which one.

Henry, too, was soon to leave home. He'd surprised everyone by getting into a small, prestigious college in the US, Dartmouth. He'd done well on the standardized tests the Americans valued so highly and anyway the school's ski team wanted him. He'd skied well when he went down to visit another older skiing friend studying there, and the coach had put in a request that the admissions office flag his file as, all other things being equal, desirable.

"Don't worry about it," Henry said. "It'll take Dad ages to find a spot. Meantime, let's do this." Ned got Henry loading the rest of his books, while Ned cleaned out his desk.

Henry tapped on Ned's back, holding up a beat-up copy of *Portrait of the Artist as a Young Man.* "This one has seen better days," Henry said. "We read it this past year with Gumby." All the teachers at Henry's school, the one Ned had gone to also, had nicknames, the more demeaning the better. "Once you get the knack of how he tells the story, it was… pretty good."

"Yes," Ned said. "You're becoming a… reader."

Henry had had trouble learning to read, and, at length, Ned had taken him in hand, set up a little school in the corner of his room, and helped his younger brother begin to decipher the squiggles on the page.

“There was this cartoon in the *New Yorker* recently—” Ned said.

“I almost never understand those,” Henry said.

“It had James Joyce's to-do list posted on a fridge. Things like: 'Pick up Nora's dry-cleaning. Buy seltzer.' And then for its final item, it had 'Forge in the smithy of my soul the uncreated conscience of my race.'”

“Ha!” Henry said. “I get it. I actually get it.” He opened the book to its final page, finding the quote.

“It's weird,” Ned said. “I never thought of us as having a race growing up. I thought we were sort of transparent. Just the norm, from which everything, every one else deviated. 'Ethnic' was other people.”

“We thought we were the shits,” Henry said.

“Turns out, we weren't, we aren't. The cartoon made me think. I've been wondering, what would the conscience of *our* race look like?”

“Ugly,” Henry said. “I'd say it'd look pretty ugly.”

Ned suspected he'd soon find out what the conscience of his people looked like, at least as far as how his college and high-school friends, and his parents and their friends would respond to his being gay. Was it even a question of conscience?

“Do you want that tree?” Ned said. He had a weeping *benjamina,* a fruitless fig in a terra cotta planter near the window. “It always made me think of the White Tree.”

They'd both loved J.R.R. Tolkien's *Lord of the Rings* trilogy growing up—one of the rare overlaps between them—and so Ned knew Henry would get the reference to a sacred tree that helps protect one of the imaginary nations in the book, Gondor. It was a source of strength, growing in the citadel of the country's great city, Minas Tirith.

"How will I get the tree across the border?" Henry said.

"If they confiscate it, they confiscate it," Ned said. "But take it, I'd like you to have it."

Truth was Henry had always coveted the tree, the way the leaves picked up the light.

"All these books," Henry said. "Like at home. I sometimes imagined the shelf in my room would come down and crush me. I hated that part of… us. Everyone always quoting stuff. Like why not say things for yourself? I want to get away from that."

"I don't know that an Ivy-League school is exactly the place for someone who wants to get away from people quoting things!"

Henry boxed up the last of Ned's books, while Ned detached an articulating lamp from the desk-edge and put it into a larger box. He collected other odds and ends, for this bigger box, his tennis and squash racquets, his sports Walkman, a clay pot their parents had brought back from their safari trip to Botswana. (Their friends also went to South Africa on that trip, but Oliver had refused, as a tourist, to support apartheid, so the Baldwins met up with them in Botswana.)

Their father Oliver came in, ready to go at it, but there wasn't much left to do. He'd been a rugby player in his youth, and was still in shape. He had Ned's fair coloring, but Henry's bulk. It was strange to see him in jeans. It took them two trips to get everything to the car, and then Ned ran a mop around the room. On the way out, he said a quick goodbye to a fellow he ran into on the quad, a guy he knew a little. None of his best friends were up yet, felled, no doubt, by the party.

"I thought that would take longer," Oliver said.

"Not much was packed when Henry got there, to be honest," Ned said. "But he just kicked into gear."

It was rare for Ned to praise Henry, and the younger brother basked in it.

"Indulge me, boys," Oliver said. "I'd like to show you two little traitors something. Your mother wouldn't like me doing this. But I find I'd like you to know a bit more about the first of us to come to Toronto." Their mother hated people speaking of their families. She had enough of that in England and came to Canada, she sometimes said, to get away from that, all that ancestor worship. "You may find you agree with your mother. Even so, I ask that you pay attention. I am only going to tell you all this once. You won't tell your mother about this, our little excursion?"

They both promised they wouldn't.

Oliver put some coins in the meter, and pointed across the road at a vast stone building, one where Ned had taken some classes. "University College," Oliver said. "As you know, Ned. What you may not know is that it is one of the legacies of my ancestor, your ancestor, Robert Baldwin. You know, I think, that you are descended from him." They both nodded. "A Victorian politician, for some time the leader of Upper Canada. Those papers, the ones I have in my office, they tell his story, in excruciating detail. Though an Anglican, he fought to have the university founded on secular grounds. He didn't quite win, but at least one of the colleges within the university was not attached to a particular faith—that one."

"That's cool," Henry said. "That he fought against the mystery cult." A few years ago, Henry had stopped going to church with his family, even at Christmas and Easter, claiming he'd found atheism. He said he got enough of all that at school, in the twice weekly chapel services.

"He was a believer," Oliver said. "He just didn't feel everyone else had to believe the same thing as him."

Oliver had an old wooden box in his office at home, full of musty old documents, ones that Canadian historians occasionally asked to see. They walked up the street named for the dragon slayer, St. George. As they walked, they passed tall redbrick houses, many with gables covered in fish-tiles, some with round corner turrets high up, rusticated or vermiculated stone on the ground level. Ned had been to parties in some of the houses, the more ramshackle ones, that had been separated into apartments and rented out to students.

"Baldwin, he sought—often found—what he called the lonely middle way." Oliver said that his ancestor, their ancestor, tried to navigate between Trinity's founder, Bishop John Strachan, on the right and, on the left, William Lyon Mackenzie, the crusading journalist who'd led an armed rebellion in 1837. "Baldwin didn't believe in the rebellion, didn't agree with it, but he defended one of the rebels in court. He was… decent. Maybe not always bold, but decent. And sometimes, to be decent, is to be bold."

"Strachan Hall," Ned said. "It's our dining hall. We didn't discuss this, any of this, when I chose to go to Trinity."

"No," Oliver said. "Your mother said you should go to the best, even if it was founded by Bishop Strachan. Plus, they offered you money." He'd won a scholarship that had been renewed each year. "Your university education, it cost us a pittance —unlike Henry's will do."

"I know," Henry said. "The tuition is ten times that of a Canadian school."

"We can make it work. It requires some economies, a little more work on my part. But we can do it."

Oliver was a doctor who worked in a public health clinic in a rougher part of Toronto called Corktown, named either, local historians said, for the massive brick distillery in it, once the largest in the Empire, or for the city in Ireland, the hometown of many of the working-class Irish who emigrated there. Oliver commuted in each day on the train from Oakville, a suburb west of the city on Lake Ontario's Northern shore. His wife, their mother Helena also worked, as a history teacher in the public high school. When the family needed money, Oliver picked up shifts at the local hospital's emergency department, and he'd likely have to pick up one a week, to help foot the bill for Henry's tuition.

They reached the Davenport Road. Above it, here, was a high-hill. At the bottom of some steps cut into the hillside was a plaque memorializing the life of Robert Baldwin. Ned had seen it sometimes on his jogs, but, after reading it once, had not paid it any attention, obeying, even in his mother's absence, her instruction that they largely ignore their ancestors.

As they climbed, Oliver talked about the compromise that Baldwin had made with the leader of the French, in Lower Canada, the gloriously named Louis-Hippolyte Lafontaine, whereby each would have some ability to govern themselves. Oliver said the two politicians had become not just allies but friends, and described the riots and uprisings in both French and English Canada that both faced in reaction to their compromise. "When everyone hates it, you've got a good deal."

This Ned had studied: Their *rapprochement* would become the basis of Canada's constitution, the *British North America Act.* But though he listened carefully to his father, much of this felt not quite relevant. Politics was more Henry's thing. In the way siblings reserve territory from each other, Ned's was the country of literature, of the arts, and Henry's was that of business, politics, and the goings on in the outer world. In Jane Austen's terms, Ned thought, he was the brother of sensibility, and to Henry belonged sense.

At the top of the hill, there was a Robber Baron's castle on their left, Casa Loma, that looked like something King Ludwig of Bavaria might have built as a prelude to erecting the turreted Neuschwanstein. And on their right, was the site of the Baldwins' ancestral home, Spadina. "'Spad-ee-na'—that's how we said it," Oliver said, "though now people say 'Spad-aye-na'. It's supposed to be a native word for top of the hill." The house had given its name to one of the city's chief north-south arteries, Spadina Avenue, around which the city's Chinatown had grown up. The dim sum house that Daniel and Ned liked was on it; Daniel's vintage store was just off it, in Kensington Market, where generations of European Jews had lived, on first arrival there, before moving uptown.

"I have this diary of a girl who grew up here," Oliver said. "She said she liked to fall asleep listening to the frogs croaking and singing and wooing, looking for a mate, in the swamps below. Yes, all that, what we walked through, that was once swamps. She evidently had a poetic turn, because she said the frogs were 'The Nightingales of North America.'"

Ned turned that over in his head. *That* he liked; *that* he would retain. They entered the grounds, and Oliver pointed out the lilacs near the gate, then in full blossom, scenting the air with their sweet aroma. The smell somehow always made Ned sad, as spring did in general. How brief their bloom was every year, how quickly this brown rot infected their flowers.

"The Baldwins planted some lilacs here," Oliver said, "maybe the predecessors of these ones." The three of them stopped at another vista point, where a gap between tall oak trees afforded a view of the city, a bit further west from downtown.

"He was a depressed for much of his later life," Oliver said. "His wife died young, his beloved Augusta Elizabeth, in childbirth—a botched Caesarian. He put this strange codicil in his will. He wanted to have a surgeon make the same cut in his body after he died, as she had in hers. He wanted to meet her in Paradise, with the same scar on his body."

"Creepy," Henry said.

"But romantic enough, in its way," Ned said. "Did he remarry?"

“No, we don't seem to be much that way inclined. We fall in love once, we stay the course, however tough it is, and then, well, that's it.”

“That's not much fun,” Henry said.

“Maybe not,” Oliver said, with a grimness that surprised both boys. Ned was glad his mother hadn't heard this.

They walked back to the top of the stairs, and Henry turned to his father. “What happened to them? To us. Sorry, but it seems so abstract their connection to me.”

“There were some scandals, a pair of them,” Oliver said.

“O, good,” Henry said, rubbing his hands together.

“Baldwin had an ambitious young man working in his office, who wooed and married his daughter. That young man rose to become the Attorney-General of Upper Canada, of Ontario. All well and good. But after he left public office, he was supposed to have used his friends in the government to procure lucrative contracts to build railroads. The beginning of our end. Our move away from public service. And there was more scandal to come. This man's son, Baldwin's grandson, Robbie Ross, Robert Baldwin Ross, went to Cambridge, where I went, to King's College. He became a great friend of Oscar Wilde's.”

“Jesus,” Henry said.

“Say what you like about him, and people did, he was very loyal,” Oliver said. “When Wilde got… in trouble, Robbie stuck by Wilde, paid his legal fees, paid for his funeral and his grave in Père Lachaise. He's buried there, too. In Paris. Or his ashes are there, in the same grave.”

Ned knew just a little bit about him, Wilde's great friend and sometimes lover. He wanted to know more, but he didn't want to seem too interested. He listened to his father's voice as he spoke of Ross—there was no disgust in it. He glanced up to confirm what he suspected, that his father's eyes were on him. Ned looked down again.

Ned wondered what he would add, if anything, to this family story. When he lived in London, he resolved to find out more about Robbie Ross. He felt within him that capacity for depression that his ancestor had succumbed to after his wife's death. The father turned to his sons and said, "And so, go away, do what you need to do, what you want to do. But come back. You have people here. Your dead are buried here. And anyway, you have us. We'll still be here. God willing."

Chapter 3:
The Secrets Of The Deep

Ned woke up early the next morning, the start of his last full day before he flew out. His mother had complained at how soon after his graduation he'd scheduled his departure, but the hell of a long goodbye was not something Ned wanted. He had the attic room in their rickety old farmhouse. It had originally been a farm built when the town supplied much of the province with strawberries, and then an asylum for addicts. An opium user had carved his initials on a window in Henry's room, or so the story went, using his diamond ring to etch the glass with his "WSH". The house was built to no particular plan, unified only by the mustard-colored clapboard in which it was clad.

There were books on most of Ned's walls. Over his desk, Björn Borg was midway through hitting a backhand, and next to the window was a framed Italian ad for the movie Manhattan. Near the middle of the room, a spiral staircase looped up to the roof. He put on a robe and climbed up, pushing out onto the widow's walk.

It was an ugly but a clear spring day—he could see the lights of Buffalo flickering across the vast lake, their inland freshwater sea. The dawn soon swallowed those lights. He leaned against the wrought iron rail and lit up a cigarette, though he didn't often smoke here, and almost never in the mornings. He'd clean his teeth and shower the smoke off him before breakfast. The smell of bacon wafted up to him. Some smoke puffed out of the chimney that gave off the back room next to the kitchen. His mother, like Ned, was an early riser, and the smoke meant she'd lit a fire so as to be cozy while reading beside it. He didn't feel like going down yet, meeting her, without the protection of others about.

He thought over his day to come, the preparations he'd need to make. Was his passport up to date? Yes, he'd checked that already. He looked at the yards around the house, a valedictory look—who knew when he'd be back next? Robbie Ross had left Canada and returned only seldom, making a career as an art critic and gallery curator in London. He was friends with Henry James, with Auguste Rodin, with Siegfried Sassoon and Lady Ottoline Morrell, with Prime Minister Herbert Asquith and, especially, with the Prime Minister's wife Margo—with everyone basically. Would Ned also manage to find his way there, gathering distinguished friends about him? Would he, too, leave Canada and seldom return?

There was a flat, sodden lawn between the house, and, beyond it, the stone breakwater that separated it from the rocky beach. In the warm months they played croquet here. Past a line of dark, tall spruces and a massive maple, both planted by the farmer, was the tennis court Oliver had built Helena for her 40th birthday. Ned remembered the card his father had given her, a deft drawing of tennis players midway through a point on a court.

The silly games of his people, of the leisure class. Ned was good at both croquet and tennis. Henry was not so good. But his younger brother was better at chess, most games involving strategy, and was, of course, a far better skier. He could leave Ned at will on the hill. Henry had guts on the hill—he'd take risks, and had once broken his leg on a slope in Vermont.

What would it mean for his parents that both of them were leaving at once? Would they heave a sigh of relief, at having got them off their hands? Probably. But there'd be something else also. His mother would find it hard. They, Ned and she, had a particular bond—they could almost see the world from each other's eyes, switching personae. Or at one point, they could. In the last few years, Ned had tried to close that often-open door between them.

He was going far away—and for a reason. He couldn't see doing this, becoming who he needed to be, near her. She'd try to stop him, and with how much power she exerted in him, over him, it was even possible she'd succeed for a time. She'd be the Dutch boy with his finger in the dike they heard about growing up, somehow keeping the North Sea from rushing in. The sea, the sea.

He'd tried to tell them before, standing on the threshold of their bedroom as they watched a Sunday night mystery. His mother was pleased she'd solved it. A gaudily colored papier maché goose that Henry had made in nursery school made eyes at Ned through the looking glass that hung on the door of their room. They couldn't see him, where he stood. And that was just as well. That evening, he realized he couldn't do it, not yet, not under their roof. He said to himself, he didn't want to spoil his mother's pleasure in figuring out the televised whodunnit. But really, he knew it was cowardice. If not then, when? He'd known who he was all along, as long as he'd known anything, as he'd told Daniel, writing it down years earlier in his diary, then tearing out the page and the one beneath it, and burning them. When he was in primary school, most of his friends had been girls. Perhaps that was one reason they'd moved him to the boys' school, Appleby, to toughen that out of him.

Once he told them, it was possible he'd become persona non grata here. His eyes swept the acre that was theirs. He'd been born inside something, something that he took for granted, but he knew he was inside. His parents were hardworking professionals, but his grandmother, after his grandfather's death, had become the majority owner of a large pulp and paper company, now run by his uncle Max. This put her in the mix with the families of the more well to do of his Trinity classmates. What would it be to be suddenly thrust outside that, to have none of the advantages he'd taken for granted, and also, vastly more important to him, to lose the affection of his mother, his father, that grandmother, his siblings, his friends, his people? His mind could run along this path only so long before panic invaded him.

He shook his head, muddling it all out of it, putting a calming hand on his queasy stomach. He crushed the cigarette on the wrought iron, putting the butt in the pocket of his robe, making a mental note to flush it down the toilet. He was sure they knew that he smoked, but there was no point rubbing their faces in it.

There were blossoms on the little crabapple tree in the front garden, the last of its blossoms still on it. Next to it was a sundial he'd bought his parents for their 20th anniversary. Inscribed on it: "I count only sunny hours."

There'd be few enough of those this day—the wind was scudding clouds across the sky and there were more where those came from, the winter was still lurking, ready to take at least one more punch. They might have sleet, they might have rain, they might even have snow—or maybe they might have all three today. Canada. England was supposedly milder, bathed by the Gulf Stream. Maybe that would suit him more. It was all he'd known his whole life, but still, how he despised the winter. He retreated inside.

He showered and changed, choosing dark clothes, reflecting his dour mood—today he'd be all Sparta, no Athens. He followed the trail of heating vents down through the house, remembering how he and his sibling had run from one to the next in the winter, the house's old furnace no match for the cold drafts, the frigid floors. ("Move on—it's my turn!") He remembered sitting at the top of the main staircase as a boy, watching his parents drink with their friends, then roll the carpets up to dance. There was much whooping, clapping and hollering. He and his brother looked at each other, thinking 'these people are crazy'. Still, there had been a lot of joy there.

When he got down, his mother was, as he'd suspected, reading by the fire in the back sitting room next to the kitchen. She had the plaid half-moon glasses she favored perched on her nose. He took her in before she noticed him there. Her hair, once brown, had gone grey when Ned was little, and, though her bridge group had urged her to dye it, she'd not done so. That seemed phony to her. Phony, petty, glib—words and qualities she didn't like. She was thin still, tall like their father, and almost as tall as Ned. Her face was also spare, but, when you'd pleased or amused her, her cheeks could rise up into little plums. Her eyes, her big brown eyes, they had all the moods in the world in them, Ned thought. No, he had to move away from his childhood idolatry of her. Was she to be an ally or an enemy going forward? Or, more likely, some mix of the two?

She, too, was already dressed; she, too, had chosen dark colors, the somber colors of leave-taking.

She looked up at him. “Oh, good,” she said. “I'm glad it's just you. I was hoping we might take a walk before breakfast. Give the dog an airing.”

“I was out, up top,” Ned said. “It's going to get messy out there.”

“Well, then, best we go now. I've cooked the breakfast. It's warming in the oven. Shall we?”

“'Let us go then, you and I.'”

“'When the evening is stretched out against the sky, like a patient, etherized upon a table.”

“Henry hates it when we quote,” Ned said.

“Yes,” Helena said.

“I didn't know.”

They, as a family, used it as shorthand between them, to allude to a relevant thought, to set a mood. Maybe Henry was right—it was a sort of laziness, using something second-hand to do so. It was, of course, pretentious, the word Ned had lobbed at Daniel, and Daniel had sent straight back at him. Still, Henry hadn't come down yet, so Ned needn't be on his guard. What delectation his younger brother took in his sleep. Ned thought of all those Christmas mornings spent watching him, waiting for him to come to.

The invitation at the start of Eliot's poem, “The Lovesong of J. Alfred Prufrock”, did the job Ned hoped it would, creating a nice intimacy between him and his mother, as if they were old chums heading out into the city for a tramp. They weren't, of course, chums—they could be friendly but never friends. She'd given him life.

Their black lab, Higgins, shook himself into a frenzy, knowing he would soon be released from captivity. There was some grey on his muzzle now, and he was thicker than he'd once been, but he still had plenty of vigor in him. The dog adored their father, quite liked Henry—and tolerated the rest of them. Still, they all had their uses.

The dog led them through the living room, looking back at them to make sure they hadn't lost sight of what was important. Ned's eye was inventorying what he was about to leave behind: the leather-bound books by Thomas Hardy and Henry James; the results of his mother's collecting mania evident with ceramic Victorian carpet-bowls and the glass insulators dotted about (their father had liberated these from various decommissioned electrical poles around the province). Through an open door, Ned peered into the navy blue dining room. On its walls were portraits of some of his worthy ancestors, wondering would he do, would he do at all? The chintz sofas and arm chairs were littered with half-done crossword puzzles, knitting projects, magazines open to half-read articles, more of his mother's reading glasses waiting push into the nether regions of anyone who sat down without checking. These were better than the other hazards, a needle or a pencil, at any rate.

In the front hall were landscapes, some trees in their autumn finery covering the slopes of some of the Laurentians; a dray horse dragging a load of logs on a sleigh through some wintry woods in the Ottawa Valley; an island in the Georgian Bay with a twisted pine, having made it through one of those winters, enjoying some summer sun. Could they, too, weather the coming cold his disclosure would cause, and reach some of those sunny hours again? He helped his mother get her navy great coat on, her vast blue scarf, her black leather gloves, a plum beret the only dash of brightness on her—on either of them as it turned out. After bundling up in the same coat he'd worn out to Three Small Rooms, he took a big umbrella just in case the clouds opened, and followed his mother out the door.

"Oh, Ned," she said, as she took his arm, and they crossed the lawn down to the lake. "It's come too soon, you leaving us."

He gave a faint nervous chuckle, for lack of anything to say. In a way, it was good it was her on her own. He'd promised himself he'd only do it with both of them there. It seemed only fair. One of his rules about it. Chief among his other rules was that he'd be with no one, until he'd spoken with his parents. Not that anyone had asked. He'd had some tepid, short-term relationships with girls—ones where he willed himself to like them. But soon enough they could see something was off, and, if he hadn't exited yet, making his apologies, they soon did.

The grass had more green in it than it seemed to from above. The cycle of life was beginning again. Some crocuses had come up in one flowerbed, a blanket of bluebells in another. And the green sword tips of the tulips protruded from the soil nearest the breakwater. "The champions of spring," his mother said.

"I was worried about the crab-apple tree," he said.

"Yes. That tree has started up early this year. But it looks to have worked out, most of its blossoms converted by the bees to little nubs. I might do jam from them this year. If I do, I'll send a jar over."

They reached some stone stairs that took them down to the rock beach. "It must feel a long way from home sometimes for you, Canada," Ned said.

"I suppose, though, as you know, I was never one for pining after lost paradises. And I had such a welcome here. From Fritzie and Chief." Chief was Fritzie's husband, Ned's dead grandfather. Or that was the name they'd given him when Ned, the first grandson was born. His grandmother had taken on a new name also, Fritzie, a bastardization of her middle name Frederica. "I'm too young for any version of Grandma." It suited her, with its crisp consonants and its playful stray into masculine territory, and soon enough most everyone a generation younger than her or more began calling her that. "It wasn't a given that they would welcome me. At all, let alone with open arms." Oliver had chosen Helena over the Toronto girl they'd more or less handpicked for their son, but they'd come around once they saw it was a firm commitment between their son and Helena.

Helena asked about Three Small Rooms. "It was such a treat for us, getting in there once when you all were young. I felt terribly guilty, but oh, we were starved for it all, the eavesdropping on proper conversations, the clothes, the food, I suppose, though I don't remember what we ate at all. I still feel badly too—that we stole their ashtray! It's not like me, you know, but I slipped it in my purse! How was it there?"

Ned tugged on the dog's leash, reining him in, as he puffed towards the lake. "It was a little awkward with both Daniel and Cameron there."

"Yes," she said. "Your great old friend. And your great new one. Curious how often one's best friends have no time for each other."

"Yes, isn't it?" This was one of the exact things he'd been puzzling over also since the awkward dinner.

"It's not simple jealousy often. It's just, you have different people in you, they come out. And they don't much like *you* in your unfamiliar guise. Nice fellow that Cameron. I'm surprised you've kept in touch, though."

"We didn't," Ned said. "He's not much of a letter writer."

"Well, nice to see him again," she said. "You once were thick as thieves."

"He wants a job, to work with Max."

"I see," she said. And he knew she did. "That Daniel. He's terribly clever. A keeper, I should say."

"If he wants to be kept."

Ned still suspected the gift of *Brideshead, Revisited* was by way of being a beautiful goodbye.

Ned had also been thinking over what his father had said about them being people who fell in love just once. It was a dangerous territory to enter with his mother, adjacent to the conversation they needed to have, but he found himself wanting to speak of love.

"When did you know, with Dad?" he asked. "That it was the real thing." He knew he'd have heard much of what she had to say before, but she tweaked her stories, sometimes adding something wholly new to the mix, as if discovering it herself, for the first time, so there might be something more he'd learn before he left them.

"Well, I really didn't know," she said. "I didn't have that sudden feeling for him that you hear about, that you read about, that they sing about. He was just this lovely friend of my brother's. I remember watching him playing rugger. He was this nice Canadian off the pitch, polite, careful, but on it, a Viking marauder by the look of him, running hard, bloody murder in his eyes, some of his opponents chucking the ball too soon, realizing he was coming at them. And then, in a pub, after one of their games, he just kept on stuttering. I couldn't make much of that, except that maybe he liked me."

"But you must have known," Ned said.

"No, not then," she said. "I was in this fog—my mother had died—he was sympathetic, solid, kind, he asked questions that my English friends wouldn't dream of asking, and then he actually listened to the responses. He wasn't afraid of my… emotions, my grief. My father was dreadful at the time, though I suppose he was going through it, in the most… awful way. Everyone said I could take the time, but I went back to College a few days after the funeral. It's what my mother would have wanted. And at the end of that term, Oliver asked me to tea at a hotel. He surprised himself, I think, by asking for my hand, and for the rest of me, and I surprised both of us by saying yes. It was shocking really."

"What's shocking about that?"

"What's shocking is I married him not entirely sure. I knew what love was—or I thought I did. There had been another before him. Something, someone not at all suitable. But grand and sudden. A reaction, in an odd way, to my mother's illness."

Ned didn't like this. He didn't like it at all. He was relieved when his mother decided not to tell him more about this other man. They reached the shore of the lake and let the dog off the leash. Higgins waded into the water and gulped at it, this although it had an unappetizingly fishy smell this morning. Ned picked up a flat circular stone, one with a little fossil in it, and he skipped it across the relatively choppy water—six before it buried itself in a wave.

Ned wasn't satisfied with her answers. "With Dad, when… how did you know? That he was more than just an escape."

"We got to Toronto. He told his parents we were arriving later, and so we had a couple of days to ourselves before the parties began, before Fritzie put us through our paces. He took me to the symphony, and it was sheer heaven to hear those familiar songs played so far away from my home. There were so many other immigrants in the crowd, also finding solace in that, though, of course, they had greater challenges than I did, not having the language, necessarily, not having a Canadian, not having Oliver to help them."

"Yes, yes," Ned said. "You've told us about the symphony."

"Of course I have," she said. "I'm reaching that age where you don't even remember when you're repeating yourself. Have I told you about the market?"

"No," Ned said.

"I suppose I wanted to keep that, for myself. So, on our little honeymoon, your father shows me the St. Lawrence Market. I remember watching the lobsters in their big glass case, sharing a silly old story I'd read about a Parisian poet who kept one as a pet, and walked it around the parks of the French capital on a leash. When asked why, he said he liked how quiet the lobster was and also that it knew the secrets of the deep. This had always somehow amused me, and I was so relieved when it did him, too."

Ned smiled at his mother. He also found the anecdote a little daffy, sweet—he, too, liked it for reasons that weren't easy to fathom.

"And then," Helena went on, "he took me to the Toronto Islands, and annotated the skyline as we looked back at his city. It was much smaller then, lower, there was no CN Tower, the needle puncturing the sky." Ned remembered when a Sikorsky helicopter lowered the top of the tower into place.

"Certainly," Helena said, "Toronto was no London then. Your father pointed out the building where his family's firm had its head office. That old bank building with these somber stone kings at each corner looking down on us. And no, he didn't mean to work there. There was the railway hotel with the green copper roof where we were staying. Above us, the cottonwood trees were shedding their spores, and there was all this white fluff in his hair—he said it was summer snow. And then, then he took me by the hands, and turned me away from the city and towards him, and he said, 'I'm so happy you've come.' It was formal, the sort of the thing you'd say to someone as they came in the door at a big party. But it was just right. I might have spooked if he'd said something more than that. I thought, do you know, somehow, I've landed in the clover. And I had. I fell for him that day—and for the lake, as we walked by it. I asked if we could live near it, and he said, yes, we could. And we did, we do. Though it was my mother's bequest that we used as our piddling down payment."

Ned and Helena looked out at the same lake together. The waves were growing, whipped up by a wind that had grown markedly more bitter in their few minutes outside. Some cold rain began to spit down on them.

"So then you knew," Ned said.

"Yes, then I knew. But what a gamble. The great gamble of my life," she said, taking and squeezing Ned's arm, as they walked east along the lakeshore. "And how it has paid off. With you, Henry, with everything." She removed her arm from his, and turned towards him. "I do hope you're as lucky as I was. I have to admit, it worries me, this country-bred girl that I am, that you're heading to London, this big, rather bad city. People can get lost there. Especially people who aren't… so practical as they might be."

"Are you saying I'm impractical?" Ned said, with a smile.

"Your head's in a cloud most of the time, and even if there's a big truck coming towards you, you don't notice. You come by that honestly, alas. One of your inheritances from me. *Tête dans la lune.* What my French mistress used to say to me. London—it's not always kind to… people like you."

This was Ned's worry also, that he'd get lost in London. He'd never even rented an apartment before. In his dorm room in Trinity, in the run-up to exams, he'd repeatedly played "Small Town Boy"—Jimmy Somerville's weird falsetto serving up a story of flight:

You leave in the morning with everything you own in a little black case
Alone on a platform, the wind and the rain on a sad and lonely face…

Run away, turn away, run away, turn away, run away
Run away, turn away, run away, turn away, run away.

This was not his situation. He had more than a little black case to his name. But it felt the same. He was leaving, taking nothing of any substance with him, trying, hoping to find his way.

He called Higgins to him and put the dog onto the leash. They left their property through a gate onto a path that passed through a public park stretching along the lakeshore. In the distance, they could see a pier with a small lighthouse on it, a glass globe on top, with a red light in it circling. They walked along a street, and up a hill, into another park. There was a bandshell near them, some large maples towering over them. Ned thought of the Historical Society picnics they'd had here, many of their family friends dressed as pioneers, vast picnics spread out, some jazz wafting about, a pony giving rides to the children. They had a photo of a miserable Henry on the pony. Both the horse and human were chubby and squat.

Helena broke into his reminiscences: “At least you'll have Cordelia meeting you.” Helena had arranged for her aunt, an author of children's books who lived in London, to meet Ned off his plane. “A familiar face.”

“It's been so long since I've seen her,” Ned said. “I don't even know if I'll recognize her.”

“I've sent her a recent photo,” Helena said. “I don't have one of her, just those lovely shots of when she was young. She'll be there. Unless there's car trouble, or she gets the day wrong. Or, or, or. But you have her address, some money for a hansom if you need it. And after, I'm so happy you and Sophie will be together.” His cousin, a couple of years younger than him, was to study fashion at St. Martin's, and the plan was, when she came to the city in the fall, they'd find somewhere to live together. “Oh, Ned. Why are you going away? There are publishing companies here, law firms, too.”

“I know, Mum,” Ned said. “I just, I just, I have to. I want to. I mean I don't want to also. But you'll come over. ”

“Yes,” she said. “We will be over. If it's not too soon, we'll come this fall, combine it with a trip to see… everyone. Each time, there are fewer people to see… And you'll be back. For Christmas, I hope. Though you haven't come out from Toronto terribly often these last couple of years. Haven't I, haven't we been good parents?”

“Yes,” he said with conviction. “Yes, yes you have.”

“You just never know what it is someone needs.” She looked down at the muddy path beneath her feet. She took his arm and turned him towards her. “There's nothing you want to say to me?”

“No, Mum,” he said. “I mean… yes, but no.”

“You know you can.”

Her eyes held his, but, after a few seconds, he looked away. “Well, then,” she said, “We'd best be getting back. Even Henry might be up by now. Do you know, I haven't told the others. About Sandy. The man I fell for too hard, before your father. A poet, visiting the university, rather a good poet. He taught us Eliot, shocking Philip Larkin. 'They fuck you up, your mum and your dad, they may not mean to, but they do.'”

“Mom!” Ned said. He'd seldom heard her swear.

“He ought to have known better,” she said. “Not Philip Larkin. He knew exactly what he was doing. My visiting poet, my Sandy. He ought to havc turned me away.” She shook her head, as her son did, trying to evict her old lover from it. But he wouldn't go. “I don't know quite why I told you today. When I ought to be asking you things, giving you solid advice. It's just you asked of love. And… and I wanted someone to hear of him. To write to him, if something, anything should ever happen. Alexander McNaughten.”

“Now you're being dramatic,” Ned said.

“I suppose I am at that,” she said, taking Ned's arm again, and smiling up at him. “When my mother died, it was this... hideous thing. Unjust. I turned my back on God for a time. Him having turned his back on me. No, that's enough of that!” She stopped herself there. “I, we'll miss you. It feels too soon.”

Chapter 4:

The World In Evening

As it turned out, Ned recognized his great aunt at once. In a photograph on Helena's dresser, little Cordelia was nude and brown, this dreamy girl photographed among some reeds in the shallows of a lake, the photo right out of Charles Kingsley's *The Waterbabies*. Inside the old woman, the girl was still there.

Cordelia wore a pink-and-green kerchief—vivid even compared to the brightly colored saris on the many East Indian women in the Arrivals Hall. When Cordelia caught sight of Ned, she took the kerchief off and waved it, and when he passed out of the controlled area, she hugged him with more strength than he imagined her slight frame could have in it. When she pulled away, there were tears in her eyes: "I could see it there, how much you looked like my Mathilda. Your mother had mentioned it, but I had never seen it so clearly before. Even if we'd never met before, I should have known you were hers, my sister's."

His heart leapt at this.

She had forgotten where, exactly, she'd left the car, and they went to several floors of the garage, finally finding it, a little grey-blue Citroën 2CV, which sank down under the weight of his two duffel bags. Helena said Cordelia was rounding the corner into her 80s, but to Ned she looked far younger, a few parallel wrinkles lining her pink cheeks, a few little ones at the ends of her green-blue eyes, some at the ends of her thin, pink, bow-shaped lips, the same ones his mother had.

They crept into London on some back roads, stopping every so often, for them both to look at the *A to Zed* Helena had given Ned. Cordelia kept turning the book of maps this way and that, trying to figure out where they were. "So clever of your mother to think of giving you hers."

Ned passed along news of Helena and the family. How Henry had won the history prize, and was working as a camp counselor for the summer, leading a long canoe trip through the wilds. ("You are intrepid, you lot," she said.)

As they whizzed around one roundabout, Cordelia turned to look at him: "Why have you come?" A version of the question his mother put to him. There were, indeed, publishing firms and law firms, in Toronto. They circled around the paved circle twice while she tried to figure out which route to take, her numbering the merits and demerits of each option. "Chiswick isn't so very far from me—at least, as the crow flies. And, of course, there's the house, which might be open. Would you like to see Chiswick House? Neo-Palladian, lovely camellias, though they're probably over by now. No, I don't suppose you want to go there. You're not here as a tourist." She veered off the roundabout in a different direction and repeated her question to him, "Why have you come?"

"I wanted, I want to figure out what to do with my life," he said, choosing the easiest answer.

"So Helena said."

"I suppose I also want to get to know London. My interests, the things I like—they mark me out in Canada. I had this hope that I'd fit in better over here. But that might not be the case. I want to get a bit of culture, you know."

"I see," Aunt Cordelia said with a sigh, evidently feeling Ned had ducked the question. "Often those who come here don't know quite why until... much later. Or if they do know, they aren't fool enough to expose their plans. The gods have a way of making a mockery of us when we announce our intentions, don't you find?"

Again, those eyes, grey-blue like her car, were peering at him, paying but scant attention to the road.

There were these curious structures on either side of the road: four 100-foot tall posts, arranged in a square, holding up, between them, four rings. He asked her what they were, and she said she didn't know. Whatever they were, Ned imagined them long outlasting him and the city around him, puzzling future generations, as Stonehenge did them.

Cordelia decided to make her next turn late, and the tiny car just about toppled over. It righted itself, and she took off along a straightaway. “Here we go,” she said, with a cackle. “Earwig Go.” It was a reference to a joke Helena had once told her children.

Ned said the punning joke's set-up line, “What did the cockney cockroach say as he went off the cliff?”

“'Ere we go. Earwig Go!” she cried out again. “O, you know that one, do you? But do you know where baby apes sleep?”

“In apricots, of course.”

“I am pleased Helena's passed those along. The great English addiction, word play. Along with opium, of course. Or in olden times, that was the thing. Now, I suppose it's all cocaine.” She gave three syllables to this last word. She gestured left at some green space they were then whipping by. “The Richmond Park. Keep an eye out for deer. They've been here since the days of Henry VIII.” On cue there, indeed, was a rather plump stag grabbing leaves off a young tree, chewing away, contemplating them with equanimity.

“More cow than deer, really,” she said. “That's what happens when the living is too easy.”

This was one of the only pastoral islands they passed in an otherwise vast suburban sea. But these suburbs had the dignity afforded them by their well-proportioned townhouses, the bright colors of the doors and their tiny front gardens differentiating them, one from the other.

"So many bookmakers," Ned said. "As befits a literary city, I suppose."

Cordelia looked to see if he was making a joke. "They're betting shops, young Ned."

This would be the first of many stumbles Ned would make, not realizing how many differences there were between the English and North American usage of the same language.

The flat was the top two stories of an old townhouse, just off the King's Road. As she pulled in to a tiny parking spot, bumping both the cars in front and behind, she said, "Chelsea used to be so Bohemian," she said, "Now it's all stockbrokers—they work so hard, the poor things."

In the flat, there was dust everywhere, the smell of tea, cat and old, slightly mildewed books. A bucket sat on the sitting room floor to pick up drips when it rained. The old junk table that Ned remembered was still there. As children, they were allowed to choose a gift for themselves from the gaudy jumble on this table. She'd been friends with the Egyptologist Lord Carnarvon so, among the cousins, there was a legend that somewhere on the table was some genuine artifact from Ancient Egypt. He scanned it now, still hoping.

She showed Ned to his room. It was full of books, with a narrow cot in it covered in a bedspread in a Moroccan motif. The room looked out over what she called a mews. There were dead geraniums in the window box, old Campaign for Nuclear Disarmament placards in one corner. One asked: "Human Race or Nuclear Race?" A cello case sat in another corner. "It's your grandmother's. My sister's. I found I had to have it. I couldn't leave it. I nicked it from John, from your grandfather." She was going to say more, he could tell, but decided not to.

"My violin's to follow," Ned said. "Once I've got a place of my own. They'll send a small trunk over."

"Well, you needn't rush about that," she said. "Finding a place."

She left Ned, saying she'd see what she had for lunch. Some of the children's books she'd written were there in the room, on a precariously hung shelf above his bed. He thought of Henry feeling crushed by all the family's books—his vision could become a reality here for Ned. He picked out one of her books. Most of her books detailed the exploits of a red train engine, and had experienced a vogue in the '50s and '60s. A radio serial was made of them, and they sold, not in the millions, but in the hundreds of thousands. Writing was something she'd taken up after her husband died, leaving her to raise two girls in their teens. Ned hoped to take a shower in a nearby bathroom, but there was only a bath, so he just splashed himself as clean as he could in the sink.

She served baked beans on toast on a table in the sitting room, with elderflower wine. For dessert, she brought out some slightly off trifle for each of them. "I made it last week, I'm sure it's still… fine. But, no, it really isn't." She whisked it away, and he got up to inspect the room's bookshelves. There were lots of hardcovers of T.S. Eliot's poems and plays, and when he took them down, he found them all signed, with affectionate messages. Her copy of *Old Possum's Book of Practical Cats* had paw-prints in the front, one with Bustopher Jones written in spindly handwriting next to it, the other with Rumpelteazer.

She emerged with Turkish coffees in pretty gilt cups, and he showed her the book's inscription. "You knew each other."

"Yes," she said. "Back when the Earth was cooling. His house published my books. Our cats corresponded. I have those letters somewhere. People have been after me to get them—a rather scandalously high offer out of some university in Texas. If only I could find them. They'd be very let down if they saw them. They're just bits of silliness."

"We studied him," Ned said. "I love, everyone loves his poem, 'The Lovesong of J. Alfred Prufrock'. You figure out a few things, but there are always more puzzles in it. I didn't know you knew him."

"Why should you? It's not important, but he was funny, he could be sharp with those he considered second-rate. And why not? He was ever so talented! Used to put on sort of greenish powder to make himself look more sickly. He was always speaking of how awful his health was. So proud of his ailments. Truth is his health wasn't all that bad. Until, then, it was. And then he stopped speaking of it, put the green powder away."

"None of your books are in the main room," Ned said.

"This is writing for adults in here. The real thing, not my little bagatelles."

"But, I—we—loved them."

"Well, thank you. They boiled some pots that needed boiling."

"Did they, how long did each take you?" He felt embarrassed. It was the sort of question you heard all the time at author readings, and it made him cringe hearing others ask it.

But she dignified it with a response. "It depended, of course. I wrote long, deliberately leaving some fat for the editors to trim. Makes them feel useful. So sometimes that took a bit, the back and forth, the getting it down to a manageable length for a bedtime story. And there was to and fro with the illustrator also. But once I had the basic idea, I was off—off to the races. The ideas would sometimes take their time to come, of course. And I'd struggle with the wrong book for months, until I'd wake up one morning with the right one, nearly written, in my head. All in all, I tended to produce one a year."

"You mustn't indulge my curiosity," he said. "Even so, I find I am curious about something else." He wanted to figure her out, and found sometimes if you asked people about their names, you learned something of how they thought of themselves. "Has anyone ever called you Delia?"

"Heavens, no."

"That's Non-U, that nickname?"

She took a hard look at him. The writer Nancy Mitford had popularized the distinction drawn by a sociologist between things that were U—that signaled an upper-class background——and Non-U. Using the term "napkin" was, apparently, U, where "serviette" was not. Or was it the other way around?

"I suppose, yes," she said. "Delia is Non-U. Delia would write to you on notepaper. But I, well, we weren't… We're neither upstairs, nor downstairs, you know. We like to work, which is good because we've always had to work. We had a house—it was neither large nor small, neither grand nor pinching. I suppose the grounds were grand, but the house itself, it was just so. Now, it's your grandfather's. I suppose what you're wanting to know a bit, is well, what this tribe over here is."

"I do want to know that," he said. "Mum—Helena—she cast a veil over it all, making it all seem that much more intriguing. It's the past—I find I'm much more interested in it than the future. Is that all strange?"

"No," she said. "Of course not."

"In Canada it is." He had not done with his inquisition. "And did you like, do you like the character Cordelia?"

She laughed. "I don't see where you're going next. Or why you're going there. Lear's daughter? You're asking me if I like her. Well, yes, I do rather. She could try being a little less blunt. She loves her father. Why not lead a little more with that? Your grandmother, my sister was thinking of naming your mother Helena that. Naming the little baby Cordelia, for me. But for all that I felt honored, I begged her not to. It's rather a burden to bear. Cordelia's always the truth-teller, even when she ought to take refuge in a few polite lies. 'Thy truth be thy dower.' In a way, it would have been fitting for Helena, but you can't know that when you're christening a child. It would have fit her better than it ever did me. She, too, can be—"

"What?"

"Direct, honest," Aunt Cordelia said. "You're a dangerous boy. I can see that!"

Her cat, a Russian Blue she'd named Bazarov, ambled in, and rubbed against his legs. Ned asked her about her time at Cambridge, and she asked him about his at Trinity. He asked her more about his dead grandmother Mathilda.

She proposed a walk, and Ned imagined some minor totter to the local grocery, her showing him the chief sites on the nearby stretch of the King's Road. This they did, but they kept on going, walking down to the Thames to see the Houses of Parliament—"Aunt Hettie locked herself here when she was fighting for the vote." She pointed at some cast-iron railing. He'd heard about a suffragette and this, he supposed, was her. Cordelia walked them up Charing Cross Road, showing him the inscription over the stage door of a grand brick theatre: "The world's greatest artistes have passed through and will pass through these doors."

"Are you a fan of the theatre?" she asked.

"Yes," he said. "The first play I saw, I felt like running after it. Just running. A production of *The Master Builder*."

"Ibsen, rather serious. How many playwrights would want that to be the reception? You're in for a treat on the theatrical front then." She said she'd give Ned the name of a hotel concierge she knew who could get cheap tickets to anything. "You'd be up in the Gods, of course, but that is no matter. You'd be there."

"I want," Ned said, "to be there. To get there."

They walked along a narrow street full of bookstores, and she described their different holdings, introducing him to a couple of the owners.

"How am I doing?" she asked one.

"A brisk trade, Cordelia."

Cordelia gestured at a red phone box. "Our cousin Giles," she said. "They were a family of church builders. And he did at least one Cathedral, lots of power stations. Those colossal ones on the South Bank are his. But it's these cheery red phone boxes he'll likely be most remembered for."

They passed the one skyscraper on their route, the Centre Point, and proceeded into Bloomsbury. With the aid of the *A to Zed*, she found the front door of the small publishing house where Ned would be working—his first day just about a week off. They pressed deeper into that district, passing the British Museum, and reaching the broad and stately square where her publisher, Faber & Faber, still had its offices. She had a key to the gates of the park in the middle of Russell Square. "It's so odd," Ned said, "for North Americans to think of a park with limited access."

"Yes," she said. "It *is* odd. They should be open to all." She opened her arms wide above her.

There were lime trees trained over a trellis, and she took Ned's arm, squiring him under an arched trellis with green vines trained on them. A fountain with jets of water coming out of a bit of pavement sat in the center of the square, and children in swimsuits splashed in it, crying out with delight when a jet spurted up and hit them.

And all of a sudden, Ned felt ready to drop. Cordelia didn't look one bit tired, but she must have noticed his fatigue because all at once they exited the park, and she hailed a black cab. "I do forget myself on these walking tours," she said. "I leave the visitors' legs just as bloodied stumps." Helena had given Ned some English cash to tide him over until he started work and insisted he should pay for everything he could. "Cordelia is poorer than a church-mouse." So, at the end of the ride, he managed to get a banknote to the cabbie before she did.

And then it all went blank, that day, his first in London. He went for what he thought would be a brief lie-down on his bed, and didn't wake up until the following afternoon.

When he emerged, Cordelia was napping in the sunlight in a caftan, with Bazarov on her chest, the animal going up and down as she breathed, casting an inscrutable but by no means hostile look at Ned, the Grand Pasha of this particular Kingdom. From an old wireless set at low volume, the BBC announced the arrest of 13 suspects in the Brighton Hotel Bombing, with a spokesman for Margaret Thatcher voicing the Prime Minister's firm intention to bring the IRA terrorists to justice. Cordelia cracked her eyes open, and gestured Ned to a nearby armchair.

"I thought I'd cook for us," Ned said. "Mum said you wouldn't mind."

"Mind? I'm delighted. You saw the extent of my abilities yesterday."

"Something simple," Ned proposed. "Maybe some chicken *piccata*?"

"Divine," she said. "I love lemony food. I'm having a lazy day. I find, with guests, I rise to the occasion on Day One, and then after that, I sink down, and it becomes rather catch-as-catch-can." About half of her sentences had the gentling modifier "rather" in them.

It was a simple pleasure finding provisions that afternoon, going to the greengrocer, the cheese monger, the butcher, introducing himself—all of them knew and liked his aunt, brightening when he mentioned her name. He asked if there was a balance on her account. They shook their heads, but changed their answer, when he said only his mother had given him some money to settle them.

At dinner, she flattered him by gobbling down her food, her gluttony not at all feigned. The plan was he'd live with her for a few weeks, perhaps a month at the outside, until his cousin Sophie and he could find a flat of their own. They talked about their shared fondness for Sophie— "she's a harum-skarum girl," Cordelia said, "I do wonder what will happen to her." He asked her about some of the authors on her shelves he hadn't heard of. Just as the past interested him more than the future, he found the company of the old, as a rule, both easier and more interesting than that of people his own age. Where would he look for solace, for perspective when he himself grew old?

In high school, he'd had Cameron protecting him, helping him to navigate with his contemporaries, and in University, Daniel usually did that same job. He'd have to fend for himself here.

There were discoveries to be made in the flat: a cockroach colony in Ned's bathroom (cuter in a joke than in reality, though they largely minded their own business), shelves of playbills from dramas past (an invitation to the opening night of *Look Back in Anger*), a gun used by Cordelia's husband when he fought, on the communist side, in the Spanish Civil War. Over all of it, all these remembrances of times past, was the dust that comes down from the cosmos and showers itself over all.

...

It is impossible he could have had a better introduction to that ancient capital, the seat, for a time, of the largest empire the world has yet seen. Two days in, he might have flown back to Toronto and still taken away a sense of London, some intimations, at least, of the city he'd come to find.

One afternoon early on, when he'd forgotten Helena's *A to Zed* at home, he got lost near Covent Garden and standing by a mysterious monument, sundials high up on a column, he thought he might not be able to locate this place again, and so he had better focus on it. He stood there, in that place, in that moment, and took it all in.

The novelty of the city at first displaced all else—the new sights, sounds and smells, the people, the accents, the noises, the vocabulary. The sudden shifts from fancy neighborhoods to rough ones. Always, the cars coming at him from the wrong direction, the step into the street and the jump back, a horn blaring at him.

Eros beckoned to him from its pedestal in Piccadilly Circus. The main city magazine had a section on Gay Clubs, which he looked at, trying to figure out which one he'd try first. But shame still held the upper hand in its battle with desire. So he went, instead, to art exhibits (The Preraphaelites) and talks (Virginia Woolf's London), to plays (*Lettuce & Lovage, Cats!*) and guided tours of Christopher Wren churches. He noticed all the city's handsome men, but he didn't approach them.

But, periodically, a sense of dread, of impending cataclysm, stopped him in his explorations. He would have to tell them.

He went for a drink with a cousin who worked at the House of Commons, for the Liberal Democrats—occupying what his father had called the lonely middle, between the Tories and Labour. Tom was the son of the man who'd introduced his parents, Uncle Miles, a rugby teammate of Oliver's. As Ned looked down from the gallery, Thatcher gave a speech about her government's decision to close 25 unprofitable coal mines, over the union's objections. Each of its general arguments she backed up with three facts, no less, no more. A formidable woman. The rowdiness of that famous chamber—the way they heckled each other, it was far less decorous than he'd imagined it would be, reminding him more of Trinity's dining hall than the seat of one of the world's oldest democracies. It was easier to like her when she was attacking the IRA than when she went after the coal miners, her own countrymen, Ned thought. She intrigued him as a human, even with her cruel streak.

Sophie came into town, bearing an extra floor ticket to Live Aid, the concert raising funds for victims of the famine in Ethiopia. She and he danced hard to it—they both liked to dance, each throwing a set of moves to the other, which the other would mimic but then throw something new back. The euphoria he felt in her company as Freddie Mercury strutted on the stage, to the beat of the deep bass groove of a song, voicing Ned's desire from up there:

I want to break free.
I want to break free...
O, how I want to be free.

His first day of work arrived, and he borrowed an old bike of Cordelia's, and took a more direct version of the route they'd walked his first day. He made sure to pass by one of the bars mentioned in the magazine: Brief Encounter, named for an old movie. One night, after he'd told his parents, he'd muster enough courage to go in.

The firm was named for its principal, the voluble second son of an Earl. He published many Canadian authors whose work Ned knew. Ned's professor, in his letter of introduction, had mentioned that Ned was savvy with computers and Ned soon realized that it was this, not his knowledge of Canadian literature, that had landed him the job. The publisher wanted Ned to teach him how to make the blasted word processor do his bidding, and to do so discreetly, so as not to expose his ignorance to the rest of the small staff—who, of course, all knew. Ned's other duties were less critical, but of greater interest to him. He'd get his share of the manuscripts that came in every week to read through, and early on in his stint, the slush pile of old, as-yet-unreviewed manuscripts, came his way—a colleague wheeled several banker's boxes into his office and deposited them in front of his desk.

He pushed through these relentlessly, authorized to send out curt rejections and some letters that declined the honor, but encouraged the author to keep in touch, to try again. When a manuscript showed more promise, he'd move it to a tray on his boss's desk, with a note as to what was alive, what, for all its flaws, was striking about the project.

The publisher often took Ned along to meetings, and Ned met the latest John Murray, whose antecedent of the same name had published Jane Austen. In the marble-floored reception, there was a bust of Byron whose work they'd also printed—an object of veneration, no longer mad, bad and dangerous to know. How he'd have hated this, greeting and dismissing all the house's visitors. Ned took notes of a meeting with the spy fiction writer John Le Carré—or the man whose pen-name was that—and sat in on the tea the publisher offered to Iris Murdoch. These would not have thrilled an individual less bookish than Ned, but they did him—these were the celebrities who mattered to him.

He was closer to where he wanted to be. It was adjacent to writing, but it had some quantifiable goals to it—there were sales targets to achieve, accounts to balance, copy to clean up, author tours to arrange. The pay, though, was poor—and London was expensive. Over her tepid objections, he'd insisted on paying Cordelia the market rate for a share of a flat in Chelsea, and it ate up the bulk of his salary. Still, there was enough room in his personal budget for a few books, and many days, after work, he'd stop at the bookstores on and just off Charing Cross Road—an evening of reading after a day of it. Bliss.

In one of the stalls, he found a biography of Robbie Ross, Oscar Wilde's great friend, his uncle a few generations back. He raced through it, hoping for tips about how he might handle it, but the author was too delicate to speak much of Ross's sexuality. And he visited some of the spots associated with Robbie—the Cafe Royal, the site of the Cadogan Hotel, where Ross had given Wilde the good advice that he should flee abroad to avoid prosecution.

On one of his wanders through the City of London, a group of three teens, all of them shorter than him, surrounding him, told him he had to give them his messenger bag. It had his diary in it. He refused. One of them hit him in the belly, another jumped up and punched him in the face. The third grabbed the bag and ripped it off Ned's shoulder. This enraged him and he started to fight back with everything he had. Not only was he able to fight them off, but he got the bag back, chasing the one who had it, until the guy dropped it. When he thought of it later, it was if he'd gone into a fugue. He knew you were supposed to let thieves take what you had, lest you end up injured, maimed or dead. But something outside him had taken him over.

As his parents' visit approached, his ability to sleep deserted him. It was a hot summer, and the flat had no fans, no air-conditioning. It was so dry that the lawns in the parks turned yellow. He also couldn't feel much that was green within him. He felt old—or what he imagined it felt like to be old. A voice in him rose, something he'd faced in his tennis matches, a sort of harsh critique of his shots, that became global. In an old guide they'd had to the psychological aspects of the game, the writer-coach spoke of the divided self, one the player, the other the critic, and how harmful it could be to one's play. But, though Ned could often ignore that voice on the court, he found it ascending in his life, taking charge, its dictums feeling authoritative.

Cordelia asked Ned several times what was wrong, but he put her off.

To make it impossible, or at any rate, difficult, for him to back away from telling his parents again, he wrote Henry a short letter telling him what—who—he was. Once it was in the mailbox, the post-box, how he wanted it back, but it was no use, it was on its way, across the Atlantic, ready to tell all—or tell much at least.

…

The plan for Helena and Oliver's trip to England was that they would spend a couple of days with Ned in London, first, then go on visits to the family—her brother Miles lived in Surrey, her sister Felicity in Dorset, her father, Ned's grandfather, with his second wife, in Somerset— and that then they'd return to London, for a last couple of days with their son.

Ned thought he'd have some time alone with them, but each time he met up with his parents, he found the party augmented by this or that cousin or an old and dear friend. He'd show up at Fortnum & Mason, his speech prepared, and there was his Aunt Felicity, in for a day of shopping. Aunt Cordelia came to a dinner at a hotel in Mayfair. They'd go to the museum made of the architect Sir John Soane's house on Lincoln's Inn Fields, and a friend of Helena's from her schooldays would tag along for the tour, and then gave them lunch afterwards in a City wine bar. He asked them specially to keep their last evening free, after they returned to London, but when he got to the restaurant, an Indian restaurant in Chelsea, Ned found his cousin (and future flatmate) Sophie was there.

“I thought I'd come in to town for a few days, to see that flat you mentioned,” she said. “I thought you'd be happy at the surprise.”

“I am,” Ned said. “Just it was… No, it's good to see you.”

He described the flat he'd scouted out for them in Islington, a Georgian house with a red door, with rooms enough for Sophie and Ned and one other, and a nice rose-filled back garden. “It has Athena in the knocker. The Goddess. In brass. A bust.” He said the owners might be willing to show it to them again over the weekend. They were, Ned explained, a young couple moving to Paris for a year so the husband could study at INSEAD.

Sophie was two years younger than Ned. She had a long nose, curly brown hair, and was slender but had what his mother called “a good figure”. The clothes she made herself suited her angular form. A portfolio with photos and drawings of them, and a finished garment or two, had landed her a place at St. Martin's, the art and design College in the heart of the West End. She was the cousin Ned knew best because she'd visited them in Canada. They'd had long late-night car-rides where much was discussed, many cigarettes smoked. Oliver had led them on a canoe trip down the French River where she'd lost her camera in some rapids—her camera but not her high spirits.

She spent most of the meal detailing a difficult break-up, not sparing them any gory detail. All the while, Ned's agitation grew. “He gave me a little glass vase at the end,” she said. “An antique, with a stopper in it. He told me it was what sailors gave their lovers to store their tears in when they sailed away. Can you believe it?”

“That's the limit,” Helena said. “I hope we've seen the last of him.”

Helena spoke of dropping Henry off at Dartmouth, before his hike through the Presidential range in New Hampshire's White Mountains. “It's quite something, the campus,” she said. “This Library that looks like Independence Hall.”

The Voice in him spoke up: *This is going to break them, your parents. Why not just keep quiet?*

Oliver said he'd heard from his brother Max, that he'd hired on Ned's old friend Cameron. "Seems quite pleased with him, as well he might." He asked Ned how he was settling in. Fine, Ned said, liking the work, enjoying staying with Cordelia.

When Sophie went to the W.C., Oliver leaned in and asked him if he was okay for money. He told him yes.

There was an elephant's head woven from rattan above their table. Ned imagined it trumpeting out an alarm. He saw Sophie coming towards the table, and Ned asked quickly if he might drive with them back to the place they were staying. There was something he wanted to tell them.
"Words to make the heart sink," Helena said. "Why not tell us now?"

Sophie sat down and Ned shook his head no. At last, the meal was over, and they put Sophie into a taxi so that she could go on to a party. Oliver and Helena got in the front of the rented Vauxhall, and Ned sat in the back, taking out the *A to Zed*, to help them traverse London, from Chelsea to the edge of the City, to get to the house they had rented. It was a National Trust property, one of the only houses to survive the Great Fire of London.

His mother filled the silence.

"'When a man is bored of London, he is bored with life.' We were always within striking distance of London—the morning train would get us in for the day—but like most country people we seldom came in. When we did come in, we stuck to our rounds, to the devils we knew: Liberty's, the Army & Navy, Heal's. Of course, the Blitz had leveled so much of it."

"You were hardly bumpkins," Oliver said.

Londoners had survived the Great Fire, had come through the Blitz, why couldn't he find his way to speak of this?

For God's sake, if you must foist this on them, out with it.

Helena carried on. "We seldom came in to the city—it seemed daunting somehow. Samuel Johnson, the bored line, not mine."

"I know. I know it was Samuel Johnson. Remember the English degree you helped pay for?" This evidently jarred, because there was a brief pause. Oliver was doing well, navigating the roundabouts and tunnels and zebra crossings of the English capital, not calling on Ned for assistance often.

"How much better," Ned said, "is 'zebra crossing' than the very pedestrian 'pedestrian crossing'?"

No one could do much with that. Ned directed his father through a few consecutive turns.

He pushed his fingernails deep into the rental car's dark blue leatherette seats. They swung past Cleopatra's needle, and swooped along the Embankment, swags of fairy lights festooned along the edge of the Thames. How cheery, he thought. He directed his father to push northward, away from the river.

This time it was Oliver who minded the gap in the conversation.

"This was before you were born, Ned," Oliver said. "When your mother first brought me over, and we came to see Cordelia. When we walked down her street, at the appointed time, we looked up and there she was cleaning the windows in her petticoats. I wasn't sure quite what to say when I met her, so I made the mistake of admiring one of her paintings."

"A print," Helena said, "an illustration for Hogarth's *The Rake's Progress*."

"And she took it from the wall and gave it to me."

"There's still a gap on the walls where it was, still the outline, the ghost of it there," Ned said.

Silence descended on them again.

Helena finally turned towards Ned. "What is it? You're not yourself."

He began, "When I dream sometimes I have no hands. I don't really… sometimes I think of what it would be like to be gone. I know that's wrong, I never would. It's just I'm—"

"What in the hell are you talking about?" Oliver said, turning his head back to look at Ned. By then, they'd reached Oxford Street and were passing in front of Debenhams, the old department store.

"Oliver," Helena screamed—a black Audi coupe had pulled from a side street in front of them. Oliver turned back, but found the accelerator not the brake. The other car got bigger quickly—and, one beat, two beats, WHAM. Their bodies hurtled forward, then were jerked backwards by their seatbelts.

After a few moments, Oliver said, "Is everyone ok?" Helena nodded.

"I'm gay," Ned said. "I've always been gay." The collision had jarred his confession loose. He couldn't believe he'd just blurted it out.

"O God," Helena said. "Just let your father deal with this."

Oliver got out and exchanged insurance details with the driver. The man's Audi had a big dent in its side and the Vauxhall's hood, its bonnet, had wrinkled upwards. Ned opened his window and heard Oliver taking responsibility for the accident. "I looked backwards. My son. He's just… Not your fault at all… Are you all okay? I am so very sorry. These are the insurance details… I have a pen, yes… This is my card should there be any problems… I do apologize."

Helena and Ned didn't speak in the interim. He could see her trembling hand, but he didn't reach forward to hold it. He didn't cry. He just sat there numb and silent. He had done it, but what now?

"Are you sure?" Helena finally said, without turning.

Oliver got back in the car. "Sorry," he said. "We've exchanged information. The insurers will deal with it. You shocked me, Ned. Can you be sure that you are…?" Oliver turned around to face Ned when he put the question.

"That's what I asked," Helena said, laying her hand on Oliver's. It was rare, such a display of solidarity.

"Gay," Ned repeated. "Yes, I am. Gay, I am gay." Each time he said the word, it depleted his reserves. "I've always, always known it."

Oliver started up the car, and drove a couple of blocks, exiting the arterial road for a side street, and found a place to park near Soho Square.

"I think you should stay over at this house tonight," Helena said, finally looking back at him. "I've been so worried about you. I knew something wasn't right. I told you so, didn't I, Oliver? You should see someone, talk to someone. Miles can recommend someone." Her brother was a doctor. "People can—people have changed. It just seems—" She lost her train of thought. "It seems to let you in for more of a tough time. And what about AIDS?"

Oliver didn't like that question. "Ned knows how to look after himself," he said.

"Does he?" she said. "Do you?"

Ned didn't know the answer to this question.

Helena continued on, "I just think it, being homosexual…" She got the word out with difficulty, but soldiered on. "They have such hard, lonely lives."

"It's not 'them', it's me," Ned said.

Somehow he had suspected that his mother, for all her liberal views on women's issues and politics, for all her peals of laughter at *The Woman of No Importance*, would have a hard time with his homosexuality. Still, he needed her approval.

"We love you, of course," Helena was saying. "We'll always love you. But why would you choose that life, Ned?"

"It's not a choice for most people, Mum. Believe me, if I had to choose, I wouldn't choose it." This didn't feel quite right. It felt too deep in Ned for him to imagine himself without it there. And so, to choose against it was to be somehow not Ned, someone else.

"It is a choice, everything's a choice," Helena said. "The Greeks did both, had wives and male lovers. You marry, make an agreement—and that way you can have children." It occurred to Ned that this was not the thought of someone truly taken by surprise. This was an argument that had been nurtured, either consciously or subconsciously, readied against this day.

"Maybe for some people it's a choice. For me, it's not."

"How could you tell us now, in this way, as we're about to head off tomorrow, just after a car crash? Of all the awful things… Do we deserve this?"

"No, you don't," Ned said. "I'm so sorry. I saw the car coning towards us, we hit it, and then it just came out. But there was never going to be a good time. And anyway, what on earth did you think I was going to grow up to be, the kid who'd play musicals non-stop on the record player. Who cooked with an apron on?"

"You got less… like that in high school."

"Yes," he said, "Because I was hiding. Because I figured out what it meant. I thought I was always one gesture away from exposing myself, that one wrong word would give me away, one inadvertent glance in the wrong direction. I tried to hide that away, to crush it. And I did try to change."

"Would that you'd succeeded in that," Helena said.

"That's not… that's not..." Ned couldn't find the words to object to this. "I don't want to lie. I want to stop lying."

"We don't know anyone like this—we don't. It all seems so… beyond the pale. Maybe you read something about it, and that made you think this?"

"It's late," Oliver said. "Let's get back. We can talk things over in the morning. You mustn't—I don't—you must not take your own life. That dream was leading you astray. I would—I would not recover."

"I would kill you if you did that," Helena said.

They smiled a little at each other—not a lot, but a little.

With Ned's occasional guidance, Oliver drove the rest of the route, along High Holborn, past the sculptures of winged lions, over the Viaduct and into the old City of London. He parked the now battered vehicle next to the house they'd rented. Nearby was an old covered market, and some men were unloading vegetables from their trucks, their lorries. Ned and his parents shambled up the crooked, winding staircases of the old half-timbered house. Oliver offered them all a nightcap, but Ned had no further discussion in him.

Helena massaged her neck. “I wonder if I have whiplash. I don't think so. Will you come see us off, tomorrow?”

Ned agreed to come to Heathrow with them.

…

The next morning, they dropped the car at the rental agency near Heathrow. Oliver gave them a thorough accident report, while Helena and Ned sat silently nearby, her seething but trying not to, Ned scared. “Just think how your father must feel,” Helena said on the shuttle to the airport.

“I’m fine, Helena. I just want Ned to be careful. Of himself, and his health.”

They checked their bags in. They reached the barrier.

“We love you, you know,” she said, as if Ned had raised doubts on that head. Again she couldn’t bring herself to utter those three little words, “I love you.” “We love you” was a long distance from “I love you.”

It may not seem like much in the catalogue of mean remarks, but her next comment stung. “It's just, Ned, I don't recognize you. You’ve changed.”

In a soft voice, he sang a snatch of a song to her: “‘Say, don’t you know me? I’m your native son.’” It was from an Arlo Guthrie song they'd all loved, his “City of New Orleans”. Surely this would elicit a smile from her, some acknowledgement of the years they'd spent together. Startled, she looked at Ned, really looked at him. It was like he had taken something of hers and she now wanted it back.

“Well,” she said with a false, little laugh, her eyes closed. “Maybe at least you’ve got some material for a short story.” She had high ambitions for each of them. She opened her eyes again, but they were no longer available to him.

Helena evidently had something more to say, because she held up one hand while rummaging through her purse with the other. Things were always going rogue in her purse. She looked up, some triumph in her face at having located her passport, which she held up. But her face darkened again.

"I know this wasn't what you wanted," she said. "I'm sure you wanted me to say, good for you, homosexuality is great, hip, hip, hooray, go with God. But I'm your mother and I'm going to tell you what I see, even if you don't like it. Even if I don't like it. And I don't, not one little bit. All I can see right now is the waste, the terrible waste of it all."

He gave his father the book he'd brought for them, Christopher Isherwood's *The World in Evening.* The title was a translation of a Berlin communist newspaper published in the run-up to the war. "Right, we'll read this."

"He was a friend of Virginia Woolf's," Ned said.

"I ruddy well know who he was," Helena said.

And with that they were gone. For a long time, he stood at the barrier, not sure what to do. He hadn't expected she'd go at him, as she had. Was it anger with him, or was she ashamed of herself for having brought up such a son? Maybe he'd kept her at a distance for too long. Maybe if he'd reached for her hand early on; maybe if he'd broken down. Maybe this would have made a difference, maybe that.

He knew her almost as well, he thought, as he knew himself. She wanted the best for him, not just as a stage mother wants a starring role for her little wonder. She didn't want to see him suffer, and for her homosexuality necessarily entailed suffering. For her, a man succeeded when he earned the following: respect in a reputable field, a worthy wife, and loyal, loving children. In that order. He was jeopardizing his chances of obtaining his due from life. These were her values: he was her son, so he'd absorbed them. A large part of him agreed with all of her objections. But what could he do?

Why couldn't he find the sweet release to be found in a big cry? Boys don't cry. He and his mother had cried together once, when he was leaving his middle school, moving to Appleby. His teacher told his mother how fond he was of Ned. Then the principal had come out, he said, to find them, to say much the same thing. From the Lost-and-Found table, they collected all the things he had lost, things he had forgotten all about. He said goodbye to a couple of friends, both girls. And then, in the car, in the front seat, Ned started to weep—and she did, too. At the sadness of even necessary goodbyes, at the passing of time, at everything. Where was that woman now? Then, they didn't have to try to reach each other.

Swimming into his head came the illustration in his children's bible of Jacob clinging to the angel: *I will not let thee go except thou bless me.* He'd received no blessing. Why should he? It had gone just about as badly as it could have gone, but, still, it was done.

He boarded the subway, the tube, and slumped down in his seat. One of his grandmother's many injunctions came to him: don't slouch. He sat back up. His faculty for noticing the people around him was still operating, though the rest of him felt shut down. There were a few punks with spiked hair, nose rings, and studded leather jackets, and a couple in their thirties with lots of luggage. They sounded Australian.

He had no one here, not really, to whom he could speak of what had just happened. He looked like family to Cordelia, but they hadn't become intimates—his fault, he'd also kept her at a distance. His cousin Sophie he didn't know well, though what he knew he liked. He hadn't told her he was gay yet either. Daniel was a long way away, just starting at Yale, no doubt busy throwing himself at the new school and discipline.

He worried about his parents, his mother especially, but at least they had each other to talk to. The book he'd given them wasn't great, but he'd read through some of the manuals to coming out that he'd found at Toronto's gay bookstore, and the writing was likely to turn off his literate parents, the cheerleading tone to bother people skeptical of simple answers to complicated questions. Still, one of those manuals would have been better, something straightforward. The title of Isherwood's book had spoken to him. Ned felt he was leaving the daylight behind, the many sunny hours of his childhood, entering a twilight world... Soon it would be night.

A handsome guy boarded the train, about Ned's age and height, but dark-haired, bearded, and barrel-chested. The guy, the bloke was smiling at Ned, but Ned did not have anything to offer in return. Still, it was something.

He was in London, a city he'd read about his whole life, and, certainly, he did not intend to be bored.

He could feel the train jerking about, and the cadence of the song they'd all loved flowed into him, slow, stately like the train it celebrated, the train named 'The City of New Orleans'. All of them in that room, that lovely yellow room that his mother had filled with her oddities, her carpet bowls, her glass insulators, her needlework, her music, all of them doing their different things, all of them in that rickety old house they'd together made into a home.

Good morning, America,
How are you?
Say don't you know me
I'm your native son.
I'm the train they call the City of New Orleans.
I'll be gone 500 miles when the day is done.

It was too late. He was crying.

Chapter 5:
This Is London

The day after his parents left, Ned made dinner for himself and his aunt Cordelia—chicken roasted with fennel, carrots and potatoes alongside. Cordelia dug in with her customary gusto. After she polished it off, she put both her hands on either side of her plate, flat on the small card table where they ate, and asked, “Did you tell them?”

“Tell them what?”

“You know very well what.”

“Yes,” he said. “Yes, I did.”

“And how did it go?”

“Not well,” he said. “My Mum, Helena, she wants me to try to change it. If I can. Which I can't.”

“Yes, I wondered if she might take a hard line on it. I am, perhaps, a little to blame for that.”

Ned was puzzled by this. “You see,” she continued, “My husband didn't die. Or he didn't die until later. He left me first, for a man. A friend of his, of ours, someone we both knew at Cambridge. Something of a reprobate. I didn't mind him being a reprobate, but he soaked up whatever money was near him—and that I did come to mind. My Charlie knew he didn't have long to live, and he said, he wanted to spend his last few months with his love, the great love of his life.”

There was so much suffering in what Cordelia said, distilled into just a few phrases. It came into Ned, causing him to shudder. “I don't… I'm sorry.”

"Do you know? I'm not, in a way," she said. "I mean he could have behaved better, but… well, so could we all."

"I didn't know that, any of that."

"My sister, your grandmother, her children, Helena, Miles, my daughters, everyone blamed him. And certainly I did at first. And, with the times, everyone decided it was for the best if we didn't speak of it. And then he died, so why would we? In the end, I thought, well it wasn't me—I did my best. And we did love each other—quite dearly. He told me so as he lay dying. Oh, Ned, sometimes… what can you do? It's not in your hands. So that was probably in Helena's mind. I am sorry about that."

"This, this is not your fault."

The autumn came and it was time for Ned to leave. The lease of his first own place was starting, but he was surprised at how sad he was. Cordelia drove Ned and his bags, careening across London in her 2CV, from Chelsea to Islington, pointing out the sights, often with neither of her hands on the wheel. The cousins' rented house was Georgian, part of a row of them, fronted by a salmon-colored door, with, as Ned had told his cousin, a brass knocker with a bust of Athena on it. A rose climbed up the railing out front, and there were more roses out back. Further back still, over a wall, sat an empty Victorian factory, where Ned would, he thought, go to read, or to play his violin sometimes.

Moments after they pulled up, Sophie threw open the door and beckoned them both in. When they'd got his bags in the door, he came back to say goodbye to Cordelia.

Next to the car, she gave him a framed photo of her sister, Ned's grandmother Mathilda, with a young Cordelia. In this photo especially, he could see something of himself in his grandmother, but it was Cordelia who shone in the shot.

"You won't forget about me, now will you?" Cordelia said to him.

"I won't. You have been… manna in the desert."

"That's rather a pretty thing to say. Though it was you who fed me, not vice versa. How much Mathilda would have liked you. Though you're dreadfully earnest. She might have teased you some—she did that to the people she liked."

He got his bed made, his clothes into a dresser, his books into a shelf, and set up the boombox he'd bought to play cassettes. On top of a short bookshelf, leaning back against the wall, he put a parting gift from his mother, the picture book *This is London*, one of the many books that she and their father had read to Ned at bedtime.

That evening, he shared drinks at the local pub with Sophie and their third roommate, Alistair, a short and ambitious young architect who was a graduate of one of the country's more prestigious public schools, and more than a little high on himself, Ned thought.

…

About midway through the autumn, Ned decided he felt ready—or ready enough, curious enough—to go out to his first gay club. The prospect both excited and scared him. At a newsagents shop on Islington's high street, its main drag, he picked up a fresh issue of a city magazine. Perhaps a guy who'd been through what he had might be found at the club for older gay gentlemen listed in the gay section. It was just off Leicester Square, in the heart of the West End, where he often went to see plays. He took a double-decker bus there, wishing it would both hurry up and never arrive—he thought about stepping off it, midway through the trip, but stayed on, watching the capital, then being pelted by rain, pass before him.

The club's entry was not marked, and he had to climb a staircase to the second story. He flapped his umbrella on the stairs and wrapped it up. The place was cozy, with theatre posters hung up, an oriental-pattern wall-to-wall on the floor, and a vocalist new to Ned singing a sad song:

Good times for a change
See, the luck I've had
Can make a good man
Turn bad.

So please, please, please
Let me, let me, let me
Let me get what I want
This time
Lord knows, it would be the first time.

He swallowed and approached the crowded bar. After all his struggles to get himself to go into a gay bar, no one seemed to notice his arrival. At first, anyway.

He got himself a G&T and lit up a Silk Cut on a barstool between two older men. He got to talking with the guy named Jeremy on his right, a tall, burly accountant with crooked teeth, maybe on the other side of 40, maybe a little older than that. Ned had never been good at estimating people's age. Three drinks in, Ned admitted that he'd been struggling a bit, that he'd come out to his parents in the fall and they hadn't exactly broken out in applause. "My Mum told me I should try to change, try to become straight."

The bald guy on his left piped up. "That's tricky, darling. Maybe they'll come around."

"Who asked you?" Jeremy said.

"Well, pardon me," the bald guy said. "I'll leave you to it."

Jeremy turned back to Ned. "You want to be careful of her. That one is a tramp."

"I can hear you, Jeremy."

Jeremy leaned in to Ned. "What's been going on? I'm a good listener… Talk to your uncle Jeremy."

Ned unfolded his story. It turned out they had certain things in common—Jeremy's father also had been supportive, his mother less so. It had been, of course, some time ago, but he'd also moved away from his family home, outside of Manchester, and also told them when they visited him in London, albeit a decade after he moved away—"I couldn't do it at home, I knew they'd throw me out." His story was a little more like the one Jimmy Somerville sang of, a lower-class kid, taking the train away from home.

"I shouldn't have spoken to them about this dream I have," Ned said. "About cutting off my hands, letting everything bleed out."

"Yes," Jeremy said. "Maybe that was best left unsaid."

"Maybe I should have waited, until I was ready, more confident. When I could comfort them some."

"Water under the bridge," he said.

"Yes, I should have waited."

"Spilt milk." One cliché after another seemed to come from this guy.

"You're skinny," Jeremy said.

"Svelte," Ned said. "Aerodynamic. Wiry. Lean. Sporty. Take your pick, but not skinny, please."

"Are you a sportsman?"

"Not organized sports, but I do love tennis. I've been cycling around the city. If I can remember the left-hand side of the road, that is fun. And sometimes I jog across Hampstead Heath."

"I bet you do," Jeremy said. "Yes, well, there's certainly lots to do and see there." He raised his eyebrows suggestively, and Ned realized that it must be well known as a cruising spot. "You don't have it, do you? That's not why you're so thin—so svelte."

"It?"

"AIDS."

"I've not yet had sex, so no, I don't have it."

They both laughed awkwardly.

"It's just, you seem so upset, so I thought maybe that was something worrying you, too. So many people do these days. I've lost a few friends already, more are going down with it. We thought it was an American thing at first—that we'd not get it. But enough of us have gone over there..."

They moved on to Madame Jojo's for a drag show. Ned was fascinated by these people, part male, part female, all performer. As a child, he'd wondered if he was part girl, if that explained his difference. In the schoolyard, when the game was Boys After Girls, he'd felt torn; the activities he liked to do, to skip rope, to make cakes in the sandbox, those were 'girlish' things to do. Once, one of the girls had tossed him from the box.

He hadn't felt that way, though, like a girl. He didn't feel he fit easily on either side of the ledger.

At this, his first drag show, he let it all wash over him, the jeers from the crowd, the repartee, the songs, the big people in high heels. One of them trilled her way through an opera aria. Another, with muscular arms poking out of a shimmering sleeveless dress, channeled the English lounge singer Shirley Bassey, delivering one of her greatest hits "Diamonds are Forever". Ned knew the song but not its originator—he presumed the performer's mannerisms, the splayed fingers carving the air, were derived from the original.

This performer reminded him of one of his mother's friends, a former Broadway actress who'd ended up in Oakville. In New York, she'd been in the chorus—in Oakville, she was a star. Among Helena's friends, Louella was second only to Georgia in Ned's affections. She was the main reason, some said the only reason, to go each year to the Oakville Club's Cabaret. On a makeshift stage set up on the badminton courts, she'd serve up, with gusto, a medley of show-tunes, new and old. A smile played over Ned's face, as he remembered her, poured into a black leotard, singing away, "Tits and ass, bought myself a fancy pair, tightened up the derriere."

"What is it?" Jeremy said. "Something funny?"

Ned didn't feel like telling Jeremy about Louella, so he ducked the question.

A guy Ned's age sat down next to him. He began to talk at Ned, but Ned couldn't hear him well, and anyway, was drunk enough that taking new information on board wasn't easy. The man had blonde cropped hair, with brown spots in it, and a leather band studded with pointed bits of metal on his wrist. He spoke some of his work, and Ned heard him say that he worked in the theatre. Ned felt he had something he could grasp onto, and spoke of the plays he'd liked, those he hadn't. The man didn't respond to any of his comments, at last saying, "You are an idiot or you're too far gone. I work in an operating theatre. I'm a nurse. I was telling you how we lost one in the operating theatre today."

Ned laughed at his error, but the guy didn't, getting up and pushing off.

"I just couldn't hear him," Ned said.

"Never mind," Jeremy said. "He looked some sort of punk. That hair—it's a look, I'll tell you. You, you're nice… and tidy. You have respect. Makes for a change from the others your age."

When the show ended, Jeremy said, "I have a flat right on the Thames—in Chelsea. It seems a shame to draw this evening to a close, don't you think?" He, too, seemed nice, or nice enough. Tidy. His cologne smelled a bit sleazy, but that was okay, Ned had no intention of getting any closer to Jeremy. If you assumed the best of people and showed them that, it was surprising how often they lived up to those assumptions. That was his mother's belief anyway.

"Chelsea," Ned said. "Where Oscar Wilde lived in his House Beautiful on Cheyne Walk."

"My building is right on Cheyne Walk," he said. "Overlooking the Thames."

Ned was drunk and boasted of his slight connection to Wilde. "This uncle several generations back, Robbie Ross, he lodged with Wilde, while cramming for Cambridge… and they became lovers."

"How scandalous. Let's have a nightcap there then? Maybe I'll ask my neighbors up. They're quite fun."

The prospect of Jeremy involving the neighbors made the invitation more appealing to Ned. In Toronto, wherever you went, it was generally easy enough to get back home. Ned was still coming to grips with London's sprawl. The raindrops on the windows of the cab blurred the colored lights streaming by outside.

Up the front of the nautical deco apartment house, lit dramatically by spotlight, was the largest wisteria Ned had ever seen, its purple flowers mainly having transformed into pods by this time of year. The vine climbed up five stories, and so did they, to Jeremy's penthouse flat. Jeremy mixed Ned another drink.

"I shouldn't," Ned said, as he tipped some of the strong drink into his mouth. "But I will."

"Are your neighbors coming?"

"I'll call them." Jeremy picked up a phone from a nearby table, and dialed a number. "No reply. Just us, then. I'll go get us some nibbles, shall I?"

As Jeremy did so, Ned admired the old London Underground advertisements on the wall. He hadn't yet seen them everywhere. He didn't know they were something of a visual cliché.

Jeremy set a cheese-plate down on a coffee table in front of Ned. Ned's head began to spin—and then Jeremy was on top of him.

"This isn't," Ned said. "I just wanted… I'm not. I've never been out before."

"This a good sign," Jeremy said, putting his elbows on either side of Ned's head, but not moving off of him. "Playing hard to get. It's good."

Ned pushed up, trying to dislodge Jeremy, but he was heavy. "It's your first time," Jeremy said. "I'll be gentle."

Jeremy took Ned's hand and put it on the pulsing bulge below his belt. "I'm pretty sure this is what you wanted. This is why you've been flirting with me the whole evening, letting me buy you drinks. Letting me pay the cover at Madame Jojo's."

"No, no," Ned tried, but failed, to slide out from under Jeremy. And here Jeremy had been adding up his outlay the whole evening, hoping to get a good return on his investment.

Jeremy spoke quietly to Ned, but again, though Ned was squirming underneath him, made no effort to get off. "Just relax. Lie back. You're in good hands. Let yourself enjoy the ride." He put his hands on Ned's belt, trying to loosen it. Ned put his hand on Jeremy's to stop him.

Jeremy took a hold of Ned's hand, returning it to his own crotch. "Here, feel it." Jeremy then undid his own belt, opened his zipper, and pulled his cock out. He used the back of the sofa to push himself up even higher on Ned, and move the pulsing thing, its head emerging from the foreskin, towards Ned's mouth. "Taste it."

It smelled rank, of the many gin drinks he'd consumed. It was angry, the color of corned beef. It needed a wash.

"Oh, no, Sorry. I don't want that." Ned finally mustered enough force to push himself up and out from under, toppling Jeremy to the floor. Ned stood up. "Sorry. I didn't mean for you to... are you okay? Excuse me a moment." Why on earth was he apologizing? He walked towards the toilet, but he didn't make it. He bent over and threw up. He looked up and there was Jeremy, his cock again in Ned's face.

"No," Ned said. "I told you I don't want that."

"Even so, that is what you're going to have."

He only saw the fist coming from above at the last moment, just enough time to turn his head sideways. Jeremy's blow glanced off Ned's temple and the corner of his signet ring cut into his skin, drawing some blood. "Think you can treat me this way? Tease me like that? You've got the wrong guy. Now suck my cock. Blondie."

A ferocious clarity came over Ned, the same mood that had possessed him in that long-ago tennis match that Cameron had seen. He pushed himself upwards with one hand and with the other arm slugged Jeremy hard in the gut, hard enough to penetrate the guy's slight paunch. Jeremy was stunned, and then Ned, now almost standing, hit him again, this time in the face, and then pushed him hard over the back of the sofa.

"Fuck you," Ned said. Like his mother, Ned hardly ever swore. He looked at his hand, felt it pulsing from the blows it had landed on Jeremy.

But then he felt a sudden panic at what he'd done. He needed to get out of there. He grabbed his coat from the arm of a chair.

From behind, he heard a different sort of voice from Jeremy, less proper than the one he'd been using all evening, the accent more provincial. "You fucking cunt. You go there looking for a Daddy, and when you land the best one in the place… you treat him, you treat me like this." What a repulsive man. Why had he spent a whole evening with him?

"I was looking for… a friend. Some advice."

"You'd best get out of here."

"Nothing would give me greater pleasure."

After some struggle, he figured out how to release the deadbolt. The night air by the Thames was blessedly cool. The rain was still bucketing down, and he tasted the salt of his blood on the drops that washed down his face. He walked towards an arterial street nearby, and a cabbie decided to stop even when faced with the mess that was Ned.

"Am I ever glad you came along," Ned told the cabbie.

"You looked a bit the worse for wear, no mistake."

In the back seat, Ned faded in and out of consciousness, the cabbie looking in the mirror, back at him, hoping he wouldn't vomit. The smell of a pine air freshener did make the nausea rise in him again, but he was able to tamp it down. Everything in his stomach had already come up. He stuck his head out the window, and let the rain pelt him, sobering him up some.

Ned took stock. He should have purchased his own drinks. He had suspected the existence of that nasty voice, the "cunt" voice, lurking below the presentable one Jeremy had used all evening, but he'd ignored his suspicion.

A voice within him piped up.

Did you imagine that a complete stranger was going to offer you a shoulder to cry on? In exchange for what? And what were you doing there, what, really, were you up to?

He had barely enough cash to cover the taxi bill. In the mirror of their shared bathroom, he gave his wound a proper cleaning. He addressed himself, “All in all, I'd say you weren't exactly the debutante of the year.”

But the chipper tone of this voiced thought was false, and his face collapsed. There was a box inside him, full of terror, of insecurities, of vicious thoughts that darted about. He tried to keep it locked. But the lid was off now.

The man's sadness and anger were so palpable, and that had all come towards Ned. He wanted to fuck Ned, yes, but he also wanted revenge, to punish Ned for all his past hurts.

His mother's words: “They lead such unhappy lives.”

...

When Ned woke up the next day, his eyes hit on *This is London* in its perch atop his bookshelf. One of his favorite illustrations in it had been one of some gents at a civilized pub. Ned paged through to it. The illustration was as Ned had remembered it. “Children are not allowed inside a pub,” it read. “But peep in and see what's going on. The grown-ups are playing darts.”

He wasn't a child anymore. If he decided to do more than peep in, if he wanted to join in the games adults played with each other, he'd have to wise up.

When he replayed it in his head, he imagined that, as he exited, he'd held up a banknote, and said to Jeremy: "This is for your expenses." And then he'd dropped it on the floor. But it didn't happen that way.

He knew—everyone said—such things weren't your fault. But he was sure that it was. In the layer of himself beneath what you were supposed to say and think, Ned knew that he deserved what he got.

He felt within him a desire to dissipate all he had. He wanted to toss it all to the winds. To let himself go, to humiliate himself, not just to let himself be violated, but to seek out violation. Maybe that's what he had done this evening.

He wished he'd not agreed to come back for Christmas. He could have nursed himself in this little room, an animal licking its wounds in its den. Or would he have just gotten worse, spending a solitary holiday here?

He mustered what he had for the journey. He'd spent too much money and time on his presents, hoping they'd provide some sort of expiation for his sins. Sins he had yet to commit.

Down in their kitchen, he made himself some coffee, and his cousin came in in a puffy fuchsia robe, her hair piled up on her head, two bunny-rabbit slippers on her feet. "You look a wreck," Sophie said.

"And you look… super. Those bunnies?"

She tapped her feet up and down, and the long ears bounced up and down absurdly.

"How was it, last night?"

"A disaster," he said.

"Oh, gosh, you're all bruised and cut up." She put a hand near the cut on his temple and he winced. "Tell me all."

And he did. And that helped.

"We have to find you someone your own age," she said. "Why on earth did you go to that oldies' club? There's this fellow in my course from Guernsey—Jersey, anyway, one of those islands between England and France. But, no, he's too skinny. You can't have two skinnies. Someone needs something to hang onto. But, at least he won't—he wouldn't rough you up."

...

On the plane, he convinced a nice stewardess to supply him with several glasses of gin and tonic. He felt giddy for a bit. But then this sense of shame descended on him. He was vile. He wrote in his journal: "I have taken all the gifts Mom and Dad have given me and squandered them—worse, smashed them up right in front of them."

As a boy, he'd often found comfort in his home. It didn't seem likely to provide him a sanctuary from the ills of the outside world—instead, it had become an unsafe place. He'd spoken to his parents, written to Henry. That was enough for now. He decided he was not going to jeopardize his precarious position there with any further unwelcome words. Every word would be as well chosen as his gifts.

Chapter 6:
The Return Of The Native

Oliver met Ned on his own at the airport, which was not a good sign as far as his mother was concerned. Usually, they both came.

Once they'd got on their way, Oliver, at the wheel, said, "You know she would have come, but she's overwhelmed with the party this year. Her teaching ended later this year, and it's sort of come on us. You'll pitch in?"

"Of course," Ned said. "Don't I always? How's she doing, you know, with it all?"

"She's struggling a little. Just give her some time. She'll come around."

Oliver asked after Ned's work, and Ned asked after Oliver's. They spoke of books they were reading, Ned of a trip he hoped to take to Paris with Sophie. When they reached Oakville, Ned's eyes absorbed it in a new way. He'd always thought of the town as ultra-English, with its croquet pitches and Club, with its tidy houses looking like so many parsonages out of Austen. But a half-year in England made him realize how American it was in many ways: his mind found glib examples (its adoption of the cocktail hour, the big cars from Detroit circulating around, the evening gatherings in front of *Jeopardy*) but it went deeper. They'd also read Fitzgerald and Nathanael West in high school, along with Dickens and Austen.

The town was torn, like Canada, between its old master and its new one. He thought of something he wanted to write in his journal: "We belong to England during the day, our manners, our quietness, our ideals—from them. But at night, we slip across the border, over the lake, to consort with our sexy, wealthy powerful neighbor." He was still working it out, some sort of pop psychology contrast between England, the source of Anglo Canada's superego, and America, the base of its id. He'd write this all down in his journal. He intended to use his diary to help him get through the holiday—he'd have at least one full ally in the celebration, one confidante to whom he could speak, or at least write freely.

His grandmother's Mercedes was in the driveway. "Fritzie's come out already?"

"She's ensconced in her suite," Oliver said. Her suite was basically a bedroom and bathroom, ones with extra electric heaters she'd had put in, so she didn't freeze. "My American blood. It's thinner." Fritzie had come to Canada for the air with her ailing father—his lungs got weakened by gas in the First World War, and then he'd contracted tuberculosis afterwards. His life became one of seeking out healthy retreats, the only job he held after that was teaching bridge on cruise ships.

Fritzie met Chief at one of those retreats, at what was then the Seigneury Club, a grand old lodge not far from Montreal. Though they were both engaged to others, they'd thrown the others over and Fritzie had moved from just outside of New York to Toronto, making a life with Chief there, learning what passed muster, and what didn't in her adopted home. She'd even become a hockey fan, so as to please Chief, adopting his sad-sack Maple Leafs as her team, too.

"You'd best go up and see her," Oliver said. "She's ready to receive you."

"Kiss the ring?" Ned asked.

"Something like that," Oliver replied.

Ned took his bags up to his own room, in the house's attic, and then descended and knocked on Fritzie's door. His grandmother didn't always get up when you came in, but this time she did. She had grey fringes on her dark, immaculately coiffed hair, Gothic arches for brows over her big blue eyes, and she, like the other women in this family, was tall, not as tall as she had been, but still not far off six feet.

"Well, there you are," she said. "What a sight for sore eyes."

After she'd hugged and kissed him, she sat down in a short armchair, and patted the one next to her. "I want to hear all about it."

He told her some about it, not all. About working with John Le Carré, about the suit he'd bought with her graduation cheque. He spoke of London generally, and she asked after her places—had he had tea at Brown's Hotel or Fortnum & Mason, had he shopped at Harrod's or Harvey Nichols? He'd been to few since they were generally more expensive than he could manage. They said "dear" for expensive, but Ned stopped himself from doing so. He did not want to be the boy who came home to Canada bearing an English accent and vocabulary. He asked after her dog, a Rhodesian ridgeback named Paisley she walked at a brisk pace through the Rosedale ravines each morning. She liked that it was a breed the Masai used to help kill lions. He asked after the friends of hers he knew. And she asked after Daniel, the little Armenian boy. She seldom forgot people's names—it was one of the good things about her. She brought out an envelope from her purse and forced it on him. "For the trip. I know, if the pay in publishing is still as bad as it once was, that you can't afford this trip. And anyway, you'll need another suit for your work at the law firm."

He'd begin that two weeks after Christmas.

"It's brave," she said. "You heading over there. But anyway, I know about young men, you want to sow some wild oats. That's why you've really gone there."

In a way, he thought, she was right. But, true to his resolution, he let that subject lie where she'd dropped it.

"You must miss him, Chief."

"Yes, especially at this time of year," she said. "Though he was the Christmas spirit, all year round. Just such a… buoyant man. Where I can be… so dark."

Ned realized he was like his grandmother that way—he always had to tamp his natural darkness down. He, too, hoped to find someone buoyant—it was a good word.

“You never thought you'd remarry?” he said.

“No,” she said. “I somehow got it right once. That was miracle enough for one lifetime.” His father's words about the Baldwins mating for life came to him.

“If you don't mind, Fritzie, there's this party this evening. And I'm a bit beat. I might just go unpack, lie down for a bit.”

She put a hand on his arm. “You look pale. You've been having a hard time. I can tell. The thing about hard times is they allow you to show other people just who you are.”

There was something comforting about this, Ned found, although it was very much Fritzie, always playing to a crowd, sure she could impress them with her character, her staunchness in the face of difficulties. She'd done much of the nursing of her husband, Ned's grandfather, herself, wanting to render him that last service—and also she was fearful he'd slip away in her absence.

“Go,” she said. “Rest. You're home.”

Was he?

He circulated around the house saying quick hellos to everyone. Helena was aproned in the kitchen getting the food ready for the evening party, and her greeting was a distracted one, impossible to read. Oliver and Henry, back from Dartmouth, tidied the main downstairs rooms. Henry's hug was warmer than usual. The tree was up, with its ornaments speaking to different people, different years, different phases in their life together. The greetings done, Ned retreated to his aerie, hoping he'd be able to nap.

He'd no sooner settled in, it seemed, than a knock came at the door. His mother came in. “Sorry, it's just chaos as usual. My mind in a million different places.”

“I wish it wasn't tonight.”

“I did tell you the date. You could have come earlier.”

“I somehow didn't register the date.” It had likely been in one of those impassioned letters, full of advice, that he'd found himself unable to read.

“We can relax after tonight,” she said. “And listen, Ned, I haven't told anyone. I… I… it just seems it's none of their business. Not yet.”

“I understand,” he said. He'd read that it could be like a smaller version of coming-out for parents to tell others about their child, that they'd have to face their own species of shame. What had they done wrong? Hadn't they been good parents, hadn't she been a good mother?—questions she'd asked him during their lakeside walk before he'd left. “I wasn't planning on making any big announcements,” he said.

He was sad at how relieved she looked. He hoped she'd have come further with it than she evidently had. She got up. “Right, no rest for the wicked,” she said. “There's so much more to do. And then, when they arrive, that's when you notice, when you remember something big, something glaring that you've missed. I'm going to head back down, put the finishing touches on things.”

It was then she noticed the cut on his temple. “What have you done to yourself?”

He decided he'd fib about it, mentioning something that had happened to him earlier in the fall, not the night prior. “I was walking along, in my own world, and these youths thought there's an easy mark. They pushed me up against a wall, and tried to take my bag. I don't know what happened, I went mental. I know, I know, you're not supposed to resist. It had my diary in it."

"Are you," she said. "Were you hurt?"

"Not much," he said. "Just one of them, he caught his ring on me."

"Well, good for you," she said. "I mean stupid to struggle with them. They might have had a knife or something worse. But having struggled, good for you for giving them what for. You got your bag back, your diary?"

"Yes," he said with a laugh. "I think it was too heavy—the bag—for them to make good speed, running with it. And you know, they were all of fourteen years old."

"London," she said. "I did warn you. What a scare you must have had."

He was glad he'd spared her Jeremy. That would have shocked her far more. After she left, he fell into a deep sleep, only to be woken up by Henry. "They're here," he said. And, indeed, Ned could hear some bells jingling outside, a car door closing, the "Cay-uuu-ga" klaxon of some family friends' car horn. The guests had arrived, and would soon assemble outside to sing carols.

"I'm on door duty," he said, hustling out.

He got up, and dressed himself in the same suit he'd worn to meet Cameron at Three Small Rooms. He put on a candy-cane tie his grandmother had given him, after one of her shopping trips to New York. If the Baldwins, this part of the family, looked sharp during the slovenly 1970s and '80s, it was down to Fritzie—Helena didn't mind a bit of slovenliness, and tended to do much of their clothes shopping at a bargain shop in Kensington, taking them all in for a hectic afternoon before school began.

Where Fritzie liked everything in her home to be tickety-boo (one of her words), every clock working, every chair reupholstered every couple of years, Helena didn't mind so much about her surrounds. She liked things to be pretty, in a vague sort of way. If she got the colors right, the big things more or less in place, she didn't mind about small ones—didn't even necessarily notice them. A large part of her mind was always on her students, her next lectures, her tennis, her books, the old South, the origins of the Second World War, the meaning of *that* sort of cloud up there… something, anything else.

There was some politics to all this. She believed in Virginia Woolf's dictum that women needed to stop being the angels of the household. She'd done her best to learn cookery, as she called it. She scoffed at the title, the *Joy of Cooking*, even while she used it for most everything, consulting the more labor-intensive Julia Child only for dinner parties. These sometimes went well, but sometimes did not—she worked so hard at it, but often lapses of attention meant something stayed in the oven too long, or, less of a problem, came out too soon. She'd once dusted a lasagna, not with parmesan but with Comet ("the packaging looks so similar"); the Cornish hens, prepared with great care for a dinner for the head of Oliver's department at the hospital, she'd left unattended on the counter long enough for their Labrador to wolf down most of them. (The bones were a danger to dogs, but Higgins, though in disgrace, seemed none the worse for wear.) But she rallied well in these instances, still making her guests feel welcomed. Oliver's former boss loved talking about that evening, the Chinese take-out they'd had instead of the quails, the fun of it, the good music and conversation they'd had.

Ned had tended to be her number two in prepping the food for these Christmas parties, and he hoped she had managed it on her own this evening. Though a part of him hoped it hadn't been managed too easily.

He assessed himself in the mirror. He looked the part, the Oakville boy making his way in the big city, but some shame pumped into him, a corresponding blush splotching his face. He was not what they thought he was, not at all.

From out the window he could hear them beginning, at first tentatively, then with greater confidence:

Joy to the world,
The Lord is come,
Let earth receive her King
Let every heart prepare Him room
And heaven and nature sing
And heaven and nature sing.

Joy—of cooking, to the world, joy. He felt none of it in him.

He exited, and made his way down two stories to the front door. They began a carol he hated, "Rudolph the Red-Nosed Reindeer", speaking of the American influence, some Madison Avenue ad guy's distillation of the Christmas spirit. Their Christmases were a battle between the secular and the sacred, with each year the secular taking more space.

There, out the open door, were the worthies of Oakville, dressed up in their holiday outfits, with as many of their kids as they could corral into coming. They were people Ned had known his whole life. The men were dressed soberly, the ties the only opportunity for flamboyance, and the women, too, had just a touch of red or green on—a pair of ruby earrings, an emerald scarf pinned down with a silver brooch. There was nothing flashy about them.

Only Louella Sinclair departed from type. She was dressed in a red leotard, a mink vest, a red ball on her long, mouse-like nose, and horns, actual antlers, attached somehow to her head. She was their Rudolph, evidently, prancing about in front of the rest, belting the song out and encouraging the others with her hands. Clouds of white breath came out of their mouths as they pushed through the song, narrating, in verse, the story of the reindeer who is at first mocked for his difference and becomes, ultimately, a hero. If only that happened in real life.

She was better, Ned thought, and also campier than the drag performer he'd seen doing "Diamonds are Forever" at Madame Jojo's.

At the carol's end, Louella pranced up the doorsteps.

"Merries!" she said, kissing Oliver and Helena. She then turned back to the crowd behind her: "Merries!" She wiggled her rump, which had a little fur tail pasted on it, and Helena waved her in.

Inside the door, Louella greeted Ned, "The prodigal returns." She kissed him full on the mouth, then used a finger to rub some but not all of the lipstick off his lips. He blushed and offered to take her vest.

"No, I'll keep this on," she said, wrapping her arms around herself and shivering. "Until I can get my body heat back up."

"The other prodigal," she said, extending her arms to Henry.

He nodded at her horns. "You've got quite a rack there," he said.

"So I'm told," Louella said.

"Henry!" Helena said.

"You've raised a very bad boy," Louella said, shaking her finger at Henry, and giving him a big smooch.

Louella's husband followed her in, greeting them. He was as subdued as Louella was flamboyant, a banker, a high-school friend of Oliver's—generations of their families had known each other, from the days when Ontario was the colony of Upper Canada on. Next came the Sinclairs' two university-age sons, who'd gone to Appleby with Henry and Ned—the boys were all friendly with each other, if not quite friends. After them, came the deluge.

They hit Ned hard, each of them bearing a swirl of complicated memories with them. Here was their family doctor who'd palpated his balls each year, checking for cancerous lumps. With those cold hands, he gave Ned an absurdly firm shake, one of the ways he tested boys, making sure they gave a firm shake back. “Still got a good grip on you, Ned,” he said. “No wet fish. Welcome back.”

And here was his pretty, petite wife, with her nice musical laugh. In came a math professor who looked like his beagle, and his conceptual-artist wife, along with their four kids, one of them, a girl he'd had chicken pox with when both were in primary school. Then there was one of Ned's great favorites, an Italian chemist who'd studied with Oliver at Cambridge, and ended up over here, following a Canadian woman over the Atlantic, finding work at a petrochemical firm.

More, there were more of them. The editor of Canada's main paper, *The Globe and Mail*, and his English wife—Ned had interviewed the editor for his high-school paper. An immensely tall lawyer whose cases were often reported in the *Globe*… in they came, relentless. Ned's mind flashed on the reindeer names—On, Dasher, on Dancer, on Prancer and Vixen—as he shuttled some coats upstairs.

These were good and accomplished people, but Ned was finding it too much.

When he came back on, the owner of the Cayuga horn, a Bay Street broker who was Ned's godfather, was crossing the threshold. Ned loathed Brian, seldom giving him the honorific, Uncle, the rest of them did. He did try with Brian, but usually he left their exchanges feeling burned. Brian had always preferred Henry to Ned—and never made any secret of his preference. They shook hands, and that was that.

Brian's wife, though, was Ned's favorite of the lot. Georgia Peele. She was old Oakville, her ancestor one of the town's founders, its first representative in the legislature. A great reader and tennis player, she was the one who'd adopted Ned's mother as a friend, bringing her into Oakville's holy of holies, her bridge club. When Ned was at Trinity, she'd met up with him for movie dates in the city, whenever a new film of an E.M. Forster novel came out. She'd gone to St. Hilda's, Trinity's women's college, back in the day, and it made her happy, she said, Ned being there.

The Peeles' two daughters followed behind them. As with the parents, one of them disliked Ned and the other liked him very much. In his final year of high-school, Ned's girlfriend had broken up with him a few days before the final formal—smart girl, Ned thought. As a favor to his mother, Charlotte had gone with him to the dance, and they'd had, Ned thought, a good time there—she was a good ballet dancer, nearly National Ballet School caliber, and they'd torn up the floor. But then Ned had dropped her off at her home, not even a peck on the cheek, and Charlotte felt used, she said. Ned wondered how much more would she have felt used if he'd actually kissed her? The younger girl, Tish, a redhead like her father, had long had such a crush on Ned that it became a joke in both families—though she was five years younger than Ned. She'd been an invalid in her youth, a rare form of anemia that had since cleared up, and he'd visited her often in the hospital and as she rested in her room at home, bringing her books and keeping her company.

At the end of the line of incoming guests—the last of them!—came the town's top realtor, Babe Mortimer, dressed in a smart red jacket. Babe was the only divorcée in their circle, and was followed by her sullen daughter, Marina, in black jeans and a black t-shirt, kohl around her eyes, a smell of cigarettes on her. The way she was dressed, that was how Ned felt. Still, he'd always felt the real rebellion was to be different, not just to dress differently.

He ushered them into the living room, where Fritzie stood to say hello to a few of them before she assumed her corner seat, and let people come to her. From within, they could hear the sound of Louella doing arpeggios on the piano, warming up for her evening of entertaining. The smell of her cigarette smoke wafted out to them, and then came a jazzy "What Child is This?" Ned smiled at it—Louella was good. The party would get a big boost from her.

Ned and Henry got all the coats up on a guest bed. They came down the stairs together and paused at the threshold of the living room. "You ready?" Henry said.

"Not really," Ned said.

"I sort of liked the days when all the kids got to hang out upstairs," Henry said. "Play games."

"Place looks good," Ned said. There were holly sprigs on all the paintings. The kissing bough, a wire globe dressed in boxwood with apples suspended in the middle, hung from the high ceiling in the middle of the room. Someone had put a sprig of holly into the mouth of a ceramic Fu dog, one of a pair that guarded the hearth, and it looked, Ned thought, like a crazed tango dancer, a rose between its lips. "Yeah," Ned said. "It looks totally presentable. The elves have been busy."

"It nearly broke me. It's a pit all year round, and then, suddenly, come Christmas, Mom wants it to be perfect. She grew up with servants, and somehow wants things to be up to those standards. Next year, I'm coming home later. That was a good call on your part."

"I was just… I… it was—Work didn't end until Friday," Ned said. This was a fib, and they both knew it.

Helena was, by then, circulating with trays of angels and devils on horseback—bacon being in the melted cheese on top of a cracker in the latter. Oliver gestured at them from the bar—he needed help getting drinks to the guests. Henry went to help him there. His first order of business would be to bring Fritzie her usual: some vodka, with a splash of Clamato juice in it, just for color. A Bloody Caesar, without all that much blood.

Ned, accepting greetings, went through to the dining room, where the food was laid out. He grabbed a long fish-shaped plate of smoked salmon on buttered bread squares, and came back into the main room, passing it around, making talk that was beyond small, that was positively picayune.

"Yes, Islington… an old Georgian rowhouse, sharing with my cousin Sophie… you remember her… over a few summers ago? Working at a publishing house… they do John Le Carré… you know the spy thriller writer… Simpson's, no I've not yet been. In the Savoy. You see the big cars pulling up there. It'd be a splurge, I know. Their steak is supposed to be great… Oh, it's all about the Yorkshire pudding? Ok."

He returned to the dining room, grabbed a shrimp ring, giving the portraits on the wall a glare. He took another pause before going back out into the fray, and his mother came through the swinging doors, an empty tray in her hands. "Sold the angels and devils, all of them. What can I sell now?" She picked up a plate with some toast squares clustered around a paté. Cameron's order at Three Small Rooms.

He followed her out, bearing the shrimps clustered around some cocktail sauce. After he'd done a circuit with that, he felt Helena tap him on the shoulder. "It's going now. It's moving. Why don't you take a breather, catch up with people?"

It was easier to be the server, Ned thought. But he parked the shrimp ring on a side table, got his own Bloody Caesar from his Dad at the bar, and found the Sinclair boys and Peele girls, along with the kohl-eyed Marina Mortimer.

"Henry was saying it was more fun when we got to hide out upstairs," Ned said.

"It was never any fun," Marina said. "I tried to weasel out of tonight, but nothing doing. Babe would not be satisfied unless I came along. I drew the line at dressing up, as you can see."

Ned laughed. "How are you liking McGill? What are you studying?"

"Majoring in history," she said. "Thanks to your Mom."

Helena had taught Marina at the local high school. “It's the hard-asses you end up liking,” Marina said. “Not the nice ones. Not the easy A's.”

“My Mum wasn't a soft touch? Now that surprises me.”

Marina snorted. “Comments in red ink on your essay longer than the essay itself. And otherwise, you know, I love Montreal, the ghost of Leonard Cohen everywhere. So many nuns.”

Helena came up to say hello to her former student, kissing her on the cheek. “It's so nice you came. How is it, being back?”

“God, it's hell. All these little crafts projects Babe puts me on, so our Christmas will be just so. I was jabbing cloves in oranges all day. I felt my young life wasting away, passing before me, as I did so.”

“Yes,” Helena said, with a smile. “Your mother brought us one. So thank you for that.”

“I mean of course they're great.” Marina did an imitation of her mother. “You just hang them in a closet, and months later you're wearing something from it, and you think, what is that lovely smell?”

Ned and Helena both tried not to laugh, out of loyalty to Babe.

Marina resumed her own voice: “Because that's what you want to smell like, cloves and oranges.”

“Now, now,” Helena said, “You're looking well. What are you doing for exercise?”

“Oh, Mrs. B., you know what I'm doing,” she said. “I'm having a lot of sex.”

Now Helena did laugh, and Ned joined her. “That's good to know,” Helena said. Her eyes darted to a cluster of napkins and empty glasses on a table, and she headed off to tidy them away.

“And London,” Tish said. You could see she was put out at the amount of space her friend Marina was taking up. “Are you… loving it? Is it terribly glamorous?”

“London?” Ned said. “Yes, all very glamorous. The Tube strikes. The late-night doner kebabs, sliced from a huge trunk of sweating meat. The dust and trash blowing along the streets. The wild-eyed dogs running amok—”

“O, come on,” Marina said. “It can't be all that bad. I mean I'm loving this, this punk version of London, but...”

“No,” he said. “You're right. It's not that bad. I just flew in yesterday, and… People from all over the former Empire. I feel a little overwhelmed by the whiteness in this room.”

Marina snorted. “Says the whitest of all of us. In all of history, there never was a whiter boy.”

The Sinclair boys looked uncomfortable. Ned decided to give some of what Marina had sent his way back to her, the chess adage, a good offense sometimes serving as a good defense.

“We used to call you Baby Driver,” Ned said. “I think it's okay to say now. Years later.” He turned to the conversation's audience, the Sinclair boys, the chorus in this little play. “My Dad once came across her, late at night, when he was driving home from a shift at the hospital's emergency ward. She was standing by her parents' car, stuck in a snowbank. She must have been all of 12 at the time.”

“Yeah,” Marina said. “My parents were fighting. They'd gone away for the weekend, try to patch things up. Didn't work. The babysitter went to sleep, and I wasn't tired. So I thought I'd fire up my Dad's car, his mid-life-crisis car, the Porsche. It was nice your Dad didn't rat me out."

"That it was," Ned said. "He's a terribly nice man." You weren't supposed to say that of your own parents—modesty about yourself and those nearest you was correct. But Ned thought he'd depart from form here—something about Marina made you want to do that.

Though Ned had always preferred Tish, Marina's best friend, to Marina growing up, he found himself drawn to Marina more now, the rakishness, the deep and raspy blues singer's voice she'd had even as a little girl.

Ned eyed the Sinclair boys, still not happy, and decided to throw them a bone. "I saw Cameron," Ned said. "Before I went over. He's starting working with my uncle." Everyone liked Cameron; Cameron was a good subject.

They nodded, the older one speaking up, "We saw him once this fall. A big group of us got together at the Madison. Have you been?"

It was a big pub taking up an old brick mansion in Toronto's Annex neighborhood. Ned had been a couple of times when he was at Trinity. It wasn't his scene, but Charlotte said she liked it. She and her Queen's friends had ended up there after the Queen's v. U of T football game. The Sinclair boys had some friends at Queen's Charlotte probably knew. So she did, and the conversation moved away from Ned.

Henry joined them, and he and Charlotte talked about whether her school, renowned for its school spirit, or Dartmouth had the wilder parties. Ned asked Tish if she'd decided where she was going to go to University yet.

"I don't know yet. I'm going about to visit a few in the New Year. Maybe Trinity. Maybe King's College at Dalhousie, in Halifax. I want to be in a city. But most likely I'll end up at McGill, join Marina there."

"Are you visiting there?" Ned asked.

Tish nodded yes.

"Dartmouth's not far from there," Ned said. "You should go down and visit Henry." He wasn't sure why he was pushing his own favorite in Henry's direction—perhaps if she liked the general Baldwin way, Henry might be able to please her more. This was perverse: he'd have felt hurt, betrayed even, if Henry and Tish became too close.

Henry had little in the way of a poker face, and the proposition of hosting Tish did not, evidently, fill him with pleasure. Though they were the same age, they'd not gotten on well growing up. But Henry recovered himself, and made the appropriate noises. "People tend to visit over Winter Carnival. It's a big deal. You could… come down then? I mean I'll be racing some, but my roommates can look after you when I am."

Tish laughed. "That's the most half-hearted invitation I've ever had. But you know, I'm curious enough about how the Americans do college, I might just say yes."

Tish, too, had grown up a fair bit since Ned had last seen her, her laugh easier, her face and body fuller. Her sister Charlotte was pretty in the sort of way Oakville admired—regular features, impossibly thin, her clothes always, always impeccable, some dancer's grace to her, an ample self-confidence breathing from her every scrubbed-open pore. But it seemed likely that Tish, so sallow and scrawny as a girl, a bit clumsy from time to time, would outshine her sister, and become an out-and-out beauty. It came and went, Ned thought, the apparent beauty of her, in a way that was both disconcerting and magical.

The Sinclair boys and Charlotte cleared off, and Tish's mother Georgia approached. She began interrogating Henry about his freshman fall at Dartmouth, taking Ned by the arm as she did so. Ned had heard much of it before, and kept only half an ear on it.

"What do you think you'll choose as your major?" Georgia asked.

"Maybe government, their word for political science. And I'm taking Russian—of all things. Gorbachev, something happening there. It all interests me, and there was a requirement that you learn a language. I mean I'm no communist, I just… thought, well, you know."

Henry was losing his confidence as he progressed, but Georgia tried to restore it.

"Of course, you find Russia interesting. It is interesting. Especially now."

Henry glowered. Something in her efforts to encourage him had pissed Henry off.

She moved on. "And have you made any friends?"

"More than I had in my whole high-school career," Henry said, stretching his arms wide to indicate volume. Ned felt a pang of jealousy in him. His brother was coming into his own a bit, even if his sulks still sometimes got in his way. His stock was rising, while Ned's plummeted. "My roommates—they've become friends. One is from Texas, a swimmer, an all-American. The other's from New York. Jewish. I only had one Jewish friend growing up here. Go figure. And there are the people from my freshman trip, a Californian girl, the daughter of hippies who'd named her Harmony. She defeated their good intentions by calling herself Harm."

Ned faded deeper—she was, he remembered, the girl who'd helped Henry respond to Ned's letter coming out to Henry. The to-and-fro between Henry and Georgia continued while Ned scanned the room, examining the old faces, wondering who'd prove to be friend or foe to him when the news got spread. "Saxon or Celt, who goes there?"

He felt safe-ish here, next to Georgia, even though she was his mother's great friend, and would, as friends do, back up Helena if called upon to do so. The friendship between his mother and Georgia began in an odd fashion, when the Baldwins were new in town. Ned was just a baby, but he'd heard the story often enough. The two women had been playing in the club tourney, a small crowd gathering on the bleachers. Midway through a tense and important point, Helena's wrap-around skirt had come unravelled, and Helena had continued the point, bouncing up and down on her Tretorns, with just her bloomers between her and the world. A couple of shots more, and Georgia collapsed in a fit of laughter, as, a few moments later, did Helena. And that, as between them, had been that. Georgia had gone on to win the match, but liked Helena's game and competitive spirit enough to ask Helena to become her regular partner.

The Bonnycastles approached—he'd missed them at the door, making a run of coats upstairs. They were keen skiers and loved to talk about their pastime with Henry. They skied out of Ellicottville, the upstate New York town where so many Oakville people spent their winter weekends. Both husband and wife were tanned year round.

"I don't know if your parents told you, but we've got a new chalet," Mr. Bonnycastle said. "If you've nothing better to do between Christmas and New Year's, you should come down."

Henry said he had to get back to Dartmouth, to practice with the team. Ned realized he had no idea what Mr. Bonnycastle did—some sort of engineering, he thought, maybe aeronautical engineering.

"That's too bad," Mr. Bonnycastle said. "It's quite a pad. It was the palace of two queens." He lisped out the end of the last word and presented a limp wrist. Ned felt himself go cold. He'd planned not to speak of where he was at, but it had come to find him.

"Is there much snow down there yet?" Henry said, his eyes getting glassy as they did when he became angry.

Mr. Bonnycastle ignored Henry's question. "The chalet was too good to miss. Right on the hill. It was the dream-place these boys had built for themselves, but one of them got sick. You know how it is for them these days. They needed to sell so…"

"Lovely taste, they had, if sometimes a little over the top," Mrs. Bonnycastle said. "I had to tone it down a bit. Gold walls in a powder room—no, thank you."

"Before we took possession, we had the place steam-cleaned top to bottom," Mr. Bonnycastle said, serving up a massive throat clear. "Seemed the right thing to do."

Ned had absented himself mentally. Henry looked at his brother, and then turned back to the Bonnycastles.

"If AIDS is what you're talking about, sir, and I think it is, the virus that causes it can generally only be transmitted by blood and through sex. So unless you were sharing a needle or having sex with them..."

"Well, I wasn't doing either," Mr. Bonnycastle said. "I just think, well, you can never be too safe."

"I think sometimes you can be too safe," Henry said.

With that, he jingled his empty glass and turned around, a soldier doing an about-face, and left them.

Georgia was the first to recover. "Well, that Henry sure is growing up fast."

"Honestly, you couldn't get two words out of him for years," Mrs. Bonnycastle said. "Send him to a fancy school, and he comes back, full of… opinions."

"The sort of thing a young man of spirit ought to have," Georgia said.

The leader of their small circle had sided with their critic, and so the Bonnycastles, bested, shuffled off. As they did so, Ned and Georgia could hear the wife saying to the husband, "What was that all about?"

Georgia put her hand on Ned's forearm, and leaned in to speak to him. "Don't mind them. They've always been silly people. Good-natured, but just not always very sharp."

He felt, oddly enough, badly for the Bonnycastles. What they'd said was the sort of thing Ned had heard throughout his childhood and youth. It was no better, nor was it worse. He had a record of all those things in him. His somewhat idle comment to Henry about the conscience of his race returned to him. He took a big sip of his drink, and, with Georgia's eyes on him, realized he needed to say something. He didn't have any more small talk to hand, so he went big. "You are a lady, Georgia, a real one. You don't meet them all that often. On either side of the Atlantic."

"That is quite the nicest compliment I've had in, well, forever," she said. Tish and her father, Georgia's husband, Uncle Brian, joined them. She turned to their daughter, "Have you told Ned how you've betrayed him?" Tish looked blank. "Have you told him about your boyfriend?"

"He's not my boyfriend," Tish said.

"He certainly thinks he is."

"If he's not," Uncle Brian said, "What's he doing always sniffing around?"

"Gross," Tish said. "Sniffing around?"

"That's what we men do, isn't it, Ned? We sniff around."

"I agree with Tish," Georgia said. "Are humans so many dogs?"

Brian went pink with anger arguing his case to Ned. "You see how I've got all these prudes around me, the only man in my house." He turned back to his wife and daughter, "In case you hadn't noticed, we're all animals, animals with needs. We're not dogs, but we are great apes."

Brian was a man most at home in the basement he'd set up to his tastes, with old jukeboxes and a billiard table in it, a wet bar with a Tiki theme. He'd come from a small town in Northern Ontario and marrying Georgia was a big leap upward. He'd done well on Bay Street, or so everyone said. Ned always wondered what he and Georgia spoke of when they were alone with each other—they seemed to have so little in common.

"Am I right, Ned?"

Ned shrugged. He realized he'd had enough of this party. He was a fully titrated solution—he could absorb no more.

There were some remarkable individuals in the mix, but this was not a setting where they got to shine. At this party, you'd never get the newspaperman to speak of being the first foreign correspondent in communist China, never find out anything about the great barrister's freedom of expression cases under Canada's new Charter of Rights and Freedoms, never hear of the artist's latest massive installation. Shop wasn't talked much in Oakville, which Ned increasingly thought a pity. As he tried to figure out what he ought to do with himself professionally, he wanted to hear people speaking about their work, digging into how they spent the lion's share of their waking hours. No, the talk would be all ski chalets and Stratford plays, all upside-down margaritas at college parties and Yorkshire puddings almost as light as air. He'd heard the Swedes, or maybe the Finns, had no small talk. Maybe that would be a better set-up. It was Ned who now jingled his empty glass and left them. He could feel those much noticing eyes of Georgia's following him.

In the guest bathroom, he splashed some water on his face, drying his hands on his pants, not on the Christmas towels hung there. Family hold back was the rule—leave the best for the guests. And these towels were for them. He found his mother, as she set out the dinner of lasagna and Caesar salad on the dining room table. "I don't have much more in me, this evening," he said. "I'm going to head up."

"Really, Ned?" she said. "Don't you want dinner?"

Ned shook his head no. "Though it all looks delicious. What a production. Bravo." He tried to put some enthusiasm into his voice, but he could hear how hollow it sounded.

"Alright, I'll make your apologies to everyone," she said.

The first of many apologies she'd have to make on his behalf, he thought. "Are you enjoying yourself?"

"That's not the point," she said. "Tonight is not for me. It's for our friends. Our dear friends."

"Tell me again, why we do this?"

She exhaled.

"You have to celebrate what there is to be celebrated in this life. We've made some terribly good friends here. For me, I came here with no one, no one but Oliver, and here, in our home, are all these rather marvelous people." She could see he wasn't convinced. "Will you check in on Louella before you head up?"

He went to see their friend at the piano in the sunroom. He picked up the ashtray (the one his mother had nicked from Three Small Rooms), her plate now empty of the snacks someone had brought her and her glass drained of Scotch. As he did so, he sang along with her rendition of Silver Bells. There were others in this side room with her singing, too, mainly fellow smokers, the bigger drinkers of the group. Her frequent partner in the club's annual Cabaret, their family doctor with the firm handshake, entered and added his strong voice to the chorus. In a few minutes, Ned returned with a glass full of Scotch, the emptied, cleaned ashtray, and another plate full of snacks for her. “You're a doll,” she said, pointing to the cigarette in her mouth. He took her lighter from off the piano and did the honors, her hand clasping his wrist, as he did so.

“So are you,” he said.

She gave him a strange look. He decided to stick around, sing a couple more carols with her.

Louella had performed in New York in her youth, until her husband, as he always said, took her away from all that, all the auditions, all the dance and singing classes, all the roommates and Murphy beds. Though they seemed to have a good marriage, Louella was by no means entirely satisfied with her exile, and she couldn't get the desire to perform out of her system. Once her boys reached school age, she'd started to do some professional acting, mainly in commercials. Every so often you'd be flipping the channels, and there she'd be wearing a robe and pajamas on the porch of some lakeside cottage, sipping coffee, getting an almost indecent amount of pleasure out of the steaming mug, or hoofing it in a Marlene-Dietrich-type outfit in aid of some sparkling Niagara wine.

She put the finishing touches on “Santa, Baby.” The song, Ned realized, was about Daddies—the arrangement Jeremy had proposed to him. And, with that unpleasant thought in his mind, he decided to make his exit.

When he reached the stairs, a sigh of relief escaped him. He would be safe up in his aerie. He heard the sound of Henry tuning up his cello behind him. He would be giving his solo soon. He should go back down to hear it, but found he didn't have it in him. He kept up the stairs until he reached his bedroom. He lay down, but found he couldn't sleep. To the sound of Henry's distant cello, he ran the conversations he'd had through his head. Why hadn't he said something to the Bonnycastles? After some fitful reading, he turned on the radio. It was all carols on the CBC, of course—and on all the other stations, too. Even with this accompaniment, the spirit wouldn't come to him this year, that feeling of the sacred entering you, lifting you up, raising your heart up to the Lord.

Henry's piece ended, and applause came up the stairs. Ned put on some headphones and plugged them into his stereo, putting on a girl-group's album, moving to the music, hugging himself, letting his arms go wide when the song came to the chorus:

Hot summer streets and the pavements are burning
I sit around
Trying to smile but the air is so heavy and dry
Strange voices are sayin' (what did they say?)
Things I can't understand
It's too close for comfort, this heat has got right out of hand
It's a cruel, cruel summer,
Leaving me here on my own
It's a cruel, cruel summer
Now you're gone...

This, spinning about to bubblegum pop, holding himself as he wished to be held, dreaming of someone whose departure would feel cruel to him—this felt better. There was some power in the quicksilver feeling in him, one that came to him when he danced. Still, what could it do in the world outside this room?

Afterwards, he went back up onto the rooftop for a cigarette.

The house nearest them had wreaths in every window, a spotlight shining up to highlight them.

Pretty, tidy Oakville. He'd loved this town as a boy, sitting on the verandah of the house opposite, having lemonade and chatting with the World War I veteran who lived there, clipping his tiny lawns with a rotary mower. He'd sometimes gone on his own for a visit to Georgia's house—he'd called her Georgia long before he should have, even when she ought to have been Mrs. Peele to him. But she didn't mind. In fact, she was sad when he discovered his error and started to call her Mrs. Peele.

Oakville. It was no country for young men. Not that many starting out could afford it these days. It hadn't been so expensive when his parents moved here, the bequest from Helena's mother, just enough for the bank to agree to fund the rest. He liked his mother's stories of the early years—the kindness of the old widow who'd sold them the place. Even though there were better offers, she'd wanted this young couple in her old home, and had left a horseshoe nailed over one door, its ends pointing upward, so as to keep the luck in. They'd been lucky enough, so far, hadn't they? She spoke of a stranger she'd met on a tramp near the railroad tracks, a woman who showed her the location of her secret wild asparagus patch, and most springs, Helena would head there and gather a few spears for the family.

They'd all been happy once, hadn't they? No, Henry had been left out in the cold when he was little, this sloppy, runty kid with bad grades and faulty eyes, with jagged teeth and acned skin. But his brother was emerging from all that. Maybe they were a family in need of a scapegoat? Maybe, glory be, that was to be Ned's role now.

There was, he knew, the possibility of an internal exile in this country, where you were allowed to stay in the land, but on sufferance. You were never welcomed. You had no vote in its elections. You were not a full citizen. Slowly, your influence waned, your relevance diminished, and you became, permanently, a guest who'd overstayed his welcome.

A maudlin wave swamped him. His first foray into the gay world, his first encounter with the community that would, by default, become his—it had been a failure. He couldn't even speak of some of his hurts now—they were beyond the pale of what could be voiced here. There was nowhere, really, that he belonged.

No, that was not a place you could go either, self-pity something his people loathed.

Below, he heard his parents bidding goodnight to Louella from the porch. They'd wave her off in the old style. On her way to the car, she trilled "It Came Upon a Midnight Clear." Despite his sour mood, her exuberance called up a small burst of warmth in him. There was still some honey in this rock perhaps. Where was that from, some part of the Bible, but which? Maybe that was where he'd find some succor and strength, in the religion that he'd found as a boy, singing in the choir, listening, actually listening to the sermons. Could he cobble the bits and pieces of it that remained in him together, and create some sort of shelter?

...

The next day, the day before Christmas, was, indeed, a quieter one, but still busy. They worked away at their respective chores for most of the day—wrapping their presents in shifts, preparing the stuffing, chopping the assorted root vegetables that always formed part of the feast, cleaning out the fireplaces, chopping wood and setting logs up ready to blaze on the day of. They put more leaves in the dining-room table, and then dressed it in white-lace table linens, polishing up the silver cutlery in a toxic but nice-smelling unguent and laying it all out.

Carols from King's College wafted through the house the whole day, and then, in the evening, after a meal of oyster stew, they read *The Night Before Christmas* in the living room, near the tree, passing the picture book, with illustrations by Grandma Moses, around between them all. They each had one gift to unwrap on Christmas Eve, pajamas and nightgowns for them to wear to bed, so that they'd awake on Christmas in something relatively fresh.

The next morning, one by one, they padded down the stairs in their new nightwear, sleepily contemplating the kissing bough. There awaiting them, in the kitchen, was a mimosa, made by Oliver with orange juice he'd squeezed and the remains of the party champagne. Oliver had been up early, setting the table in the breakfast nook, preparing a proper fry-up. There were kippers and eggs, sausages and bacon, a long cooked oatmeal, cut-up fruits, fresh-baked croissants. After breakfast, they went to the front living room, near the tree, lit the fire, and opened the stockings, and crows of "Thank you, Santa" came from all quarters.

This year, they'd each done one other person's stocking. Ned had Henry, and had stuffed his brother's sock with some hair pomade from a gentleman's shop on New Bond Street (his brother was absurdly proud of his hair), a Christmas-tree ornament of a skiing hedgehog, some of the chocolate bars Henry had loved as a child and a Canadian flag tuque. "Just so you remember where you're from."

Oliver had been assigned Ned's stocking, and filled it with a tennis-playing turtle ornament, some Earl Grey tea, a couple of second-hand whodunnits with lurid covers, and a selection of the Yardley soaps he liked. The smell of the toe tangerines signaled the end of the opening orgy. They all breathed out.

Then Helena set to trussing and stuffing the requisite massive turkey, before shoving it in the oven. "We did goose in England," she said, "but I've grown to prefer turkey." A party, without heathen Henry, headed over to St. Jude's. Snow had fallen overnight, a dusting, not a big drop, and the sidewalks between where they parked and the church, though wet, weren't icy.

The nave of the church above them looked like an upturned ship—as befits a church in a former shipbuilding center, all blonde wood, sitting on pink-and-white brick walls. It had stained glass windows done by a famous Victorian-era artisan—an angel all in white pushing aside the stone where Jesus was interred. The Lion and the Unicorn, the beasts of the British Royals, sat in a crest, above a side entrance. Over the altar were the words that once chilled Ned with their majesty, "Reverence My Sanctuary, I am the Lord." They gave him a small shiver today, as he knelt down to pray.

In pews near them there were families they knew, some of whom had been at their party. There was a solemnity among them on this morning—all of them wanted to start afresh, all of them wanted to be forgiven.

The sun's rays lit up the rose window at the rear of the church, the Holy Spirit entering into the building. The opening hymn *O Come, O Come, Emmanuel,* was a favorite of his, but still, he felt nothing, no inner trembling as he often did.

Georgia did a reading, her aspect humble, but her back ramrod straight.

"A reading from the Gospel of Luke," she began. The words were ones Ned could recite himself, in that they were used by Handel in his Oratorio the Messiah, which Ned sang every year in the choir: "For unto you is born this day in the city of David, a Savior, which is Christ the Lord..." The stable and manger got their mentions, the angels came in at their usual spot, bringing, they bragged, glad tidings of great joy. He looked over at the Peele party—Uncle Brian was absent, which struck Ned as odd. If he had to guess, their marriage was in trouble. Still, you'd never know that from Georgia's presentation here. She ended her reading with the usual incantation—"The Word of the Lord"—and the congregation responded, "Thanks be to God."

The minister had aged markedly since Ned's days in the choir—he now had a streak of white through his dark hair. He was a tall, thoughtful man, funny and warm, with a widow's peak and a lantern jaw. The boys in the choir in his day made fun of everyone, all of the parishioners, all of the older members of the choir, of the kind organ-master and his gentle wife. But, as if by general agreement, they did not mock the reverend—there was a tragic air to him, below his jokes, as well as some sort of cool—and they all felt it.

The pulpit was carved out of maple, and red Christmas banners hung from it. The priest's vestments matched these banners. He held up his hands in the pastoral way, and bid them Merry Christmas. He spoke today of God's decision to enter the world in the person of his son. And of his efforts to be heard by us. "One of the psalms has God saying to His people, 'Call out to me in the day of trouble, I will deliver thee.' Through that son, born today, he tells us, 'Come unto me, ye that labour and are heavy laden, and I will give thee rest.'"

These words seemed to a tired Ned spoken to him.

The priest spoke of how nearly the baby who became that man came to getting killed, by Herod in the Massacre of the Innocents. "The prophets said there was a king among them and Herod feared the coming of a new king." In the sermon, the priest laid out the chief milestones in the progress of the baby who survived to manhood, from babe to king, and then of what his kingdom ultimately consisted. "It was pain, suffering He took on for us on the cross."

The sermon continued, but Ned's thoughts wandered away from it. As a boy, he'd always had a strong sense of God near him, in him, that he could hear the almighty and make himself heard. But that, lately, had left him. His belief in some sort of providence, some sense that there was a shepherd caring for this flock, a flock that included Ned—that, too, had left him. He wished to hear again, to feel again, some presence. But, even here, in this sanctuary he revered, he could not hear Him, could not feel Him. He again eyed the motto in bricks, "I am the Lord!" If you are, Ned thought, then show yourself. Take better care of this wounded world. But then he crossed himself at his presumption that he, Edward Cawthra Baldwin, knew better than God, the King of Kings, what should be done.

His job, he knew, was to submit to the will of this omniscient, omnipotent being. His mother always said this was the hardest part of their faith for her. "Submitting has never come easily to me." He tried to do so, submitting mentally to his idea of God, some mingling of the old Testament firebrand, the jealous Jehovah, and gentle, but radical Jesus. It did give him some sense of comfort—he was not in charge. But it didn't last long.

The curate, a bald, mournful man, walked them through the prayers leading up to the taking of Eucharist. "The blood of Christ given for you. The body of Christ. The gifts of God for the people of God." Insofar as the wafer was the body of Christ, you held it gently on your tongue, not allowing it to touch the sides of your mouth—that profaned his flesh—and then you let His blood wash it into you. Were they the people of God? Ned thought not.

At the end of the service, at the church's front door, Ned gave the priest a warm handshake. "I admired your sermon."

"You were off in a dreamland," the priest said. "I well remember that look."

Ned laughed. "You set me off on a journey."

On the walk to the car, Ned took Fritzie's arm. He asked her how she'd liked the service, and she said, "A bit too much Jesus in it for me, and that man, he is ever so sad. On today of all days, it would have been nice if he'd been a bit more… upbeat. You know, the flowers were pretty. The music was lovely. But do we have to talk about infanticide today of all days?"

After they got home, they unwrapped their presents. Ned had given Helena a Liberty's scarf in baby blue and gold. "I was thinking," he said, "you always came in from the country to go to Liberty's growing up."

"That was for wallpaper, dear. No, it's very nice. They're not colors I'm used to wearing, but I'm sure I can find an outfit to go with it." He was crestfallen and looked it.

Henry had given her some minimalist salad tongs from the MoMA store in New York. "I need a pair at the cottage, and these have such clean lines. 'An elegant plainness'. Who said that? Was it Mies?"

"Yes," Ned said. "It was Mies."

Henry groaned. Ned glared at Henry—it was enough, him objecting to this all the time. Henry gave Ned's glare back.

They did the final preparations for the feast. They burnished the crystal glasses, running their fingers around the rim to hear the music note the glasses served up. They boiled and mashed the root vegetables. They took a rest to listen to the Queen's Christmas message. Then they figured out which dishes would go in which silver chargers. Helena distributed the place cards at the table, and laid out the Christmas crackers.

Their labors done, they sat down, candlelight illuminating their faces. Oliver carved the bird at the sideboard and asked who wanted white meat and who wanted dark. From Fritzie, "Honestly, Oliver, I'm your mother and somehow you don't know after all this time that I prefer dark?"

Then came the usual Latin Grace, the compliments to Helena's meal—"You micromanaged your helpers ruthlessly," Henry said, "but you got results."

There were rude comments about the portraits of the ancestors all around them and thanks to Fritzie for the Pouilly-Fuissé with which they toasted all the absent and the dead, Helena's mother Mathilda, Chief (at which Fritzie dabbed away a few discreet tears). Out of the Christmas crackers came the paper crowns and the bad jokes—"What does Santa suffer from if he gets stuck in the chimney? Claustrophobia".

Lights down: Enter the flaming plum pudding.

Oliver's toast to the highlights of the year just past did not include the car accident in London, or Ned's unwelcome disclosure afterwards. Instead: Henry's admission to Dartmouth, Ned's landing not one, but two jobs in far-off London, and Helena's teaching award.

After dinner, Fritzie declared, "I'm going to love you and leave you"—and she did.

Once the dishes were done, Oliver and the boys settled down to work on the jigsaw, of a Turner seascape Ned had purchased at the Tate's gift shop and brought with him. They set it up on the bridge table, Oliver sorting through the pieces, finding all the edges, the brothers working on separate sections, always separate sections. The dog collapsed next to them, and began snoring. They completed the border. Helena came in, watching them work away for a few moments.

“Got one!” Oliver crowed, fitting a piece into the section he'd started working on: the orange sunset. Ned was wrestling with bits of the angry sky, Henry the moody sea.

Oliver looked up. There were some wrinkles around his eyes, but his cheeks were still smooth and pink, the cheeks of a younger man. His expression asked Helena, did she need anything?

He gestured at them. “Feels like old times.”

“Does it?” Helena said. “I'm going to retreat also, to live to fight another day. Thank you, everyone, for a lovely Christmas.”

It had been, Ned thought, a merry Christmas, but not a particularly happy one. They'd gone through the motions, but the spirit wasn't in them. Emmanuel had not come to them this year.

…

The family moved through the days after Christmas, at once let down and glad that Christmas had passed. They ate turkey sandwiches, all of them preparing theirs in their particular ways. Different combinations of Baldwins walked the dog down by the lake, venturing out onto the pier, all the way to the lighthouse at its end, when it wasn't too icy. On one walk, Ned asked Henry if he was okay with his new situation. “I am, you know,” Henry said. “It doesn't change anything. I still hate you as much as I always did. Joke, right?”

…

At home, they all found their own distractions: Henry and Fritzie watched the Leafs, Oliver read the books he'd been given, sometimes helping Ned work on the jigsaw, and Helena marked student assignments, writing out those comments in red ink Marina had mentioned.

Once Ned came into the living room, his mother was doing her needlepoint. She looked up, and he could see distaste for him seeing her face before she hastily revised it to reflect a more correct and neutral expression. "How are you today?" she said. "Did you sleep?"

They were always concerned about each other's sleep—especially when one had been the cause of the other losing it.

There was a book laid open beside her. His eyes went to it—he always wanted to know what people were reading, sometimes bending down on the tube to find out what books strangers had in their hands. She lifted it up, "Hardy—a reread, *Far From the Madding Crowd.* That set," she said. "It'll come to you."

Ned couldn't bear to tell his mother that he didn't love Hardy and didn't want to be saddled with a leather-bound set of them, however much they meant to her. The author too often seemed to have it in for his characters, allowing a letter written by one of them to clear up all misunderstandings to slip under a doormat, never to be found. Life felt cruel enough without a spirit intervening to make it worse. The gifts they had to offer each other were not the ones the other wanted.

The first to leave the holiday gatherings were Henry and Fritzie. On her way to her own home in the city, their grandmother would put Henry on a train at Toronto's Union Station, so he could get back to Dartmouth, to get ready, with his new teammates, for the ski season.

Ned wasn't slated to fly out until the New Year, a holiday that Helena and Oliver usually rang in at their cottage on a bay off the St. Lawrence River, up near Kingston.

On the day of their departure, she started moving food from the refrigerator to a counter with CBC radio on at a medium volume. She moved some of the Stilton, another bit of smoked salmon, some salad makings, some frozen lamb chops. Ned was sitting near the fire in the back sitting area that adjoined the kitchen, a book in his hand. He kept rereading the same sentence, his typical focus absent.

She asked him if he wouldn't mind going to the basement to get a cooler for the food.

"You know the one," she said. "It's behind the thing." She did try to be specific, but that was somehow never easy for her.

"No, I don't know the one. Remember, I no longer live here."

"Oh don't be stroppy," she said. "It's the one we've always used."

"It's a mess down there," he said. "It's not easy to find anything."

Nonetheless, he went down and found it. It *was* behind the thing.

"Here it is. Happy?"

"Moderately. Now if you wouldn't mind washing it out, please."

He took it to the laundry room, rinsed it out in the big sink there, dried it, and put it on the counter beside the assembled foods.

She began to fill it up.

Without turning towards him, she said, "So, you've definitely decided you're not coming with us?"

Ned looked around the room for someone, anyone with whom he could share his disbelief. "You were the one who suggested I stay down here to catch up with everyone." His Trinity friend Daniel was hosting a big New Year's Eve bash in the city.

"I said I thought you might like to do that, but I didn't suggest it."

He sighed hard. "Fine. Do you want me to come? I will. I'll go pack."

She opened the fridge and surveyed its contents. "I didn't say that. You have to make up your own mind."

"Mother, what do you want from me?"

"What do *I* want from you? You've made it crystal clear these last few months that what I want for you is irrelevant. The way you're choosing to live, it has consequences."

"I can't do what you want me to do," he said. "I'm not going to waste time trying to find a cure for what supposedly ails me. I'm sorry, I just won't do that." But he wasn't sorry really. He was angry. So was Helena. "It's not fair, this—the way you're shutting me out," he said.

"The way I'm shutting you out? You who've shut me out for years. How many times did I ask you what was what—and you finally answer, after a car crash… in London."

The jaunty theme to one of Canadian Broadcasting Corporation's morning news programs came on the radio, and they each held their tongues while it played. She was wearing the Liberty's scarf tied at her neck—there was a reason she seldom wore those colors, they didn't, as she'd said, suit her.

The dog was barking at the sliding door between the kitchen and the back yard, and Ned went to let him in. He felt a wave of pity for his mother. He knew she was struggling not to think something along the lines of "I gave up the best years of my life, for what? For this?" He could see that through the door still ajar, not quite closed between their psyches.

For her part, Helena realized Ned probably wouldn't forgive her for her resistance. When he returned to the counter, she was tossing some carrots into a zip lock bag. "Anyway," she smiled furiously in his general direction. "There's nothing I can do about it. I'm an old woman, useless, irrelevant."

"You're not... you're not useless. Or old." There was some of the former Ned in him, at any rate, because he'd automatically leapt to minister to her hurt.

Still, neither of them would give way to tears, to false hugs. They had reached no rapprochement. Perhaps they wouldn't. This struggle between them gave them some last gasp of the intimacy they'd once had—now theirs was an unpleasant intimacy, but it was intimacy nonetheless. And then she—they—were gone, and Ned was left alone in the house. He tried to muster enough energy to get in to Toronto to Daniel's party, but he found he didn't have it in him. Instead, he smoked and drank, ate turkey sandwiches and left-over lasagna. He couldn't sleep, but he also hated being awake.

Chapter 7:
Resumé

On the plane, Ned tried to lessen the sense of a danger he felt inside him, to guard against it, to medicate with music. He put the music of his summers up at camp into his Walkman. Neil Young. He did all of *Harvest,* and all of *After the Gold Rush.* As he left his home country behind, he had one of its bards in his ear, keening about loneliness and addiction, questing after a heart of gold, telling tales of burning castles, of queens and knights in armor. No, that wasn't helping. He put in a mixed tape Daniel had sent to Oakville, for a Christmas present. "Clubbable" his dandy friend had called the collection, that adjective for a man one could take to one's club. Yes, that was better.

He arrived, went through customs, and followed signs to the Underground, the same portal he'd taken after seeing his parents off on their flight in the fall.

The club hits on Daniel's tape got Ned from Heathrow to King's Cross—techno New Order giving way to fey Howard Jones, one older boy, the Culture Club's Boy George succeeded by some younger ones, the Pet Shop Boys.

Sometimes you're better off dead,
There's gun in your hand and it's pointing at your head
You think you're mad, too unstable
Kicking in chairs and knocking down tables

In this stew of jaunty beats, his mind veered from one extreme thought to the next. Nothing cohered, there was no narrative, no through-line could be found in them.

He wanted to lie down and never get up.

He wanted to dance, to move to the rhythms of some of these songs, in a crowd thick with big, burly men.

He wanted to kill himself.

A virgin still, he wanted to be taken and to take someone—whatever that, in sexual terms, meant.

He felt sad, near to tears, but he couldn't get the relief of an actual crying jag.

His mind twitched about, like a cat held hostage in a rough child's arms.

There was this constant flow of critique within him—they were his thoughts, but they almost seemed to come from without, the devil at his shoulder, as in those old Saturday morning cartoons Ned and Henry used to watch. This had always been in him, but somehow it had become more insistent. Ned could almost hear it sometimes, the voice of one particularly harsh aspect of his own consciousness.

You're such an ass, a stupid ass. Why didn't you at least apologize for telling them then—right after a car accident?

This new arrival in his life, The Voice, sometimes adopted his mother's arguments, but gave them its own nasty twist.

Why won't you go see someone, a psychiatrist? Why won't you do that? You're clearly sick. A disgusting, perverted person.

It wasn't, he didn't think, like the voice that some schizophrenics report hearing. It didn't come at him, as radio reports on the world at large. Instead, it was more of an unimpressed theatre director, giving him non-stop notes on his performance.

Navigating the tiled labyrinth below King's Cross, he followed the "Way Out" signs to get up out of the netherworld. That was what he wanted, a way out.

A cab swung into the taxi stand and whisked him to his rented home. It was dreary weather, the city made sodden by heavy rain.

Not faithful to his down mood, his eyes strayed, letting themselves be charmed by the many novelties in this Leviathan of a city. He'd never noticed that one row house had this splendid green door. What a grotesque and enormous armoire they'd put up in the window of their local junk shop. The sign on the old pub, The Angel, had one of those heavenly creatures painted on it, something he'd also never noticed. But Ned's eyes weren't able to infect the rest of him with any pleasure.

The rose climbing up their front railing had already begun to put out new shoots in his absence, something it wouldn't have dared to do at this date in Canada, in the thick of the winter. In London, Athena was still in the middle of their brass doorknocker, looking sternly out over the stoop, the goddess of justice preparing to make her ruling.

You let everyone down... Cameron. Of course, you haven't heard from him. What would he want with you now? A guy like that doesn't stay friends with... a faggot. A faggot not yet fucking.

That word, "faggot," that was a word he would never feel okay about. People tried to take back words, remove their sting. But that wasn't one he wanted to take over. Its sting could not be excised.

Daniel, Ned thought, Daniel still likes me.

How would you know? You didn't go to his party. You chickened out. He's probably pissed off.

In his messenger bag, he found his key. Some thumps from within, someone bounding up the stairs from their downstairs kitchen, Sophie, Cousin Sophie, squealing.

“Here you are! Here you bloody well are!” They hugged. She had an all-orange outfit on, with a white tie-dyed sun bursting from her chest.

She noticed him noticing it. “I made it over Christmas. The fabric was my main gift. What do you think?”

“It's bold,” he said, as she turned. “Vibrant.”

“Don't you love, love, love it?” She flicked on the hall light and spun again.

“Wait, the top is not entirely opaque,” he said. “I can see… I have a very plain view of… You're not wearing…”

“Yes,” she said. “Isn't it naughty?”

Ned was glad to see her, but she felt a lot to take. He served up brief responses to her questions about his Christmas, and asked her nearly nothing about hers, down in Somerset. Misery made him impolite. Their other roommate, Alistair, the architect-in-training, was out. Ned was relieved not to have to exchange pleasantries with him.

“Long flight,” he said. “I might just have a lie-down.”

“I hope you're hungry,” she said. “I thought I'd cook up a rack of lamb. The recipe's from the *Larousse Gastronomique* you gave me. Such a princely gift!”

“I'm so glad you like it, but I'm afraid I'm not terribly hungry,” he said. “I don't feel altogether well. I'm not myself, in fact.”

"The lamb will keep," she said. "It's in the freezer. Until you're feeling better."

In his room, he closed the curtain on the rain, but could hear it battering relentlessly on the roof. The owners had left him a narrow bed—which he had dressed with a duvet in Provence colors, grey-blue and bright yellow—and a small bookshelf—which he'd almost filled up already with his Charing Cross Road finds.

One of them was a collection of Dorothy Parker's work. He took it down and opened it to her poem "Resumé", numbering out the inadequacies of different suicide methods:

Razors pain you,
Rivers are damp,
Acids stain you,
Drugs cause cramp.

He'd also found a biography of hers, and read about how she'd tried to commit suicide a few times, but never succeeded. Maybe her frequent attempts gave her the right to be glib about killing oneself.

Just do it, get it over with. You will not be missed.

But his father. Tish. Daniel. Even Cameron.

He lay down but he couldn't get comfortable on his bed. He thought over how he would do it. He would get the Ginsu knife that Sophie and he had purchased in Selfridge's in the fall. The chef had demonstrated its sharpness by slicing tomatoes in the air, by cutting through a rope. Yes, Ned would run a nice warm bath, and the blood and life would drift out of him.

Just do it.

He had some respite when Sophie came to the door with a tray supporting two mugs of soup. She sipped hers quietly, while he got down as much of it as he could—not because he wanted it, but because she had brought it.

"Do you want to talk about it?"

"No," he said. "I don't really. You have been—you are such a super flatmate." That was, he said, just in case.

"What are you like?" she said.

She left him alone for a few hours, and he paced his room and then tried, but failed, to nap. She banged on the door early evening. "We're going down to the pub."

Sophie had been to a girls' school, one of the private schools that they, for some reason, called public schools. But she, like many children of her class and generation, larded her rather U-accented speech with many non-U expressions, as if to give two fingers and an "oi" to her parents. In one sentence, she could move swiftly from Upstairs to Downstairs, from *Brideshead Revisited* to the working-class soap opera *Coronation Street*. Ned noticed, though, when she was on the phone, wanting someone on the other end to do something, her proper voice, her BBC newsreader's accent, was the one she used.

"Get dressed," she said through the door. "Come join us."

"Sod off," he said. "I need some sleep."

Henry. He hates you. You've been a bad brother to him. Why don't you just end it?

When they were out, he snuck down to the basement kitchen, and grabbed a bottle of Bombay Sapphire gin from their drinks cupboard. The Old Queen on its label resembled the rendition of the Empress in stained glass in the parish hall of St. Jude's. What on earth was he doing? He took the knife out of the drawer. It gleamed. He hastily put it back in the drawer.

The gas oven—hadn't Sylvia Plath just turned the gas on, stuck her head in, and waited?

Just do it.

He retreated with the bottle of gin and a glass to his room and drank it neat. He could hear his cousin return from the pub. She knocked on his door again, a post-pub giggle escaping her. "You alright?"

"Fine. Just trying to sleep."

He had this strange desire to crawl under the bed, and to live there, shut away from everything and everyone. He also wanted his body to melt away, to diminish to a speck of dust. To disappear as if he'd never been. He didn't want to cause anyone any bother, just not to be here anymore. His mind, on autopilot, took this theme and riffed on it. Maybe his substance could all draw down to a single point—as the universe was supposed to do, a reversal of the Big Bang.

No, that wasn't it. That was phony, as so much in him was. He felt disgust, a palpable feeling that he was foul, his actual nausea mixing with a bigger feeling of self-loathing. He'd wasted his efforts—he'd wanted to be loved. It was pathetic really how hard he'd worked to be loved. And he'd failed.

He smelled himself—he didn't smell good. What on earth was he to do with himself? Was there any easy escape from this hurt? Was there no way out?

When the house quieted, he snuck back down to the kitchen and took the knife out. Their only loo was also in the basement, in an extension on the back of the house. It was tiled in white with a cherry-red line around the room's edges. Over the toilet, Sophie had placed a poster advertising an exhibit of Joan Miró's work, one with the same red in it. The tub was surrounded in a cedar frame that gave off a pleasant scent when steam hit it.

Alistair's vast collection of liquid soaps filled a shelf attached to the wall next to the bath.

Sophie loved to mock their roommate for them. "Smelling good, Alistair. Let me get a waft of you. I think it's chamomile, I'm getting, with some peony in the mix, maybe a bit of grapefruit. Certainly, some citrus. Is that about right?"

Ned got his first-aid kit out, putting it on the counter. He ran the bath, putting the knife within reach. The gin made his head spin, and he knelt next to the toilet and threw up the soup and the remains of the airline meal he'd gotten down on the flight.

Just do it.

His mind, a whirl of thoughts. This would show her. What shame, what anger would follow this. He needed to know he could do this, that he could exit if he wanted. It would just be a trial run. He'd never even had sex, proper sex. Would he die a virgin?

Just do it.

"Razors pain you." It didn't take such a deep cut for the blood to start flowing. The water was so very warm. The gin was still strong in him. The blood ran over his wrist, making rivers and tributaries, smaller creeks, little brooks. How pretty the patterns it made on his skin was—how like the maps he'd taken on canoe trips through Ontario's north country.

He felt, what did he feel? He felt … relieved. He turned his head to the side and saw an apricot exfoliating astringent, idly noticing that it had a different brand name than its North American equivalent, but the same graphic design. He drifted off.

What would have happened if the owner of all these soaps hadn't banged on the door? "I need to use the jakes," he said.

Ned awoke with a start.

"I've got to take a slash."

A slash. Their word for a leak. The bathwater was the color of his grandmother's Bloody Caesars, even a little darker. The cut on his wrist had gone deeper than he'd intended. He had to avoid detection, that was his first need. "Go outside for your slash, Alistair," I said. "I'm in the bath. I just got in."

"It's pouring out there," he said. "But alright. You owe me one."

Ned heard the back door open, and he leapt out of the bath and opened up the First Aid kit. He gasped when he dabbed disinfectant on the gash, and he used a needle and thread to suture it up, wincing each time he drove the needle through his flesh. He had remembered what he'd learned at camp, the basic training they got before taking their campers on long canoe trips: three deft stitches, and the wound was closed. He put a large band aid over his handiwork—a sticking plaster they called them over here. His mind was cycling still, throwing irrelevances up. He wrapped his wrist in a tensor bandage. Until it healed, he'd say he'd fallen and sprained his wrist.

Shame flooded into him. He had done this—to himself, and it might have traumatized others. He drained the tub and used toilet paper, to clean it, the sink and the bathroom floor. After he'd heard Alistair retreat to his room, he took the knife to the kitchen and cleaned it thoroughly.

The blood loss left him weak. He swayed a bit on the tall stairs back up to his room, but he didn't fall.

He didn't sleep at all that night. Why hadn't he prayed to the God he supposedly believed in? Did his friends and family deserve this? Oliver. What if his cousin had been the one to find him in there?

The next morning came—and the sun came out, drying out all the rain. And, then, at last, he slept. And slept, and slept, and slept. After her classes, Sophie brought him some more soup. He was relieved he hadn't blundered into his own death, but he couldn't focus. He couldn't speak to her about it, but not to speak to her also felt false. What Alistair had said, about Ned owing him one, he'd never know how true that was.

On the second day afterwards, he rose again, bolting awake to the sound of the bottle of milk landing out front. He got up, and took off the robe he'd had on, the night he did it. It had bits of blood on it. He put on some pajamas, and his slippers. He went down to get the milk from the stoop—that decadent yellow cream top on it. There was Athena. The sun made her face look gentler. Today, she was the goddess who fostered a golden age in her city, Athens, not the fierce and implacable goddess of justice. 'You've had a close call,' she seemed to say.

He took the milk down to the basement, and put the electric kettle on. It was just builder's tea that he brewed himself that morning, throwing a tea bag into the hot water, waiting, then adding lots of the creamy milk and sugar. But it tasted superb, like ambrosia. Or how he imagined ambrosia tasted.

A marmalade tabby cat visited each of the houses on this row, promiscuously bestowing its affection on anyone who fed it. He mewed outside the kitchen window. Ned poured some creamy milk into a small bowl and took it out onto the back terrace. They called him Orlando, but he had, no doubt, a different alias at each establishment he visited. He rubbed up against Ned's legs and purred his thanks for the milk. Ned knelt down and petted him, as the cat lapped at the bowl.

Ned went back in, and heard a rap from the knocker on the front door. Who could be calling so early? Some religious fanatic, no doubt.

No, it was a boy in overalls who wanted to know if they needed any manure. "It'd help with your garden. My father has a lorry with lots of it on the flatbed." He looked towards the truck, and his old man was standing at the ready on the truck bed, a shovel in his hand. There were boys of varying ages trying to make sales on several other stoops.

“Yes,” Ned said. “We would like some dung.”

He went to retrieve some cash, and by the time he came back, the boy had carried a large garbage bag to the door. The smell of the countryside. Ned paid him and walked it through the house and set it down on the lawn out back. The roses would thank him.

In this calm after the storm, over another cup of tea, he made some decisions. He'd call up the law-firm where he was scheduled to start work in a couple of days, to see if he could put off his start-date by a week. He was in no state yet.

The Voice intruded: *You will never be quite right. You are a faulty part. You should be returned to the factory for a refund.*

“Shut up,” he said aloud to The Voice. “Shut the fuck up.”

Sophie rubbed her eyes as she walked into the kitchen in another robe new to Ned, an orange kimono, the bunny slippers below. She turned the kettle's boil function on again. “I know peculiar runs in our family, but who are you telling to shut the fuck up?”

The second half of the Parker poem came to him:

Guns aren't lawful;
Nooses give;
Gas smells awful;
You might as well live.

Chapter 8:
Plenty

A few days after what he began to call The Slash, Ned managed a walk around the neighborhood, reaching its vegetable market, and bringing home the makings of a mushroom-potato soup. "I might have met him then," Ned later said. "He lived right on that street. But I didn't."

Towards the end of the week, he got on his bike, and wobbled his way up the hill to Hampstead Heath. Jeremy had intimated that men cruised for sex here, and maybe Ned would try that at some point, but he didn't feel ready. Instead, he enjoyed a more childish pleasure, allowing his bike to pick up a little more speed than was quite safe on the ride down, lifting his hands at one point as if he were on a rollercoaster.

Fritzie had given him some money for a new suit. Sophie said he might make the gift go farther if he bought some fabric and asked a fellow on her course, a tailoring prodigy, if they found the fabric, if he'd make Ned not one but two. So, they took a bus to a famous fabric store in the East End, and, with her advice, bought the material for two suits. The man liked Sophie and made quick work of the suits, one charcoal grey, and the other navy blue. They looked respectable, but how they felt, on him, was somehow special. They were made just for him. He decided if he couldn't be impeccable, he would try to look it.

He wore the charcoal one on his first day, with a shirt with slightly long sleeves, to make sure the bandage over the wound on his wrist wouldn't show. It pulsed as he presented himself at the front desk of a mid-rise modern building not far from the Guildhall. His needlework, his own tailoring had been decent, though, and it looked like there wouldn't be much more than a ridge left over on his wrist. Though the building was post-war, constructed in one of the many holes left in the cityscape by the German bombers, the firm was old, a member of the so-called Magic Circle.

Ned's job would be to paper the transactions by which American and Japanese companies raised money on the London market. Under the supervision of a lead lawyer, he'd essentially take massive agreements from the firm's database and its precedent library and amend them to reflect the agreed-upon terms of a new deal.

He was determined to understand all the clauses that he came across, looking up every Latin and French term in *Black's Law Dictionary.* His office-mate was a glamorous, red-haired New Zealand lawyer, who'd fled to London after a messy divorce. She said Ned was like one of those three-year-olds for whom one question leads to the next. "Why is the sky blue?" He was lucky with her—there was little she didn't know about these agreements and she allowed Ned five questions per day, sometimes relenting and letting him pester her even more. She also saved Ned from offending his Japanese contacts at the closings, telling him to inspect each business card, toggling his face between the card and the executive, that frequent minor bows never went amiss, that "No" was a word Ned was to avoid saying, substituting, instead, "Let me speak to the head of our group about that."

But both of these colonials sometimes found themselves at a loss in navigating the English. Ned was once taking notes at a meeting with senior counsel whose names were out of Wodehouse: Simon De Courcy-Wheeler, Brydeston Forbes-Bethell, and Philip Mortimer-Smith. One was exulting that his mother had been appointed a judge at Crufts. Ned said, there probably still weren't many females on the bench, which prompted general merriment. Crufts was a dog show, and not just *a* dog show, but *the* dog show, and being asked to adjudicate it was a major social honor.

Another partner who billed his time out at £500 per hour, once took nearly that amount of time to show Ned how to roll up an expensive umbrella Ned had bought, in his pursuit of the impeccable, on a soggy day at James Smith on New Oxford Street. "It was a travesty, an insult to it, the way you had it rolled."

But apart from these niceties, what was Ned learning? Was this the life he wanted? The puzzles in these agreements interested him, and the fast pace appealed to him also. And the long hours? Well, what else did he have to do? It didn't hurt that he found he wasn't bad at it—few errors slipped past him. Among the young lawyers-in-training, the articled clerks, he started to make friends. One of his new friends was an enthusiast for the theatre, and together they went to the brutalist South Bank Centre, to watch a drama by a writer new to Ned named David Hare. It was called *Plenty* and centered on a woman who'd worked for British Intelligence in the War. For her, nothing compared to the stakes of that time—and how could it? Bored and bitter and anyway a perverse soul, she became bent on sabotaging her diplomat husband's career and taking her own plentiful gifts and squandering them.

The writing and the performance both hit him hard. To bear witness to the playwright's words made flesh by a superb actress, to read books written in this spirit, maybe someday to write one—this, this was what to live for, this ferocity, this honesty. "What was that all about?" his work friend asked after the applause died down.

"Decline and fall," Ned said. "It was about decline and fall. The British Empire's. This woman's."

"What a downer," he said.

The character's trajectory was downwards, but the ride was even more exhilarating than Ned's ride down the Hampstead Hill.

A letter from his mother arrived towards the end of January:

Helena Lucy Fitzroy Baldwin
The McBride House
Oakville, Ontario

Dear Ned,

The holidays seem such a long time ago—as they are. And I kept meaning to sit down to write, but I wasn't sure quite what to say.

But first things first. Thank you for coming home for the holidays. I am sure it was not the Christmas you hoped for. I was trying to hold my peace, while I sorted out my thoughts, but then, there we were, in the kitchen, having it out. I said a few things that trouble me now, but there's no unsaying them, is there?

I am sorry that we don't see eye-to-eye on this. I am doing my best—I know it can't seem good enough to you. If I cared less, it'd probably be easier for me to say the right thing, to tell you just what you want to hear. But I find I can't and I do worry—about your health, both physical and mental, about your happiness, about your future prospects.

After I'd recovered from Christmas, I began to think seriously about coming over, during March Break, or, even, in late January, in the short pause the school has between semesters. But your father insisted I wait. He said it was best to leave you be for a bit. "There will come an answer, let it be." He so rarely insists on anything that I found I had to give way to him.

But I wonder, would you be amenable to a visit late in the spring, after I've done with school for the year? I'd go see the rest of my family, my father and Cora, see Miles and Felicity—if they are about. I'd take a room at a hotel in town and see you only when it proved convenient.

I did finish Christopher Isherwood's book, The World in Evening, *and frankly it made me sad. No one in it seems to be having such a good time, or to be experiencing the joy that this life offers as a compensation for all its difficulties. My friend Josephine at the library has also kindly ordered me some books on... homosexuality and "coming out", so that I can at least try to understand a bit more what you've been facing. (I think she thinks it's me, that I might be coming out...) I don't promise a volte-face in my attitude, but I do want to learn about it.*

It's been a sad time on this end for other reasons also. If you'll excuse me, I find I want to write to you at some length about this. With your special relationship with Georgia, I know it will matter to you, at least I hope it will matter to you—and for me, there's no one here, apart from your father, that I can speak to about this safely. And somehow there are things about it that you'll understand better than your father does. I know you'll be discreet about this.

It seems that Georgia and Brian are splitting up—and in a dramatic fashion. Brian has fallen for one of his younger colleagues, an employee, I suppose, a rather brassy woman named Siobhan. She, too, has been married to someone else.

This sort of thing, of course, happens, and we always knew Georgia and Brian were so different—but it gave you hope, somehow, that a marriage between such opposites could thrive.

Their girls are taking it as best they can. They are quite angry with their Dad, not just for the affair, the betrayal of their mother, but for the financial predicament he's put them in. You see, he's had a bad couple of years in the markets. He borrowed money from some of our friends so that he could cover his losses and keep his firm afloat. Your father wisely refused to lend him anything. Anyway, the funds Brian borrowed are gone. His firm is filing for bankruptcy—it's often been in the business pages, making Georgia's situation, their situation, that much more public. To pay everyone back, and as part of the divorce, they're selling their house, the cottage, and much of their art. She brought so much of that into the marriage and is leaving with so little.

Georgia and Tish have been living with us for a bit... Georgia's in the Fritzie suite, and Tish is in your room—I hope you don't mind. Georgia simply hated to ask the small favor of living with us. She leaves almost nothing for Maria to do on her days here. As I write, I don't think there's one unlaundered piece of clothing in the house.

She's also applied herself to finding work, at once landing a job as an orderly at a senior citizen's home. She's figuring out what she needs to do to re-qualify as a nurse. And then she'll leave us behind. Though I admit, I can't bear the thought. Mainly it's what happens after a divorce. People leave town. La bella figura*—you have to keep it up here. How tiring that can be!*

Unfortunately, the split has also divided our friends.

But enough of all that. I hope your new job goes well so far. I trust that whatever happens on the other side of life, the social side, that you will make a success of your placement there.

In other news, Henry did rather well in his first term—he's come some distance from the boy you taught to read! We intend to visit him down there for parents' weekend in the spring. I find I am curious to see how the Americans educate their young—so far, whatever they're doing, bravo.

At the risk of beating a horse so dead it's now fossilized, I do think you should consider seeing the distinguished doctor Miles kindly tracked down for us. You are clearly in some sort of funk—much of that, I know, is down to me. But whatever the cause, I suspect he can help. I don't say that his remit should be to change this part of you that you seem to feel is immutable. What you do in there would be up to you and him. Miles speaks very highly of him, as a sensitive listener, as a brilliant and altogether humane individual. Why not, at the very least, set up an appointment?

Please give my best to Cordelia. I am glad you've gotten to know her a bit better. She was one person I was unambiguously sad to leave behind when we shipped over to Canada. I am also so pleased you and Sophie are living together. It sets my mind at ease, knowing you're with her. Somewhat! Be careful, won't you?

With our love, as ever,
Mum

He filed the letter in the antique captain's box he'd found at a stall on the Portobello Road. June was some ways off. He'd figure out how to handle her visit nearer that time. He both wanted her to come and dreaded it.

...

Pursuing a quest he'd set himself, to use his time in London to, as he'd told Cordelia, get some culture, he went with her to a lecture on William Blake's mysticism in Soho's Swedenborg House. He found a violin teacher in Knightsbridge and took a class on the Bloomsbury Group at the Inner London Educational Exchange. When the weather permitted, he played tennis with a young Frenchman doing a *stage* at his office. He was not quite as good as Ned, but still, able to push him some.

But there were bad days, ones where he just dragged himself through the work he had to do. He'd always found articulating his thoughts easy, but then, on bad days, or when he was nervous, he began, for the first time, to stutter. Perhaps that was something that came to him from his father. He thought of young Oliver stammering through an early meeting with Helena.

There were weekend days when, rather than heading out into the city, he'd retreat to binge on books, eat prepared meals he'd purchase at Marks & Spencer and write long entries in his journal, the same one he'd saved from those young toughs. In this time, he had the first of what he'd later learn were called panic attacks: hours where his pulse and brain raced, his heart beat hard as if he were facing a physical danger and, even gasping for as much air as he could, he could never get enough.

And then he'd calm down and advance back into the city. Luckily, Aunt Cordelia's concierge friend took a liking to Ned, and helped him land cheap tickets to many of the shows. He collected the playbills—*Les Liaisons Dangereuses, Les Misérables, Waiting for Godot*—in that antique wooden box.

He was far from bored with London, but all this culture, although congenial to him, was not really why he'd come. As Fritzie had intuited, he was there to sow some wild oats.

Through her fashion studies, Sophie had met many gay men. She'd tried to set Ned up with the one she'd mentioned, in her course, from the Channel Islands, but Ned found the man did nothing for him—and it seemed Sophie's friend felt much the same. They had a pleasant dinner at a Greek restaurant in Notting Hill, and that was more than enough.

Sometimes Sophie's gay friends would invite Sophie out, and Sophie would bring Ned along. The two cousins loved dancing with each other. One would try an absurd set of moves, then throw to the other, who'd try to outdo those and go a bit further. They were both good physical mimics, and would incorporate moves they'd seen on others into their own repertoires. Although they often danced to amuse each other, they were dead serious about it—there was even some sex between them when the music played.

Luca wasn't at the Fridge in Brixton (with its pounding dance-punk music and dance floor filled with ultra-fashionable lesbians) when they went there, nor was he at the quaintly named Brief Encounter on Charing Cross Road (where a stranger squeezed Ned's ass). He wasn't at Heaven, the cavernous, subterranean club beneath Charing Cross station. Nor did they meet each other at another late-night, early-morning hangout named the Troubadour in Earl's Court (with its lutes hung high up on the walls). It would have been hard enough to tell his parents and Fritzie that they met in such places as these, but it was utterly unimaginable to say they met where they actually did.

Sophie was the one who took him there, telling him, beforehand, that there'd be a mixed crowd assembling at an old warehouse in East London. She knew about it because her classmates were the ones transforming the warehouse into an arty S&M club. This was an acronym Ned didn't know, which stood for Sadism & Masochism. A particular friend of hers was doing up a tableau, and she had to attend. For the occasion,

Sophie sewed them both bodysuits out of black PVC. Ned's was a little tighter than he would have liked.

"If anyone asks you if you're dominant or submissive, you'd best say you're dom and say it with conviction." She made him practice. "Go lower. More bass, a little less tenor—certainly a lot less soprano. Be gruff, be forceful."

The warehouse was in a rough part of the Docklands, and Sophie had to turn on her proper accent and her charm to get the cabbie to take them there. As they got out of the cab, they saw a big rat waddling down the road. They took what looked like the warehouse's main door, and some stairs up a storey, to what he'd call the second floor, and they, the Brits, called the first. When they got to the top of the stairs, he almost turned tail. There, facing them, seated on a tiny chair was a large woman, wearing leather knickerbockers with straps going up around her exposed breasts to her broad, meaty shoulders. The only light in this anteroom came from the thin candles lodged in pierces in her flesh, slowly burning down towards her skin. One sizzled as it hit her body. Ouch. The sweet smell of poppers—he'd smelt them in other clubs—wafted toward them. Sophie saw Ned's dismay at the whole scene. She strutted over to the woman, and lit a cigarette off one of the candles. "Thanks for the light," she said. "Ta, ever so."

"Make yourself at home," the human candle said, as if welcoming them in for tea and crumpets. "Through there is the labyrinth."

"Is there a minotaur?" Ned managed to squeak out.

"Don't you wish."

Sophie slid open the big door ahead of them. Inside was a passage with an electric light shaped like a torch at its end. Here there was a choice between right and left. The maze was custom-built from wood painted to look like stone, lit with occasional electric torches in sconces on the walls. In the dark parts, strangers would grope or gently slap them or grind against them. There was constant moaning in the maze, punctuated by occasional screams.

The narrow passages would periodically open up to reveal an illuminated set piece. The first was a woman in a black PVC catsuit like theirs with a mask covering everything but her eyes and mouth and blonde ponytail. She was using a horse crop on a hairless young man in leather chaps. In another illuminated alcove was an old man with a white beard stuffing masses of cut fruit from a silver platter into the mouth of a young woman in a tennis outfit. She was strapped to an Eames chair, and would masticate the fruit and then spit the cud of it back up, with the juices and pulp draining away down her chin and onto her formerly white, collared shirt.

"This," Sophie said. "My friend did this."

"Did what?" Ned said.

"He conceived it."

"But what skill was involved?"

"Thinking," she said. "Props, Costuming, Casting."

"Casting? People auditioned for these roles?"

"You'd be surprised."

They emerged from the maze, and there was sufficient light ahead of them to see a small door. When they opened it, light and sound flooded through. There was an elevated dance-floor, strobes pulsing, illuminating, in flashes, a crowd that was rough and various, tattooed, pierced, shaved. It looked to his Oakville-bred eyes like some vision of Hell painted by Hieronymus Bosch.

The music was, at any rate, familiar. They were playing mainstream tunes that had some submission or domination in them. When they got in, the Stones' *Under My Thumb* was on. Then came a song they could dance to, Depeche Mode speak-singing about playing at being masters and servants.

Sophie and Ned started shaking it. She became Ned's mistress, his dominatrix one moment, and Ned took charge as her master the next.

Then a song came on that Sophie and Ned loved. She screamed, lifted her arms, and together they exploded with delight as yet undisciplined into dance. Their faces, until then impassive, filled with pleasure when the chorus came.

Bring on the Dancing Horses
Headless and all alone,
Shiver and say the words
Of every lie you've heard
First I'm gonna make it
Then I'm gonna break it
Till it falls apart
Hating all the faking
And shaking while I'm breaking
Your brittle heart.

They reached a point with each other when their moves were merging. They were no longer throwing it between them, but both moving in a loose sort of tandem. Others began to cluster around them, as if drawn by some gravity in them. Ned looked around—an army of lovers they were, all pulsing to the same beat. He felt in the middle of something grand. So many of them were coming from tough places, places far tougher than Ned's—some of these boys and girls didn't even have a little black case. But many of them knew what it was like to be alone on a platform, heading away from all they knew. And here they were all giving what they had to the song. He tried to take it into him—he wanted to keep this inside him. But, of course, the song ended.

One of the songs from Daniel's cassette, “Do You Really Want to Hurt Me?”, came on, and Ned and Sophie dragged themselves around, their arms hanging limp by their sides, unenthused, until the song picked up—and they gradually did, too. Sophie raised her eyebrows at Ned and threw her head at the space beyond him. Ned looked back. He expected it'd be someone wearing something extreme, even for this crowd. But the man wasn't—or, in a way, he was. This stocky guy with black, slightly curly hair had on a light blue suit and a floral tie. He looked like he’d just come from admiring the hydrangeas at the Chelsea Flower Show: he was wearing a boutonniere constructed around a single, white rose. The guy could dance, but he wasn't showing off like he and Sophie were.

A couple of numbers more, and Ned and Sophie exited the floor to an area near a makeshift bar. She lit up a cigarette. The man in the blue suit came off the floor and approached them.

“I saw you, in the foyer, lighting a cigarette. Nice move.”

“Oh, that.” She sized him up and decided he was more likely to be Ned's type than hers. She introduced herself and then her cousin. “This is Ned. Seldom Edward, never Ted.”

“Hello, Ned,” he said. “What about Ed or Eddy?”

Ned smiled. “G-g-god forbid.”

This foppish man bowed, he actually bowed. “Luciano Emanuele Carlo della Torre at your service.”

“That's a whole lotta name,” Sophie said.

“You can call me Luca.” Luca's cheeks were round and sat high, giving him a permanently amused look. His eyelids sat low, often hooding his blue-grey eyes. His hair was black, short on the sides, big on top—the length and curl of it not unlike Henry's at the end of a summer, but the cut was stylish. Ned estimated his age as maybe a decade older than his. He was not nearly as old as Jeremy, but not a kid just out of college like Ned.

"N-n-ned Baldwin."

Sophie excused herself to go congratulate the tableau-producing friend whom she'd spotted across the room.

"A drink?" Luca said.

Ned nodded yes and they approached the bar together. When they got there, Ned paid for both drinks. He wouldn't be beholden to this guy.

"Well, thank you," he said. "You needn't have. But thank you. Your cousin, she is very elegant. In a way that is rare in an English girl."

"She's part F-f-french," Ned said. Her mother, Helena's sister Felicity, had married a French ex-pat.

"That explains it. And you, do you stutter, regularly?"

"Not usually—just recently. And you, do you always ask s-s-stutterers if they stutter regularly? Do you find that makes them feel less self-conscious about it?"

Luca answered Ned's pointed question with another. "Don't you find people are often dying to get the chance to respond to the question everyone else is too polite to ask?"

"I was always quite… a talker. The stuttering started happening a few weeks ago after…"

"After what?"

Ned fingered the lump on his wrist. This time he wasn't going to reveal too much, too soon. Also: He wanted to impress this man. He didn't think showing him his scars would help.

"You're not from here," Ned said, and offered him a cigarette.

He took it between his lips and let Ned light it for him. "Where am I from? *Milano*—I'm from Milan."

"God damn, this is h-h-hot," Ned said. "I've never worn PVC before. I'm liquid under here."

Luca cocked an eyebrow. "Well, why not take it off? No one here would mind one little bit." Ned blushed. "This isn't really your scene, is it?"

"N-n-not really," Ned said. "My cousin, some art-school friend of hers did one of the tableaux. This is not your scene either, judging by your outfit."

"O, I could dress this part," he assured Ned. "And to a certain extent, it's everyone's scene. We all dominate; we all submit."

This somehow struck Ned as funny, and some of his drink shot out a nostril. He put up his hand. "Sorry."

"What?" Luca said. "This party, these are children playing with knives."

The ginsu knife. The Slash. A shudder hit Ned, and he cast his eyes down at the floor, touching the ridge on his wrist.

"What is it?" Luca asked. "Should we get the hell out of this hole?" Ned asked him where to. Was this to be a rerun of the Jeremy situation?

"We would go wherever you wanted." When Ned failed to propose a plan, this man, this Luca suggested the Fallen Angel, a bar in Islington.

“I've been there,” Ned said. “It's not far from our home.”

“Kismet,” he said. “It's not far from mine either.”

Ned checked in with Sophie on the other side of the room, and she said there were still more people to see, songs to dance to.

When Luca and Ned got out into the cold, clear night, Luca said he'd driven here and wanted to chauffeur them to the bar.

“Are you okay to d-d-drive?”

“You're not so lucky-go-happy, are you?” he said. His English was impeccable, much better than that of most native speakers, but sometimes his idioms were a trifle off. Ned later realized, that often Luca knew very well what the correct expression was, but enjoyed playing with the words.

“Smell my breath,” he said. “I haven't had very much to drink.”

Ned leaned in close. “Fresh as a rose, no?”

“A daisy,” Ned said. “Fresh as a d-d-daisy.”

“A rose is a nicer flower,” he said. “Less plebeian.”

“But one with thorns,” Ned said.

Ned wanted to be kissed, and Luca, after smiling for a few beats close to Ned, did so. He tasted smokey, but good. Neither of them closed their eyes. Luca pushed his head around the side of Ned's, and nibbled at his earlobe, breathing warmth into his ear, and massaging his neck. He whispered in Ned's ear, “I want to get that suit off you. I want it so very much.” This sounded to Ned normal enough, but then Luca's imagination went in a more perverse direction. “I want to leave you here, to make your way home, wandering nude through the streets of London.” And then Luca pulled abruptly away from Ned. Luca was good at making you want more of him.

There was a slight burn on Ned's skin where Luca had been—the stubble on his face, rubbing Ned, pushing into and chafing his skin.

Luca had wedged his little, old white Fiat 500 between two trucks, two lorries parked near the factory. He unlocked Ned's door first, then his. Once they were both in, Luca took some glasses from a case in his jacket and put them on. "I should wear them always, but I am vain, so I do not."

"Could you see me at all?"

"I could see enough."

Whenever he wasn't shifting gears, he rested his left hand on Ned's thigh. That felt presumptuous, but also just Italian. "You are not a plebeian, I don't think," Luca said. "Not a daisy, but a rose."

"I am Canadian," Ned said. "So I guess that makes me a plebeian. We have no nobles. But my grandmother—she aspires to that, the condition of nobility. She's American originally, but she subscribes to *Majesty* magazine. She has opinions on Charles and Diana. It's absurd. But I'm part English. And my great-aunt—my mother's aunt, she lives here. She says we're somewhere between Upstairs and Downstairs people."

Luca moved the car speedily through London's East End.

"M-m-maybe," Ned said, trying again, "in Soviet terms, we're maybe intelligentsia? Lots of writers and architects and s-s-suffragettes."

Luca chuckled. "That's rather a lot, what you've said."

Ned worried he'd revealed too much too soon, and his face fell.

"No, that's good," Luca said.

"And you," Ned said. "Are you plebeian? D-d-daisy or rose?"

"A bit of both. My father was, he is—the rose side. And he married a commoner, a daisy. It was a great love affair."

His mother waited tables at her family's restaurant, not far from La Scala. Everyone, in both families, rejected the match.

"My father's family was grand," he said, and then rubbed his fingers together. "But no money. And my mother's family, it was the reverse. Anyway, my mother and father, they didn't care. Until later, when they realized they had so little in common that they had almost nothing to talk about. Still, I am happy. I know, I can tell I was conceived by two lovers. I am a lovechild."

"That's not," Ned said, with a chuckle. "That's not what lovechild means! It means a bastard, born out of wedlock."

"A bastard," Luca said. "Well, I can be that sometimes."

Ned told Luca the Fallen Angel would seem to his mother an appropriate name for a gay bar.

"There was no welcoming committee when you came out?" he said. "No tape-ticker parade?"

"Hardly," Ned said.

Luca parked the car outside Ned's house. "Now I know where you live, you'll never be able to get rid of me."

Ned ran in, nodded at Athena, peeled off the catsuit, showered and put on an outfit that Sophie had chosen for him, not as formal as Luca's but not, in Fritzie's words, slovenly. Then Luca drove them down some back streets and over an old canal to the bar.

“So if that scene didn't turn you on,” he said. “What does?”

“I don't yet know. This sounds maybe priggish but I don't want to dominate or submit, but a relationship where neither bows down to the other.”

“You're right. That does sound priggish. Even the word 'priggish' sounds priggish.”

It was good, Ned thought, a point of overlap, that Luca was interested in words.

Luca wedged his car into another tight parking space, and they walked the few blocks to the bar. There, Luca ordered two mineral waters—“Let's keep our heads as clear as possible,” he said. The bartender gave Luca some keys, and they went up a couple of steep flights of stairs. One of them opened a door, and they went out onto the rooftop deck. With another key, Luca took a padlock off a chest, and removed some blankets from it. So this, Ned thought, was where he was going to lose his virginity?

The night was cool, with illuminated snatches of London all around. “My house at home, in Ontario, near Toronto,” Ned said. “It has a widow's walk up top—where I go to read, to think, these days, to smoke. On a clear day, I can see all the way across the lake, the mist from Niagara Falls, the lights of New York state.”

“Toronto. Buffalo. Niagara Falls.” The way he said them lent them a pleasant exoticism. It was impossible to imagine him in the places where Ned had grown up. Ned tried to picture him in yellow rain gear on the *Maid of the Mist,* the tourist boat that bobs around below the Falls, but he couldn't quite.

Luca turned on two nearby propane heaters, which began to warm the air around them. Luca gestured at a bench facing south, towards the relatively tall buildings of the City of London, the financial district where Ned worked. When Ned sat down, Luca sat next to him, covering both of them with a blanket. His hands began to rub over Ned, but they didn't stray near his privates. He touched more tentatively, on his side, the leg nearest him. Ned also let his hands stray. Luca was so hot to Ned's touch that Ned wondered if he had a fever.

While their hands wandered over each other, Luca told Ned a long story about an extended family they knew in Italy. Its members agreed on very little except that they all passionately hated the matriarch. The old lady got ill, perhaps mortally ill, and they all piously pretended they were reluctant to take her off life support, but still, they did so at the earliest opportunity, voicing regrets that none of them felt. Ned didn't want to laugh—it was wrong to laugh—but he couldn't resist Luca's mimicry of these assorted hypocrites.

He didn't know what to say to this story, which, though funny, scandalized him. “Euthanasia,” Ned said. “I once was asked to do a presentation on it, at Appleby, and I thought it was Youth in Asia, you know something on young Chinese and Japanese and Filipino people.”

“No, you didn't,” Luca said. “It's clever, but untrue. And thus it's not interesting. I am hungry to know true things about you, not clever falsehoods. Tell me more about your family,” he said. “Would you ever pull the plug on your Fritzie?”

“Never,” Ned said. “My father, he's a doctor. Fritzie's his mother. He has a superego the size of Manhattan. He never, ever does the wrong thing.”

“How tiresome,” Luca said.

“You say,” Ned said, “That your parents hardly talk.”

“My father has his mistress for that,” Luca said.

“How convenient for him,” Ned said.

"And convenient for my mother," Luca said. "She doesn't have to worry about looking after him. He is taken care of."

"That's one way to think of it."

"Are you a Puritan? One of those moralizing Americans who won't face the facts of life?"

"I suspect I am a bit," Ned admitted.

Luca pondered that, and, for the first time that evening, he looked dubious.

"You are very young. You can grow out of that."

"Are you always this… condescending?"

Ned got up from the bench they were sharing and went to the edge of the roof. He tested the railing, and it felt secure enough, so he leaned gently on it. He looked out over the city, and called out: "Quite excellent!"

Luca came up behind him. "What was that?"

"My friend Daniel and I, we used to say it, to call it out, when we liked something."

"Was he—is he, was he your lover?"

"No," Ned said. "I've not had a... lover. I've kissed a couple of guys, in the clubs. But…" He tried to see if his inexperience was a problem, for Luca, but the light was too dim to make his reaction out. Ned turned back to the city.

"I love the chimney-pots," Ned said. "I don't quite know why, but I do."

"Yes," Luca said. "They're one element of the beauty of the roof-scape. You need regularity for beauty, and then some departures. The sea of chimney pots, they make the steeples look good. Both need each other." He sounded professorial, and Ned wondered if he were a teacher. In Toronto, strangers invariably asked each other what they did right off. Ned decided to leave Luca's profession unknown, at least for that night. Butcher, baker, candlestick-maker, Ned didn't care; actor or operating-theater nurse, he didn't much mind.

Luca turned Ned toward him and kissed him again. Ned squirmed in his arms.

"Basta," Luca said. "That's enough for one night."

"But," Ned said.

"You have to go slow with things like this."

Ned offered to walk home, but Luca refused to allow this, dropping Ned off, with kisses and touches that left Ned unable to sleep, with the *My Fair Lady* song "I could have danced all night" in his head.

...

Luca telephoned Ned late the following morning, greeting Ned as if they spoke on the phone all the time: How had Ned's morning been? Had he eaten yet? What had he eaten? He'd had his coffee in the garden? What was in the garden? Which roses?

At last, Luca's curiosity about mundane things satisfied, he proposed that they meet for lunch on the Islington High Street. "If you're not otherwise engaged."

It was rainy, and blustery, and Ned walked there with his fancy umbrella to protect him. On his way to the restaurant, he'd worried that Luca, by the light of day, would be ugly, somehow unpleasant. But his worries disappeared at once when he saw Luca.

Luca had on a brown leather jacket with some beat-up black jeans and a black Polo shirt. The leather was suppler than any Ned had seen, tight to Luca's torso, with a look of melted chocolate to it. Ned had aimed for impeccable this winter, and dressed carefully for lunch, but Luca's ease in his clothes was something Ned realized he just didn't have in him. His eyes were as blue as Fritzie's, something Ned had not noticed in the dim of the night before.

"No boutonniere today?" Ned asked.

"No," he said. "No more fancy stuff. This is me."

When they sat down, and Luca took off his jacket, Ned noticed Luca's nipples pushing the fabric of his shirt forward, the tight curly hair covering the top of his chest.

Once they had ordered, Ned asked Luca the usual Toronto question. Luca worked for a firm of architects specializing in theater design—"Which is ironic, given that I hate the theatre. Just for old people." Ned's face fell. "Oh, you're a fan? Well, I have much to learn, too. Maybe… you could teach me about it."

"Why do you do that," Ned said, "if you don't like the theatre?"

"The music in these same halls, that's my passion." Luca spoke of the high mysteries of acoustics. "There are formulae and rules, to be sure, but there's a ghost in the machine. We still don't know why some halls have the most extraordinary warmth and resonance, and others—they echo too much, or the sound is dead."

He said he was finalizing the arrangements to marry an American woman in his office who needed European papers. Maybe they'd have a child. Why not?

In Luca's world, possibility was all; the rules that seemed fixed in Toronto were irrelevant here. If you just tweaked everything a bit, you could make anything work.

Luca sent back his eggs *meurette,* but did it courteously. When the waitress had gone, he said, his eyes glinting. “I didn't realize '*meurette*' was French for cold.”

Luca said Ned should start his *lyonnaise* salad, but Ned refused—more because his appetite had deserted him than to be polite.

“And so there is this Fritzie,” Luca said. “There's this admirable father, who wouldn't ever pull the plug. And there is your mother who thinks her little Ned is a fallen angel. Are you an only child?”

Ned told him about Henry, his brother, taking Russian and history, at a college in the US.

“So you both left them,” Luca said.

“Yes, I suppose we did. For a time.”

Another plate of eggs *meurette* arrived, and Luca took a bite and nodded his approval to the waitress. There was no residual embarrassment in him that he'd sent food back. Still not hungry, Ned began to pick at his salad, and the conversation moved to food more generally. Luca said he'd lately decided to do a number of guest appearances on a friend's radio cooking show. He'd cooked his way through architecture school, at an Italian restaurant Ned had heard of in West Kensington.

“Your rose, last night,” Ned said. “I thought when I saw you of *Der Rosenkavalier.*”

Luca brightened up.

"The concrete stairs from my street up the apartment, they have great acoustics. I sing there. And I sound fantastic. But it is you who are the *Rosenkavalier*," he said. "You are the young one the old princess must give up, when the boy finds true love, a love his own age. The young have all the power, always. Is *Der Rosenkavalier* your favorite opera?"

"It's one of maybe three I know," Ned ventured. "But maybe my favorite of the three is *Madam Butterfly.*"

"Better than *Butterfly* is Puccini's *Turandot,*" Luca said, that pedagogical tone entering his voice again. "You pronounce the 't' at the end."

"I've only seen one opera, *Boheme,* with Fritzie. And she's more interested in observing who's there than in the music. Her season tickets, she's been maneuvering to get these seats for years. She said she had graduated from the rabbit and fox stole section where she sat as a young married woman, and she's now well into the mink, full-length."

Luca nodded his approval. "That is a big part of the opera. Who is there. Who is not. Who is with whom. I did that right, yes? Who is with whom? Now, I am curious, what were your plans for today, if I hadn't called, if I hadn't whisked you away?"

Ned said he'd have gone for a bike-ride, and said he was trying to make sense of W.H. Auden's poem about Sigmund Freud, so he'd probably have spent the rest of the blustery day reading, indoors. "Lame, I know. Pretentious."

"Why do you apologize for reading poetry?" Luca said. "Why wouldn't a young man read poetry? My ex-boyfriend, my flatmate, he owns a red-satin waistcoat that once belonged to Auden. Tim went to Oxford, so what doesn't he know? His friends are awful—they think they're so cosmopolitan, but they could be nothing but English. When you make dinner for them, they push all the different things on the plate together onto the same fork. If I'd wanted them mixed, I would have mixed them up in the kitchen."

Although Luca had chosen to live here, had come here for his architecture studies and stayed, he didn't have the highest opinion of the English. "Luckily, in London, you can spend as little time with them as you like." There was a sharpness to his opinions that made conversation easy. There was something to respond to, agree, disagree he didn't care much.

"You're a reader," Luca said. "You should meet Timothy. He is the editor at a literary magazine. It seems to be a big deal, I'm told it's a big deal but I never see it on the newsstands. You… you can come to our next dinner party. When Tim gets back from New York. He… he left last night. I dropped him at the airport before coming to that silly party. He… Tim, he has AIDS. I do not. But he does. We aren't… we aren't having sex anymore. But he relies on me, being there."

"H-h-h-ow is his… h-h-health?"

"He was bad last summer," Luca said. "The sweats, the white stuff coating his mouth, the thrush—strange, a bird name. And the purple lesions, he had those, too. We thought he was a leaver. Is that how you say it?"

"A goner."

"But he came back."

A shiver ran through Ned.

Questions swam into Ned's mind: Luca said he and Tim weren't sleeping together, but were they still a pair? They lived in the place they'd shared as lovers—did Tim still consider Luca his man, his property? It felt too early to ask such questions, but then afterwards, somehow it seemed too late. Or maybe he just didn't want to know the answers.

Luca spoke of his *nonna.* "She doesn't speak much, mainly plays the piano. She went a bit *pazza*, a bit crazy in the War. Our home was occupied, by the Nazis, as well as some local *fascisti*, officers in *il Duce*'s army The family was allowed to keep a few rooms. They would speak to her sometimes, ask her questions about the house, but she never responded. She utterly refused. She just played the piano, Chopin, the Nocturnes."

"Nothing has ever happened where I'm from."

"Something always happens. Of private importance, if not public. You said it didn't go well when you came out." Ned must have looked uncomfortable because Luca said, "I see. I'll show you mine, before you show me yours?"

Ned hadn't realized that was what he wanted, but when Luca said it, he realized it was true. He nodded yes.

"My mother was cutting up tomatoes and basil," he said. "Because what else do Italian women ever do, but chop tomatoes and basil for their marinaras? She was chopping, chopping, chopping, when I told her I like boys, mainly. And then, and then, she pointed the big knife at her chest. 'Kill me now,' she said. 'I do not want to live any longer.' She then took to her bed."

He'd told it as a caper, and so Ned laughed. "We didn't," Ned said. "We didn't have access to that emotional register."

Luca waited, and Ned, his mother's son, minded the gap in the conversation, and eventually filled it with his own story. Luca crowed with laughter when Ned laid out the circumstances—his revelation right after a minor car accident on Oxford Street. But also, as Ned plodded along, he asked a few questions about how it had all been. It felt so much safer than it had with Jeremy. As Ned spoke, Luca nodded, he thought about it, he commiserated, he made a small joke or two. "You're doing well," he said. "You're making all the right moves."

Then came The Voice into Ned's head: *Bollocks are you making the right moves. Don't listen to him. What does he know, another faggot like you.*

And yet, Luca was more powerful than The Voice. If he said you were making the right moves, you were making the right moves. Ned also found he seldom stuttered around Luca.

“What is,” Ned started. “What is Timothy doing in New York?”

“He has to cover a big writing festival for his magazine, and then he'll take a class, he'll workshop a novel he's drafted. He's tired of just writing about other people's work—half of whom he doesn't think much of. It's time for him to take his shot. And he wanted to do so in the privacy of New York, where fewer people know him. He wants to try to leave… some legacy. But good critics don't always make good novelists, do they?”

Luca invited Ned over for lunch the next day. “I'd like to cook for you. You need fattening up. I won't give you cold eggs, I promise you.”

“If you do,” Ned said. “I'll just send them back.”

“You'll get the wooden spoon from me then.”

“I can only hope.”

…

The next day, an aproned Luca met Ned at the bottom of his resonant staircase, his singing staircase, and kissed him. He sang an aria Ned recognized as being from *Der Rosenkavalier* as Luca escorted him upwards. He then gave Ned a quick tour. The flat took the top two stories of a row house on a street with the pedestrian market where Ned had gone to get soup vegetables after The Slash. The interior was spare, all white plaster and glass, with contemporary art and Russian communist posters from the ’20s. Everything rolled, everything moved into different configurations. A single amaryllis, with its graciously arced leaves, and erect, phallic flower stem, sat on a windowsill in the main room, nearly ready to burst. This was what sophisticated gay men did. Ned made a note to himself—he intended to have one of these flowers in his place, every winter from this point on.

"You'll like this," Luca said, leading Ned up to the roof. "Like our own widow's walk." From it, they could hear the street vendors' cries from below, and they could see some of the chimney-pots and steeples they'd spoken of their first night. Timothy had the master bedroom. Luca's bedroom was smaller.

He gave Ned some red wine and settled him on an armchair in the main room, while he finished preparing the meal. On a coffee table was an advance copy of a book Ned's former employer, the publishing house, had put out, presumably sent to Timothy in the hopes that he would review it. One of the tall rolling chrome shelves had many other books on it, piled and stacked in no particular order.

Luca brought the meal out to the large table in the front room. First, came snails in garlic butter. The snails had been sourced from a nearby alley and Luca had put them on a cleanse, Luca said. Then came some of the linguine with a pinkish sauce on it, and chunks of sausage in it.

Ned had seen it hanging from a wire, in his walk by the kitchen. "Who makes their own pasta?" Ned said.

"The sauce, what are you tasting?" Luca said.

"There's a tomato in it, some creaminess, but also, some licorice?"

"Good boy, fennel. In the sausage also, and from the tarragon."

"I've never had Italian sausage," Ned said, keeping his eyes on the table. He could feel a flush traveling up his cheeks.

"Oh," Luca said. "It is a dirty, little one. Well, you'll have more than you can handle of that. Soon enough. But not just yet. I've worked too hard on this meal to waste it."

Luca wouldn't allow Ned to come into the kitchen, and so Ned sat in the main room between courses, taking its measure, standing up and paging through the books strewn about. The contemporary fiction was often signed with affectionate, personal greetings.

After the linguine came a dash of arugula, which Luca dressed at the table—this green Fritzie had introduced to Ned when it was a new thing in Canada. Rocket, they called it rocket in England. Then came an *osso buco,* Luca's mother's recipe, he said, one of the family restaurant's most famous dishes. The fat that they knifed out of the crevasse in the bone was salty and decadent. "Peasant food," Luca said. Then, at last, came a pine-nut gelato he'd made.

Luca asked Ned if he wanted a coffee. On his tour, in the kitchen, Ned had seen a big brass Gaggia espresso machine, a nozzle for steaming milk, all of it topped with an eagle. Ned asked for a cappuccino.

"No," Luca said. "No, this is a morning drink."

Luca brought Ned an espresso, with a lemon peel next to it, and then a shot of grappa.

Ned looked at his watch. "Four hours. I've never had a meal last four hours."

Ned jumped up, intending, at least, to clear these last few dishes, and wash the ones that must have accumulated in the kitchen. He'd been half-hard most of the lunch, and the outline of his cock showed through his pants, his trousers. His hand instinctively went down to cover it. Ned blushed.

"Should I?" Ned said. "Clean up the dishes first."

"Leave them," Luca said.

"But I—I want to be a good guest, to help. You've gone to such lengths."

“O, don't be so bourgeois,” Luca said. “It is a favor. Receive it, give thanks for it. Do not attempt to pay it back. We won't be keeping accounts, you and I.”

“But—”

Luca reached across the table and put a finger on Ned's lips.

“Enough chatter,” he said. “Enough food.”

He beckoned Ned to sit with him on a low couch. He put his hand on Ned's neck, massaging it, moving in closer. “It tickles,” Ned said, shrugging Luca's hand off his nape.

“Good, you must always tell me.”

They kissed, and Ned was again surprised at how Luca's stubbled face chafed on his—and how he liked that slight burn. He also liked the taste of cigarettes, Luca's particular cigarettes, on his tongue, as well as the red wine they'd lately shared. In Ned's head: The blood of Christ, given for you.

He pulled away from Luca, stopped by this passage from the liturgy and a thought. “We're told all the time how unnatural it is. A man and a man. But it just feels, kissing you, it feels normal, correct.”

“Normal? Correct? I hope I can get better reviews than that.” Luca leaned around the side of Ned's head, and kissed his ears, whispering into them. “Oh, I've waited for this. How much I want… to fuck you.”

When Ned nibbled and breathed on Luca's earlobe on the other side, Luca's breath quickened markedly. “Yes,” he said.

Luca pushed on top of Ned, and kissed him again, and then pulled up and looked at him, watching him, as he ran his hands over Ned's chest. Ned's nipples were bursting through the fabric of his shirt, and Luca lingered there, taking each between his thumb and forefinger. Ned's breathing grew short and his cock even harder than it had been. “This,” Luca said. “This you like. I could see them, throughout our meal. How much I wanted to reach across and pinch them.”

Ned groaned. “Those are like electrical switches for me.”

He pushed Luca off him, and rolled him over, and began to push on top of him, but Luca put up a hand.

“Do not rush,” Luca said.

“I'm in a hurry!” Ned said.

Luca laughed. “There is no measure to you. No… no calculation. It is on or off.”

“Shut up, Luca,” Ned said, kissing him.

Luca pulled away. “Okay, we'll hurry… just this time.”

Ned undid Luca's shirt. He took the firm mounds of Luca's chest in his hands, the heels of his hand kneading them upwards. How much more of him there was than there was of Ned. This, this is mine. Luca could tell that Ned liked his chest, and breathed more air into it. The hairs on his chest had mostly curled into tight circles, and they tickled Ned's tongue. His nipples were dark, and had a ring around them. They had a ball at the end of them, that Ned took into his mouth.

“Bite them,” Luca said.

Ned pulled away and laughed.

“It's not flattering,” Luca said. “To laugh. While we are…”

“Why,” Ned said. “It's weird, isn't it? Silly.”

“Maybe it is,” Luca said. “Now bite.”

Ned took one into his mouth tongued it back up into a ball, and bit around the ball, into it, Luca moaning his appreciation.

Luca lifted his arms, and Ned kissed him there. Luca moaned some more.

“Those,” Luca said. “Those are my switches. Under my arms.”
Ned returned to Luca's chest, and licked down the narrowing trail of hairs, licking the mound that had come up below Luca's belt. Luca pulled him up, and kissed him.

“My turn,” he said, undoing the buttons on Ned's shirt, pulling it off. It was Ned's best shirt, made in Italy out of Egyptian cotton, and Luca turned to the side and deftly folded it.

“Forget the shirt,” Ned said.

“It's not much, the shirt, but still, we shouldn't destroy it. At least until you get some better ones.”

As Luca continued to fold it, Ned leaned over to Luca's ear. “Come on! I'm hungry.”

“After that big lunch, he's still hungry,” Luca said, his hands taking ahold of Ned's nipples again. “How crazy can I drive you?”

He stood up—“This couch is the worst,” he said. “Shall we head to kitchen? There's a counter there that I...”

Now it was Luca's turn to laugh. “I am the joker now. The look on your face. What a prude it is.”

He took Ned's hand and led him up the stairs to a small bedroom, some architectural drawings on its walls, five watches sitting in cases on a low dresser. On a table beside the bed there was an ashtray. The decadence of that, Ned thought.

"Now," Luca said. "Now we begin."

He undressed Ned entirely—"I wanted to see you, under that cat-suit."

"You wanted to leave me, naked, on the streets of London to make my way home."

"It's a good fantasy, no?" Luca said.

He was naked before Luca.

"Turn for me. Around."

Ned did so, his cock bouncing up and down.

"You are so white," Luca said.

"Am I okay?"

"You'll do," Luca said. He took a hold of Ned's cock, and massaged his soft hands up and down it.

He pushed Ned down onto the bed, touching and tonguing Ned watching Ned's face, feeling his body's reactions, for signs of pleasure and displeasure, looking up to ask Ned, with his eyes, if it was good—and it was. He not only sucked Ned's cock, almost to the point where Ned came, but his toes. "Don't," Ned said. "They're ugly."

He had short curled toes, so many snails at the end of his feet. Luca took each of his ugly toes into his mouth, and Ned squirmed on the bed, looking down at the spectacle of a grown man sucking on his toes. Again, he laughed. He was surprised to find his toes, too, were connected to the electrical system attached to his nipples. Ned began to giggle, but stifled it.

Luca turned Ned over, licking up the back of his legs. Ned moaned as Luca hit the pale area behind his knees. He moved up further, licking between Ned's legs, behind his balls. Again, a shiver pushed through Ned, until, oh, he felt Luca's tongue on his asshole—and then inside. He was revolted at the thought of it, but it felt good.

He wriggled and moaned. Luca's tongue lapped at the small of Ned's back, and up his spinal cord.

"You don't sweat," Luca said.

"Not much."

"And me," Luca said. "I become a pig. Wetter than a water buffalo."

Ned felt a slightly sweaty arm come around his neck, as if he were going to take Ned into a chokehold. Luca did a jokey squeeze there, as if about to strangle Ned. One of Luca's hands took a hold of Ned's shoulder from behind and Ned could hear and unzipping. He felt a big, hot lump on his backside, pushing, exploring.

He thought Luca would try to push into him, but he didn't. "Yes, that will be," Luca said in Ned's ear. "That will be nice."

Where everything in Ned had balled itself into a no with Jeremy, here it was different, right. He felt he was floating.

Ned rolled back over. "Now it's my turn. I get to... study you." Luca peeled off his pants, his trousers. The first thing Ned studied was Luca's cock. It was hooded, with a purplish head, large, thick. The sight of it made Ned breathe faster—he did not know what to do with a cock that was uncircumcised. He ran his hands over the rest of Luca. He again kissed

Luca's chest, lifted Luca's arms and licked him there. He moved downwards on his torso.

"Am I," Ned said. "Is this okay?"

"Shh," Luca said. "Try it all."

"It's just," he said. "I haven't done this."

"Shh."

Still avoiding Luca's puzzling cock, Ned followed Luca's lead, and passed on below it, sucking Luca's toes. He came up off them. "Now, these toes, these are some toes worth being proud of."

"My feet are perfect," Luca said. "Everyone says so." He held them up in various angles, and Ned had to agree.

Luca's body had some vestiges of his cologne on it, but Ned liked the smell of Luca under that—sort of a citrusy, musky smell. Luca was beginning to sweat, not much but a little. If Ned's paleness excited Luca, Luca's darkness somehow turned Ned on. How much darker his cock was than his body. How interesting the way the hood and cock worked, the hood now stretched along the sides.

Ned licked all around Luca's cock, holding and stroking, palpating Luca's balls until they tightened up into a big sphere, like one big plum. Luca's cock was ticking time next to him. He took it inside his mouth. He'd read about how to do it, to make a man crazy—in a women's magazine. Eating ice cream just beforehand had been involved. That all drifted away from him, as he got to know the contours of it. He kissed it, and lapping at it, and then tried to fit it inside him. His hands gripped Luca's ass-cheeks. How strong and meaty they felt. He could hear Luca's breathing coming faster, and he felt proud that he was bringing Luca closer. Then, then, Luca pulled himself out of Ned, and shot over Ned's shoulder. Ned could feel some of it on his back, hot.

"I wanted you," Ned said. "To do that in me."

"No," he said, "You wouldn't want that. Not yet."

"Maybe I know what I want."

"And maybe you don't. Not yet. I wanted to wait, but… I couldn't. When I looked down at you."

Luca pushed Ned down onto the bed, drying him off on the bedsheets, and then began to suck Ned, taking him all the way in, his hands fingering Ned's nipples. With a groan and a "Jesus" he came. Luca took Ned's cum inside his mouth. And then he began to move his hands up Ned's body.

A warmth moved through Ned. We have done it. But then a shudder, as Luca's hand hit one of Ned's nipples.

He pushed Luca away. He wanted to be away from Luca at once. Ned squirmed to the edge of the bed, turning his face into a pillow. It almost made him nauseous, what he had done. He felt oddly sad, too.

Luca's hand was on the nape of his neck. Ned shrugged it off and the hand moved down onto his shoulder, giving it a squeeze.

"So now the Puritan emerges. You are ashamed, now?… Turn over."

Ned did so. "Do not do this," Luca said, putting a finger on his lip. "It's not good. It's a bore."

"I can't… help it," Ned said.

"Yes," Luca said. "Yes, you can." He leaned down and kissed Ned. He pulled back. "You are a good boy. You are a very good boy. *Bravo Ragazzo*. You know that? You know that?"

Ned nodded. Luca took him in his arms.

"Leave the shame to us," Luca whispered.

Ned pulled away a bit, and Luca could tell he hadn't understood. "Leave it to the Catholics. We are the experts. We know how to handle it. We do something, we feel bad for it, we confess it, in great, loving detail, we say the Hail Mary's, we give the money to the church, we purge it. And then we do it again. Maybe a little differently so we have something fresh to say about it."

Ned felt tired. He felt very tired. Luca kissed him again, closing Ned's eyes with his fingers. Ned's fading mind thought of how you did that to corpses, if they died with their eyes open. Luca kissed Ned on his eyelids. There was a rain of kisses on his face, on his nose, his cheeks, his forehead, his chin, again on his lips. Luca's lips barely touched Ned's skin, but he could feel them, a bit of moisture left where he'd been.
"Sleep, little prince."

Ned could smell a cigarette's smoke wafting through the room as he drifted off. He was still on top of the covers, he realized. He should get under them, but he didn't. It was warm in this room, and he didn't mind lying there, on display again for this man, his lover.

When he awoke, the covers were on him. There were three cigarettes in the ashtray. There was light coming through a band of clerestory windows high up, ones he hadn't noticed the night before with his focus almost entirely on Luca and what he would do to Ned, what Ned would do to him. Ned turned over, and Luca was still asleep, on his back, some gentle whistling coming out of him whenever he exhaled through his nose. These wheezes were sweet, somehow. Ned leaned over and kissed him on the cheek, and Luca's hand came to his face, cupped Ned's cheek.

He'd done it, finally. He'd been with a man. With Luca. He wanted to tell someone, maybe Sophie, that it had happened. But what could he say? It was strange, so much of it. Had he done okay? There had been easy moments, and uneasy ones. But desire throughout, in every bit of it, the drive towards him, towards his flesh, towards his lips, towards him. He wondered, throughout, what a man like Luca was doing with him, but Luca's careful exploration of his entire body kept him from worrying about this. In fact, worry—his constant companion—seemed to have departed for a time altogether.

And then, afterwards, when the shot of shame downed him, Luca had revived him. It had helped what he said, that he could simply refuse to feel it. That it was a bore. And then, in the few seconds before he'd fallen asleep, he'd felt the rightness of it all—how natural and correct it was. He'd waited his whole life for this, and it had come, and it was good. He'd never been able to fall asleep when he felt unsafe. And here he'd fallen asleep at once. He still felt safe. His cock went hard, as certain parts of it replayed in him.. Did he, did they have time to start again?

The digital alarm clock on the side-table told him he was late—a little not a lot. He had to get to work. He'd bike home, shower there and change into his office clothes, prepare himself to meet the demands of a busy Monday. He felt ready, ready to go at things, whatever they were.

He got up, and turned to look at Luca. He wanted to remember what his sleeping face looked like.

An eye came open. The blue of it. Luca yawned and stretched and put up his hand to stop Ned, while he found some words. "In the bathroom, don't use Tim's razor to shave. His has got a bone handle. The virus."

"I, I, I hadn't p-p-planned on shaving here," Ned said, dressing quickly. His shirt he'd have to get from downstairs.

"Did you have a good time?" Luca said.

"Yes," Ned said. "Yes, I did. It was—"

"The overture," Luca said. "It introduced the themes. Now we will separate them out, play them more slowly. We will do it all properly, the next time. Or maybe the time after that. We will find it."

Ned felt relieved that Luca was proposing a next time—and a time after that. And yet, the razor—the threat of death so near them.

Luca flashed the blanket off himself to give Ned another view of him, raising one perfect foot in the air. Ned kissed it, and then he scurried out. As he put his shirt on in the living room, the dishes scattered about the table, he smelled Luca on him. He lifted his arm to his nose. Yes, Luca was there.

Their bodies had come together. They'd had their releases. Was it more than that? Was it ever more than that?

...

Since Ned had, at least, some interest in the opera, Luca took him to Covent Garden on the occasion of the Queen's birthday, for a command performance from Placido Domingo. Ned liked an aria from *Tosca*, *E Lucevan e Stella* most, and he asked Luca for a translation of the lyrics in the intermission: "And the stars were shining, and the earth was scented," Luca said.

This was how Ned thought of this time; these were the words, this was the musical soundtrack for this idyll.

They tramped often on Hampstead Heath, watching as the short winter gave way to a long spring. Each plant got its starring moment; it was not just one raucous, two-day fiesta as in Ned's part of Canada. First came some wild crocuses at the edge of the woods, then a hill filled up with pale yellow narcissus. Then the magnolia near the manor house bedecked itself in white snowdrops, followed by the bluebells and the forget-me-nots. They saw a falcon once on a fallen tree–nature was not just a garden made for their pleasure, but a hunting ground. Sometimes, in the forests, they saw lots of single men wandering about.

"Do you like him?" Luca said once. "You could go into the woods with him now. You see he's eyeing you."

"No," Ned said, "It's you he's undressing with his eyes." Ned couldn't imagine any person meeting the two of them, and wanting Ned more than Luca.

But then he circled back to Luca's proposal that he go with this stranger. "Wouldn't you mind if I went into the woods with him?"

"I would a little, I think," Luca said. "Which surprises me."

It was never jerky, their sex. It moved, Luca moved it, from one thing smoothly into the next. Where they'd taken turns their first time, soon they weren't. There was both domination and submission throughout. And Ned found he liked both. He wanted to push into Luca and to be pushed into—this, though, they did not do. Not yet, Luca said. When Ned spotted Luca on the street, he gladdened, he brightened, something quickened in him. Sex was like that, only more so. Something that made him feel warm and glad, and it was wrapped up in Luca.

Ned found he was a person of sudden wants, strong needs—sometimes they left restaurants before finishing their entrees. He was always the man in the rush, while Luca was always the one taking it slower. Luca liked to do it once at night, then in the shower the morning after. The kitchen counter proved an idle threat. After they'd showered and had sex, if the weather permitted, they ate breakfasts on the rooftop, with the hawkers crying out below: "Diapers, forty-eight for 50p." Luca's robe falling open to reveal that thick, now hooded, olive-colored cock.

Three weeks in, Luca gave Ned a copy of Plato's *Symposium,* inscribing it, "The ultimate party, a conversation filled with big ideas, sex always coloring their discussion—delicious food, lots of wine, it had it all. Our parties, my parties pale by comparison. As you shall see."

Ned noted Luca's use of "our", but he ignored it.

Luca had decided, he said, to have a dinner party to mark, he said, the end of their first month. Luca insisted that Ned bring someone to the party. "Why?" Ned said.

"Then your host doesn't have to worry about you."

Sometimes, Luca felt like a younger version of Ned's grandmother Fritzie, with specific rules on what flew and what didn't. Ned knew Fritzie's rules—and many of them were outdated. He trusted Luca to tell him what was what. So Ned brought Sophie along.

When the two of them arrived, bearing a big bunch of irises up the resonant staircase, Luca eyed the bouquet. "No," he said. "Then the host has to do something with them."

"That's what I told him," Sophie said.

Luca got them drinks in the kitchen and made a chore out of getting the flowers in a vase. He gave it to them, to put somewhere in the main room. Ned felt a wave of uncertainty come over him.

You're in over your head, buddy-boy.

Ned stuttered his way through the aperitifs, Sophie taking the lead in conversation.

When everyone expected had arrived, Luca seated them all. He knew he would not be seated next to Luca. Luca had told him: "I don't believe in that. So boring to seat lovers together. Either they coo or quarrel. They know already what each other has to say. And anyway, why not make each of them a little jealous of the other?"

Ned was at the opposite end of the table from Luca, between a young BBC presenter (agreeably foul-mouthed off the air) and a philosophy professor, over from Italy, a family friend of Luca's. The prof was less interested in Ned's hesitant attempt to speak of *The Symposium* than his thoughts about Post-Modernism. Luckily, Ned had learned the basics of this developing school of thought at Trinity, in a class with the English department's token radical. At the middle of the table was a tall Nigerian pop singer with deep lines in his cheeks, a Canadian heiress next to him—Fritzie knew their family, but they were richer by far than the Baldwins. When Ned and she spoke before dinner, Ned found he had no wish to find acquaintances in common. Luckily, neither did she—she only had eyes for her singer.

On either side of Luca, at the other end of the table, was a swimsuit designer for model Jerry Hall's new line and a fat American comedienne, who was bigger in England than she was in her home country. To Ned's annoyance, somehow she managed to transfer some of her loud lipstick to the collar of a new shirt he'd bought for this occasion.

To Sophie's delight, Luca had seated her next to an older Frenchman, a reporter for *Le Figaro* over on assignment in London, and across from a handsome young Dutch photographer—he did author profile shots for Tim's magazine. As these three all spoke fluent French, that part of the table did so.

After dinner, the philosopher asked, “Won't there be any games?”

“No,” Luca said. “Games are Tim's thing. This one” - he pointed at Ned—“He likes to dance. So that's what we'll do. Bad pop. That is what he likes.”

This was true, Ned thought. His younger brother had good taste in music—or what passed for that in this time; Ned liked the gawdy, pretty songs, the maudlin ones and the euphoric ones. He knew when a song had a good hook, and he poured his own thoughts and feelings into the lyrics. However vapid, they became file folders containing particular moods, people he'd been with. Even if they weren't Auden, they mattered somehow.

And so, that evening they danced up on the rooftop. Midway through one song, Ned looked out over London, and then up to the dark sky, dipping his head down as he'd been taught to do when he addressed his God, whispering, "Thank you." Though he gave credit to someone, something benevolent up there, beyond the clouds that blanketed London. Ned felt, somehow, this evening had come about as a result of him dancing by himself after the family Christmas party, hugging himself as he spun. Maybe that was the prayer, and this was its answer. After the party ended and everyone had departed, Luca's arms felt better, far better wrapped around Ned than his own had. Of course they did.

...

But the next day, the Voice went at him—and he tried to rebut the accusations mentally:

You're talking to this great expert in post-modernism, and there you are, prattling on, based on what? One class you took? What an ass you are. What a stupid fucking ass you made of yourself. Why not ask him to tell you his thoughts?

"But h-h-he wanted mine. And I did ask."

Look at all these people going places, many of them already there, and you, you have nothing set up. You're going nowhere.

"True. That at any rate is true."

Over Christmas, Oliver had recommended that Ned at least put in applications to do graduate work in a field that interested him. Since it was his father who'd recommended it, Ned decided, on that day, that morning after, he'd at least, apply to various law schools and to masters' programs in literature.

...

Luca and Ned fought seldom but fiercely: about whether Kafka was funny or not (Luca thought so, Ned did not), about Ned's failure to make time to help Luca pick out new glasses.

“I had no idea you were so vain,” Ned said.

“To pay attention to how you look,” he said, “it is to show respect for others.”

Here Luca and Ned's grandmother felt the same and used almost exactly the same words.

The most serious fight came when Ned mentioned a study he'd read about which suggested that cigarettes and AIDS didn't mix.

“I know T-t-timothy smokes...”

Luca's face was never hard to read, and it darkened. “If you ever mention that in Timothy's presence, I will not—be happy.”

“I just read about it,” Ned said. “I wasn't planning to… when he gets back. But I thought you could.”

“Children shouldn't play with knives.” This was evidently a go-to metaphor for this cook.

“I'm not a child.”

“Sorry,” Luca said. His face went a bit limp. “I've been so angry. I lose my temper with shop-girls, cabbies, waiters. I am not this man. I snap at my boss—not a smart move, though he is extremely irritating, it is widely known. Do you say 'mad as a hatter'? Is that what you say?” He flashed Ned a grin. “I am mad as a hatter.”

“Not exactly,” Ned said. “Not quite. That's a different sort of mad. As you very well know.”

In the late spring, the day before Tim's return from New York, a few days before Ned's mother's arrival, they had what Ned would long think of as The Perfect Day. They both took the day off from work. Luca wore that same blue jacket he'd had on at the warehouse party, another boutonniere, this one with a red rose at its center, and a long, striped scarf.

They went to find one of the places where Robbie Ross had lived, on the poetically named, Half-Moon Street in Soho. The house was gone. Never mind—Ned read aloud a description of it from a recently released biography, and showed Luca a picture of the tidy, little man in his Moroccan-themed interiors, a big signet ring on his pinkie. Over lunch at a simple sandwich shop, the pair of them planned a trip to Paris, which included a pilgrimage to Wilde's grave in Père Lachaise cemetery—his great-uncle's ashes were also buried there, in this sphinx Robbie had commissioned a sculptor friend to make to sit atop Wilde's resting place.

In the afternoon, they biked along the path next to the Serpentine. As the water glittered next to him, Luca chattered away, speaking to Ned about the different levels of nobility in the different European countries, both of them swerving around pedestrians, the walkers plodding, while they soared, barely earthbound. It turned out Luca would, when his father died, become a Marchese. "Which is very grand indeed."

Ned laughed. "You don't say that about yourself. About your own family!"

"Why not? It's the truth. To be false about it, to grovel before others. That is strange. Is that a Canadian thing?"

Ned supposed it might be. He asked Luca, "Don't they want you to continue the family line? To have, I suppose, h-h-heirs?"

'They do. But I… I won't. I don't like children."

Ned laughed again. "Not at all?"

"Not at all. Not even when I was one. And my younger brother—he will have many. You can see that. That will make him happy. That will make everyone happy."

Their second destination was the London Zoo. In the Gorilla House, Luca told Ned strange facts about the primates, while a chimp masturbated mournfully near them in its vast cage. "Just going through the motions, poor thing," Luca said. Outside, under a cloudless sky, Luca talked Ned through how a Russian architect had designed the sleek, deco Penguin Pool, as they waddled over a long curvy bridge over the pool.

"Do they know they live in an architectural masterpiece?" Ned said.

How much Luca knew—and how much Ned liked being around someone who knew so many things, and could convey them in a sort of gossipy way.

The two of them stopped by Aunt Cordelia's for a rather slapdash tea. She said she'd quite taken to Luca—"he's such a terrible flirt." Luca got her to tell them about her dead husband's time fighting in the Spanish Civil War, and their joint time protesting against nuclear proliferation.

Then, they went to a Persian restaurant on the King's Road run by a chef friend of Luca's who sent them out dishes, with names new to Ned, like Tah Dig and Kuku Sabzi. Luca asked Ned about Henry, the member of Ned's family he'd heard least about so far. Ned told him about his excellence in chess and on the ski-hill, how the two of them didn't really get along, though they had when they were both little. "When did it stop working between you?"

"I don't rightly know," Ned said. "I did my own thing for a long time. I was trying to figure things out. And I just—I didn't pay attention to him. He didn't interest me that much. But he does now, a bit. I might have missed the boat on that one. He's studying Russian. Of all things. Working at his campus's newspaper. At Christmas, he kept talking of this girl, this

Californian. Seems she's some sort of campus activist. She helped him write this letter back to me, his response to me coming out to him."

"His girlfriend?"

"I can't rightly tell. The way he says her name, you could hear how much he liked her."

"Say my name," Luca said.

"Luca," Ned said. "Luciano Emanuele Carlo della Torre."

"I hear it there. Ours is a love like my parents had."

"Is it?" Ned said. "Or is it more like what your father has with his mistress?"

Luca scowled, and his eyebrows pushed down over his eyes.

"A joke," Ned said.

"A joke should be funny," Luca said. "It's not like that with you. It's not like that at all. In a way, I wish it was, but it's not."

That last bit troubled Ned. But he pushed past that. On the bike-ride home, he thought of that play, *Plenty*, the sad play with the nice title. How long he'd waited for something like this, and yet it was more than he expected. This was the man he'd wanted, even better than the one he'd imagined for himself. Luca could mock or jolly Ned out of his bad moods—or just listen to him in a way that made things feel better. He didn't propose solutions. Sometimes, he just shrugged. Some things are the way they are.

Ned had always thought too much wit, too much attention to fashion—these were things that undermined a man's masculinity. He tamped those things down in himself. But with Luca, these things just increased his appeal.

Back at work a few days later, Ned paged through the faxes that Luca had sent Ned. They were written in Latin, something both of them had studied in school. Sometimes they arranged an evening meeting, sometimes they were just dirty ones, sent for the pleasure of shocking Ned. It didn't matter to Ned that most of the lawyers could read Latin. Anyway, Luca never signed his name. Here was someone who wanted Ned, and Ned wanted him, too. Did Ned love him? Yes. It wasn't hard to love Luca. Did Luca love Ned? It seemed so. That felt enough. That felt like plenty.

They'd had their month. Now their connection would have to weather further scrutiny—from a returning Timothy, and from Helena.

Chapter 9:
To Be A Pilgrim

Oliver dropped Helena at the airport. When he took her suitcases from the trunk, he groaned at their weight. "Are you leaving me? By the looks of those suitcases, you definitely have enough in there to start a new life."

Helena usually packed light, but had been uncertain what to bring. It was a symptom of her general uncertainty. What role was she to play now in her son's life? Avenging angel? Sweet and supportive non-entity? She didn't know what costume to put on until she knew the role. After Christmas, she'd borrowed the videotapes of the miniseries *Brideshead Revisited* from the library. How different to see it a second time, when, alas, the issues had become personal. How much she sympathized with that fierce, uncompromising mother, stretched between the commands of her faith, Catholicism, and what her flamboyant son Sebastian asked of her. Helena's own faith wasn't so driven by thou-shalt-nots—she was Church of England, after all, not Catholic—but it wasn't irrelevant.

"I know… you," she said, then paused. "You still don't think I should go. That I should leave him be."

He nodded his head to confirm that he still thought that, that young adults must be left to their own devices, to find their own ways—or not. A redcap porter approached and Oliver gestured at the bags, and handed over to him payment for taking them in with Helena.

As the porter put the cases on his dolly, Helena said to Oliver, "But I find, I just can't. I have to see if he's well, or at least managing."

On the plane, she numbered through the clothes she'd packed. For all that she'd put in half her wardrobe, she didn't feel she had anything appropriate to wear for her meal with them. What do you wear to meet your son's gay lover, an Italian architect-chef? She wanted somehow to impress upon this man—what, what did she want to impress upon him?

Sleep wouldn't come to her on the overnight flight, so she read through the whodunnit she'd packed. It was the nurse in the old-age home who was behind the killing spree, she was pretty certain of that from about the middle of the book. But perhaps that was where the writer had led her, with a series of false clues.

The customs agent, looking at the birthplace printed in her Canadian passport said, "Welcome back." She still retained her British citizenship, but hadn't bothered to renew her papers in years. Anyway, she felt more Canadian now.

The hotel was a treat from Fritzie for Helena's birthday, a once grand Bloomsbury dame a bit down on her luck. The facade was a fantasia in brick, terracotta friezes, wrought iron and carved stone, with a lion and a unicorn over the grand, arched entry, turrets up top as well as Jacobethan gables. Within, most every surface was covered in veined marble, the more colorful the better. The materials for this hotel had come from all over the empire on which, at the time this hotel was built, the sun never set.

The bed had been turned down, and a mint placed on her pillow. Often when she arrived back in England, she got out there at once, jet lag be damned! But this time, though it was still morning, she threw herself down on the bed. It was such a luxury to have the bed to oneself. She and Oliver shared a four-poster barely big enough for two. His snores and tossing often disturbed her. So, she slept, and then slept some more. When she awoke in the early evening, the message light on her phone was flashing. It was Ned, welcoming her, hoping she'd have a nice dinner with Cordelia, and looking forward to seeing her the next day to introduce her to Luca. His tone had some cheery bravado to it at first, but rapidly became more tentative as the message proceeded. Still, it was his voice.

She took in the room more. At the writing desk, there was an uncomfortable-looking chair, an intricately carved imitation of an archbishop's throne. All that Victorian propriety concentrated in the steep vertical thrusts of a chair back and a building facade. Do not bend; do not yield. It reminded her of her father. It was the sort of chair he would have gravitated towards, assuming, if there were just one of its kind in the room, that he had the right to occupy it. Ned had asked if he could accompany her on a visit down to see her father, his grandfather. He was curious, he said. Well, so be it. Let his curiosity be amply satisfied.

She pulled herself together for an evening with Cordelia, putting on some navy slacks and a silk shirt with wild paisleys all over it. Its controlled anarchy she knew her Bohemian aunt would like. They met at the flat, which hadn't changed much. There were some moribund zinnias in a vase near a window. Cordelia had evidently fluffed up the cushions on the couches, but the stench of her cats had, it seemed to Helena, grown more powerful.

"When Ned was here," Cordelia said. "It was ever so much tidier. We had a nice little run, I must say, your son and I. A lovely cook. At least compared to me. Which is not saying that much!"

Helena smiled, and her stomach gave a little twinge, in remembrance of meals past.

On the street, on the way to a vegetarian place Cordelia loved, she took Helena's arm, and Helena felt warmth come into her. It would all be fine. The restaurant was lofty, in an old banking hall, the prices low, the smell of lentils and cumin almost as overpowering as the feline smell in Cordelia's place. They were the oldest people in the restaurant by many years.

At dinner, Cordelia spoke of her fondness for Luca. "I suspect, I hope you'll like him. He has some charm to him."

As far as Helena was concerned, charm was an overrated virtue. Cordelia took Helena in. "Now, don't purse your lips that way. Don't set yourself against him. You know, it may not be a match for the ages. They're both so young. Well, Ned is at any rate."

"What, is he ancient?" Visions of a decrepit old man taking advantage of her young son swam into her.

"Not at all," Cordelia said. "Just a few years older. And somehow younger than Ned, in spirit. Anyway, he's not a waste of Ned's time. And Ned isn't wasting this boy's time either."

"It all just makes me think of…" Helena said. "Of you, and your hard time."

"Yes," Cordelia said. "But it's not the same. And anyway, do you know, he loved me. In his fashion."

The poem she was referencing came into both of their minds: *I have been faithful to thee, Cynara, in my fashion.*

"We had," she carried on, "we have our children. It was no Greek tragedy, the whole thing, though it seemed that way at the time. He just, at the end, he wanted to be with the great friend of his youth. His lover, yes, but also his friend. Just as I was."

Helena let that sit there for a time. Cordelia had reworked the story. Or, the story had reworked itself in her, the good bits of it wrestling the bad down, pinning it to the mat. How kind a person's memory could be, taking the sting out of old hurts, editing out foul periods. At least, it could do that work, if you had a generous disposition like Cordelia's.

A waiter came to the table, bringing their herbal teas and the cheque, which Helena pounced on.

"It'll be fine tomorrow," Cordelia said, shifting the focus back to Ned and away from her old grief.

Helena took her cue. "The strangest thing is that I've been worrying over what to wear. I never worry about what to wear. But this boy, this man, he's from Milan, the world's fashion capital. I remember Mother saying, 'You dress like who you are, but you stretch towards the occasion. People shouldn't pretend to be something they're not. If you're from the provinces, then you wear your provincial best.' So what should a middle-aged schoolteacher from an unimportant suburb of a lesser North American city wear for such an occasion? What is my 'provincial best'? In my day, I could look… like someone."

"Don't worry overmuch about that."

"That's a great help! Every so often, I'll see a rather bold hat, and I'll think of her hats, the absurd *folies* she found to wear for the village fetes." She did her mother's voice, "Some color, always some color!"

"Good gosh," Cordelia said. "You really can do it. Her voice. A shock to hear it again. It feels so recent, losing her, but it isn't. I suppose it will always feel recent."

"We're going down there," Helena said. "To the house. To see Father. Ned is intrigued by him. The ogre, the selfish giant in the backdrop."

"Oh, dear," Cordelia said. "He does go in where angels fear to tread. It's atrocious that your father hasn't invited the boy down. Atrocious but typical."

"Yes, he was always a hard-working man, in his job," Helena said. "But ask him to do anything that requires any labour outside it, any non-legal labour? Ask him to have a single encounter with any emotional uncertainty to it, where he'd have to work at that, pay attention, take care? He balks. Do you know what he told me when I called? He told me he has more interest in my other son, in Henry. 'The scrappy little number,' he called him."

"Sees a bit of the old Nick in the boy, I suppose."

"I suppose. But who told him he got to pick and choose?"

"No one has ever told him anything. Mathilda did try from time to time, but he didn't, he wouldn't listen. You'll find her there, in that house, in the grounds. She's there, still, I feel. I know it's nonsense, but… It was a long time ago I was there last, but she was still… in residence."

Helena walked Cordelia back to her flat, noticing that her aunt's once vigorous stride had shortened, that her once erect back had curved some, that her shoulders were slipping down the side of her body. How nice that her dreamy pleasantness had remained untouched. You'd thought life would have curbed this tendency in her, made her pay attention more, but it felt like that part of her had, instead, brought life to heel. Good girl, Helena thought. She felt a century older than her aunt.

Cordelia told Helena to come up and in. Helena settled herself on a chair without too much cat hair on it, while Cordelia scuttled off to another room.

She came back bearing Mathilda's cello. "I stole it from the house. The only time I was back there on a visit. I was giving a reading at a library, and I mean it was my house, too. I thought the least he could do, after he dispossessed me, was to stand me a meal. But no, he asked me for drinks, some cheesy bites. And after I'd had my fill, I nipped upstairs, nicked it, took the maid's staircase down, left without saying goodbye. It did feel marvelous. I'm so glad the car started!"

"Good for you!" Helena said. "I did wonder where it was!"

"It's for you," Cordelia said. "Your Henry, he plays. I gather he's rather good."

"He *is* rather good," Helena said. She opened the case up, and looked at the old instrument, the source of so much of the music of her childhood. "This is very special. I can almost hear her playing 'Sheep may safely graze' on it, as I look at it. Are you quite sure?"

"Receipt of stolen property," Cordelia said. "It's a crime. You may get done for it. Anyway, none of mine want it. They don't... they don't remember her as well as they might do. I have told them all about her. But in their own rights, they don't remember her well. They were so very young. As were you."

"Yes," she said. "But thankfully I was a scrappy little number, too."

...

Helena awoke late the next day. It was a chilly, soggy one. The way it gets inside you, the cold and damp of England on such a day, Helena hadn't missed that. Fog shrouded the square beneath the window and, when she got out, water beaded on her trench coat. She paced briskly down Tottenham Court Road, en route to the Portrait Gallery near Trafalgar Square. She walked by Heal's, where her mother had purchased incidental furniture, continued through Oxford Circus, past the lone skyscraper, the Centre Point, in the no man's land between Soho and Bloomsbury, and then on to the familiar, congenial territory of Charing Cross Road.

Some impossibly young boys, one with double-dyed hair (black over blonde) and white plastic trousers, poured out of a doorway on the Soho side of the street and into a waiting cab. Were they gay? Indubitably. Were they coming from the sort of club that Ned frequented? Such unattractive creatures. They were cackling.

In the museum, she stood a while before the Holbein portrait of Sir Thomas More. In her English history class, she spent a lot of time on the Tudor period, a time when the essence of Englishness was being defined. What a cast of characters! If you can't make that period come alive, she thought, then best to call it quits.

In her classes, they tended to cover More briefly, the church prelate who would not assist his friend and sovereign Henry VIII in the campaign to throw over Catherine of Aragon for the comely, young Anne Boleyn. More would not push the Pope to allow Henry to get out of his marriage to the

Spanish princess, who'd given him only a daughter for a child, not a male heir. Sometimes Helena would show her students the film of the play about More, Robert Bolt's *A Man For All Seasons.* The film made him seem an admirable man of principle, but by other accounts he was a stubborn pedant, who refused to make the necessary adjustments to the drift of the times he lived in. Somehow both men—the hero and the prig—were in Holbein's portrait.

Should she adjust her ideas, her views as Ned wanted her to do? Or should she remain staunch? Here I stand, I can do no other. That was Luther, she thought, another stubborn man. At a cafe underneath the church of St. Martin-in-the-Fields, she had a salad for lunch, wandering through the church proper after it, kneeling to pray for a few minutes, asking for guidance in the days to come. The church was the source of much of the classical music she listened to on the radio in Canada, and a choir was rehearsing in the complex somewhere, wafts of music coming into the nave, presumably whenever the door to their practice room opened.

By the time she got back into the open air, the day had brightened. In the end, back at the hotel, she chose an outfit she'd bought for the theatre, a white silk blouse and a Houndstooth suit, in black and white. In recognition of her mother's dictum, she tied a green scarf around her neck in what she hoped was a jaunty attitude. She inspected herself in the mirror, added a bit more make-up to her face than was usual, and ran a brush through her hair. Should she have gone to a salon for a quick trim and set? Too late now.

She took the bus from the hotel to Islington, sitting on the upper level as it lumbered along. Why anyone would sit on the lower level had always puzzled her. She liked to walk and take transit when she traveled, finding it pleasant to stretch her wits by navigating in an unfamiliar place, and, anyway, one sees so much more. But this was not a pleasure trip.

A few seats in front of her, there was a young mother trying to comfort a fussy baby. What a long haul it was, bringing up children. The little things didn't realize it; they just assumed it was their right to ask all of this of their parents, especially their mothers. And fair enough: they hadn't asked to be born. How tiring it all had been. And your best, it was never quite good enough.

She stepped up to speak to the mother. “It's not easy,” she said. “I remember. But you'll get there. You will.”

The woman laughed, and held her baby up and spoke to the little thing. “We must be making a right scene, with strangers coming up to express their sympathy, mustn't we?” The baby looked up, trusting at Helena, curious about her.

“And then,” Helena said. “Like that, a second later, they're good as gold. And you never want to be parted from them.”

“That's about right,” the mother said.

The bus pulled into the stop nearest the Angel, the tube-stop named for the old inn. Here shops and hostelries had been congregating from at least the Middle Ages on. She got off, and found her way to the agreed bistro. It was cheery, surrounded by tables with umbrellas advertising French liqueurs. She was early, so she went into a bookstore, found herself a mystery by a strong British crime writer who was a former coroner, so she knew a fair bit about death's manifestations.

She then browsed in some antique stores in a small glassed-in mall. Was there something nice and particular she could find for Ned's place? No, there was not. It was not a part of London she knew at all, but she liked what she saw of it. Ned was lucky to live here.

When she walked back to the restaurant, she spotted her tall, thin son out front, next to this shorter, thicker man. Her spirits lifted some when she saw Ned. It had been too long, and their last meeting so hideous.

Ned spotted her and waved. She waved back, hers more fervent than his, as if seeking to overwhelm the caution in his. She gave Ned a hug, squeezing for good measure this body, which had come out of hers.

Luca's greeting to her was courteous without being obsequious. “Ned's mother. Mrs. Baldwin, what a pleasure!” He extended both hands to her, and it was clear, he intended to kiss her, one cheek, two. He did it deftly, so it didn't feel awkward. She took in his strong nose, olive cheeks. She liked his mouth, the dark pink of his lips, the way they turned up at their extremities, as if he spent much more time laughing than crying. He looked still young, but yes, he was maybe a decade older than Ned. He had on a dark suit, one that sat well on his solid form, a white shirt, a tie the blue of his eyes, and some rather too avant-garde spectacles framing them. For his part, Ned looked glum, one of Henry's wives en route to her beheading.

“Buck up,” she thought, “I've only crossed the ocean to see you.”

She looked back at Luca, and that mouth formed into a smile, his head dipping in acknowledgment, it seemed to her, of the length of her journey, the importance, for him, of the occasion. He gestured her into the restaurant. This man, at least, knew what to do, how to reduce the necessary awkwardness of such a meeting as this.

They were given a corner table, on a slight ledge, overlooking the rest of the restaurant. It was the one Fritzie would have wanted. The hostess seemed to know Luca. They took their seats, Ned between the two of them. She fluffed her scarf up.

“I do prefer a busy place,” Helena said. “And there's hardly an empty table in here.”

“It's been popular from the start,” Luca said. “I do hope you like it. It was too loud when they first opened, so I told them about these panels.” He pointed upwards. “They deaden the noise.”

“That's what he does,” Ned said. “Acoustics. Or architecture that deals with acoustics. It's part science, part art.”

Luca put up his hand to stop Ned. “Let's get ourselves a little settled in, shall we? Get ourselves equipped with a drink.”

A nod from Luca, and a waiter came to the table. Helena ended up with a white wine, Luca with a red, and Ned with a gin and tonic.

"Yes," he said. "I work, in a junior capacity at an architectural firm which deals with theaters and concert halls. Building new ones, refurbishing old ones, trying to get the acoustics right, correcting them when they're wrong. So many of the ones that have gone up in the last twenty years, the sound quality, it's a disaster. Like, what did you think you were building, a sculpture, a monument to your ego?"

"I was thinking of that, of acoustics, today," she said. "I ate lunch at the cafe at St. Martin-in-the-Fields and then I went into the church. Why is it the music from there… why does it resonate so? I don't, I don't have the vocabulary. But it seems… warm. Even a choir rehearsing somewhere in the bowels of the building, it was… special to hear. It sounds a specialized area, the one you work in."

"Yes, yes, it is." He left it there, and she found she was relieved he didn't dive into it, that she didn't have to assimilate enough information about his trade to ask at least one follow-up question.

The menu was large and awkward to hold, so she put it down, the better to absorb Ned and this man separately, and then to take in Ned and this man together. Luca reached over to point out certain dishes he particularly liked on the menu, and ones to avoid

And then Ned began to chatter, speaking of a performance they'd seen at Covent Garden, of Sophie's new boyfriend (a young Tory city counsellor), a bike-ride he and Luca had taken through London to the zoo, alongside the Serpentine. His sentences were full of stutters, and he looked ready to broach another subject, when Luca put his hand on Ned's. It was another effort to get him to slow him down. It took some adjusting to see a man's hand on Ned's, but she could see it settled him. It didn't revolt her, seeing Luca's hand there. In fact, it seemed rather nice.

Ned saw her noticing it, and extricated his hand from Luca's.

Luca turned to her, "“I suppose he's always spoken more when he's nervous, not less?”

“Yes,” Helena said. “He always has.”

“And how was your d-d-dinner with Cordelia?” Ned said.

She worried about the stutter. It was new, and she hoped its stay with Ned would be short.

“Godawful,” Helena said. “The food. This vegetarian place she likes.”

“My sympathies,” Luca said. “Yes, we've been there.”

“She speaks very highly of you,” Helena said.

“She is a doll. Do you say, a poppet?”

“You don't say it too terribly often,” Helena said. “But it works for her. She *is* a poppet.”

“But that flat! How could Ned have lived there?”

“I know. It's septic, positively septic.”

“I loved it,” Ned said. “One of the best times of my life.”

“Such a high recommendation, don't you think, Helena?” Luca said. “One of the best times in his long, long life.”

“Don't patronize me,” Ned said, but with good humor.

She wondered who was the stronger of the two of them. Not who did what to whom in the bedroom. She couldn't let her imagination take her there and anyway it didn't interest her that much. But outside the bedroom, who had the more power? There were the rules between men and women, and you knew what they were. As the woman, you gave your man pride of place, or you were trained to do so anyway. As often as not, she breached the rules in this regard, but they were there, they gave you a framework. These two, they didn't have as much of one to rely on. She realized she envied them that, the ability to improvise more. Though perhaps that group, the one Ned had chosen to join, the one he'd felt impelled to join, perhaps the homosexuals had their own rules. Again, that didn't interest her overmuch.

After they placed their orders, Luca pulled out a pack of cigarettes, opening the pack and pulling a cigarette out. "Helena?" he said, as he offered it to her.

"I quit years ago," she said. "I find I'm tempted, but it was so difficult to quit. I used to sneak them next to the fireplace for a time."

Luca laughed. "I realize I'm already calling you Helena," he said. "You don't mind, do you?"

She found she didn't and told him so. She asked him where he lived. He lit his own cigarette up.

"Not far from here, so that's… convenient. We live in a flat over a market. It makes for a rather raucous awakening on the weekends." He imitated some of the hawkers' calls.

"You don't live alone?" Helena said. Ned looked uncomfortable.

"I live with an old and very dear friend," Luca said. "My flatmate, he's –"

Instead of going on, he asked her about her hotel.

"In Bloomsbury," Helena said. "Rather old-fashioned, but nice." She turned to Ned, "Fritzie's treat. For my birthday."

"Oh, yes," Ned said. "Happy birthday. I sent you a card, did you get it?"

"Yes," Helena said. "But I was rather hoping for a call."

Ned blushed and his expression turned to a pout. He'd seldom pouted as a boy. That was more Henry's territory.

Luca said he'd heard some, about Fritzie. "Your mother-in-law," he said. "She sounds formidable. She might not be an easy mother-in-law to have?"

This made Helena laugh. "Wait," she said. "At this early stage in our acquaintance, you're asking me to share my feelings about my mother-in-law?"

Luca nodded yes. Helena liked that he didn't withdraw or qualify the question. "Fritzie, you know, she wasn't easy at first. This random Englishwoman stealing her son away while he studied at Cambridge. And the wedding, the small wedding we somehow pulled together. My mother had just died. It wasn't much of a wedding. It certainly wasn't the one Fritzie had in mind for her firstborn. She had in mind some fashionable London church on Hanover Square. But we've made a go of it, Oliver and I, and Fritzie and I have too. She likes my children, so that helps. And now we live and let live, the two of us. I do a lot of pretending not to hear things. I'm sure she does the same."

"A wise approach," he said. The waiter came to check in—was it all to their liking? Luca's voice became abrasive, "It all is fine."

After the waiter left, he turned to them. "I hate it how they do that, the check to see if all is well. Don't you? If it's not fine, I will certainly tell you."

"Yes," Helena said. "I thought it was just a North American thing."

"No, it's come here. Not to my country, not to Italy yet. There they watch you, they eavesdrop, and they know if it's not fine. And for you, being back, in your own country, in England," he said. "How is it?"

"Well, of course, London isn't England," Helena said. "Though much of the world thinks it is. For us, it often seems like a carbuncle on the otherwise healthy body. But each time I come, I feel something more has gone out of this country. It's not what it was. A nation of bed-and-breakfasts, of twee pubs and cutesy teashops. We, who were warriors once."

"'A nation of shopkeepers,'" he said. "Ned says you like to quote."

"I can't seem to help it. It's a tic really."

"That is Napoleon, correct, calling England a nation of shopkeepers?"

"Yes," Helena said. "In our family we called him The Frenchman. To pronounce his name, it was still bad form. As if you might yet conjure him up. Yes, his dig about us as shopkeepers. Yes, the Frenchman got to see what we were. At Waterloo and at the Battle of Trafalgar. He had time to think about it in his long stay on St. Helena, where we imprisoned him so he couldn't make any more mischief."

"Your saint," Luca said.

"Yes," Helena said. "I didn't think of that when I thought of the island. Constantine's mother. Evelyn Waugh wrote a rather awful book about her. About how she and her son wandered about Asia Minor looking for remnants of the true cross. It was no *Brideshead.*"

Ned perked up at this mention. She told him that she'd found the miniseries made of the book at the library, and re-watched it. She watched him taking that information in.

He asked after her trip to visit Henry at Dartmouth there over parents' weekend. She mentioned how much she'd enjoyed meeting his friends.

“Henry's friends,” she said. “Those sweet words, 'Henry's friends.' Plural. I didn't get to say those words much when he was high school.” She turned to Luca. “Ned was a hit at his school, a hero in his schooldays, dearly beloved of the masters and students.”

Ned ran away from this, his mother speaking of past triumphs, speaking of an exhibit they'd seen at the V&A.

They set to eating, and Luca told a story of his own brother's visit to London, how his brother had somehow gotten on the wrong bus one day, ended up in a rough part of the East End, lost his wallet somehow, as well as misplacing Luca's phone number and address. “He knew only that we lived on a market not too far from Hampstead Heath. This publican took pity on him, fed him a nice meal and tracked me down. My brother is that person. Utterly helpless and everyone can see it, so people go out of their way to do things for him. Me, they take one look at me, and say, you're on your own. You seem competent enough, you go handle it. So I do. Handle it. Him, he sort of bats his eyes at them—you say that, yes—and it's all taken care of.”

“It's a lucky thing to have,” Helena said. “That quality.” She thought of Cordelia. People wanted to do things for her.

“I guess,” Luca said. “But when he gets older, less handsome. He'll have to learn better to cope.”

“I suppose he will,” Helena said. “Still, 'Sufficient unto the day are the evils thereof.' There it is again, I suppose. My reliance on things other people have said. Anyway, he'll find a new strategy when that one stops working.”

“No doubt,” Luca said. “Listen, I gather that you haven't been having an easy time with Ned's… sexuality. It certainly is not easy.”

Some food went down the wrong way and Helena coughed it up a bit. It remained caught in her throat, and Helena took a sip of wine to make it go down. It did. She then put a napkin to her lips, and some of her lipstick came off on it, the shape of her lips on it. How thin her lips were, not the sensual ones you saw on movie stars. She tried to open herself up to what Luca wanted to tell her.

And he continued, at ease, she thought, where he ought to have been nervous. “My mother was far from happy with it. When I told her, she was in the kitchen, making dinner, one of the recipes from their family restaurant. She took out a big knife and held it to her chest. 'Kill me now,' she said.” Helena knew whereof that woman spoke. “And then she took to her bed for months. And my father! I could do nothing with him. Why had I done this to him, to my mother?”

“I'm sorry,” Helena said. “That sounds difficult.”

“It was… tough. For a time. I told her, ‘Mamma, at least now you know you will always be the most important woman in my life.’ It's the same for you, Helena, you will always be the most important woman in Ned's life.”

Helena smiled in spite of herself. “I hadn't thought of that, Luca. I admit it was a shock when Ned… came out to us last fall. On our last night here. But I'm… I'm getting there.” She ventured a glance at Ned, who was keeping his eyes on his plate. She reached over to put her hand on the same one Luca had grasped. Ned looked up, surprised she'd done so, by no means pleased. “I'm trying. Really I am.” She turned back to Luca. “And how are they now, your parents?”

“My mother is good, but my father, he is not. Oh, look, he's no longer angry with me, but he's still not happy. He hasn't made his peace with it. I'm not sure he will.” Helena understood exactly. She couldn't change Ned's mind, she accepted that now. It was possible to love Ned still, but she had to stop seeing this thing as a parasitic attachment, drawing sustenance from his soul. That word she'd used about London, a carbuncle. No, she had to see it as part of him, coming from within him, perhaps born into him. Like a birth defect. No, not like that either. She found she didn't yet know how to think of this.

"And how did you two meet?"

"At a club," Luca said. "It was this strange warehouse, that they'd done up—"

Ned interrupted him. "It was through Sophie," he said. "We went to this place, done up for the evening by some of her art-school friends."

The bill came and Helena insisted on paying for the meal, and Ned and Luca let her. She and Ned firmed up the arrangements to get down to see her father, which had Ned renting a car, and picking her up at her hotel the next day, them trying to navigate out of the city and towards the West Country in the late morning.

They took her to the taxi stand, and waved her off. It all had gone fine, though there was some sense of anticlimax to it. A part of her had hoped for some sort of grand showdown, for the opportunity to speak of the big emotions that had roiled her this year past. "Kill me now!" How satisfying it would have been to say such a thing.

She longed for the bed in the hotel.

She liked the man, she decided. He had some largeness of spirit to him. He could make a conversation move, saying the things you did, but in his own particular way. But he could also make it slow down. He wasn't afraid of speaking of the real things, of difficult things. He didn't belabor them though; there was no desire in him to wallow in misery. You nodded at it, tipped your hat, 'Hello, Misery', and then you moved on.

That, the wallowing, that was more Ned's thing. Or these days it was. He'd been such a happy child, so easy to please. What a shock it was then, when colicky Henry came. She thought, with sympathy, of the mother on the bus.

There was something strange about the way Luca had described his flatmate. And there was something Ned didn't want Luca to say about where and how they'd met.

On the whole, though, Helena was satisfied with the way the evening had gone, pleased that, as Cordelia had said, this man was not a waste of Ned's time. She had made it through this day. She dreaded the next one, but put it to one side. As she'd said: Sufficient unto the day. Even more than her bed, she found she craved that cigarette Luca had offered her. Funny how that longing never quite left you.

...

On the way down to her family's home in the West Country, in Somerset, they stopped at Stonehenge, and wandered through it. Ned asked her why they'd visited her father so little. She decided he shouldn't be overburdened with her views of her father, but that some explanation was called for. "We didn't always see eye-to-eye," she said. "And, I suppose, with Cora filling my mother's spot, it just… it was hard. I should have, I could have overcome my reservations more. But he never tried to bridge the gap either. I've invited him over many times. He never comes."

They made good time in the second part of the drive, arriving at her old home in the middle of the afternoon. The house was a symmetrical stone house, eight windows across, three high, on a small rise. There were the stone pineapples on the gates that Ned found he remembered from a childhood visit. "The symbols of hospitality," Helena said. "Something my parents believed in. My mother, she made people feel at home." The hoops and colored posts needed to play croquet had been pushed into a close-clipped, lime green lawn next to the house. Two roses climbed up a trellis in the front. Helena sighed as she took it in. Across a pond to the house's left was a gazebo. "We did theatricals there," Helena said.

Cora came to the door. “Hallo, you two. You got out of London.” In the manner of all country people, she spoke of getting out of London as if it were the same as escaping from the clutches of a dangerous beast. She had on a nautical suit. Parallel blue stripes at the bottom of the flared white skirt, to go with the stripes at the ends of the jacket sleeves. She looked, Ned decided, more of a sophisticated divorcée from a drawing-room comedy than a county judge's wife. The skirt was tight, showing off her slender legs and it was cut high enough to allow her ankles to be seen.

The hall was tiled in black and white, a painting of a somewhat bovine woman in front of some flags on one wall, and a big jar to the right had the fancy and sometimes fanciful handles of assorted umbrellas, walking sticks and canes sticking out of it. He looked up the stairs at the end of the hall, expecting his grandfather to come down.

“He's napping,” Cora said.

“God forbid he should depart from his regular routine,” Helena said. “I've only come from Canada to see him.”

Cora's lips narrowed. “You weren't expected for some time. He's hoping, once you're settled in, that we might play some croquet before dinner. He thought you might enjoy that after the long drive.”

This time Helena kept her thought to herself. This, also, was part of his daily routine, only today, he wouldn't be playing with his usual cronies, but with Helena and Ned. What a concession he'd made for their visit!

Helena had her old room, which Cora had redone with some godawful Laura Ashley wallpaper. The bed was the same, though, the views, similar, if the oak tree of her youth had grown taller, the principal boughs now a few feet above the window, not right there. Now, instead of a mass of green leaves, you saw a small orchard, and the pond off to the left.

Ned found himself in the room where Sophie's mother, his Aunt Felicity, had grown up, one that looked out over the croquet lawn. After he'd got himself washed up, he saw his grandfather down below, taking practice shots, his whippets trotting about him. Ned opened the window, leaned out and waved, but his grandfather didn't see him.

"Augustus, get out of there!" Just below Ned, a dog was rolling around in some manure that had been spread around the base of the roses. "Come here!" The whippet reluctantly moved towards his grandfather. He pulled the dog by its collar towards a teak table next to the lawn, picking up a newspaper from it, and swatting the dog with it. "You know better than that, Augie!"

Only then, did the man look upwards. "Oh, hallo, you," he said. He and his wife had evidently agreed on hallo rather than hello.

"Ned," Ned said, putting his hand on his chest, since it seemed his grandfather might not have remembered his name.

"Yes, of course," he said. "I know your name. I'm not past it yet."

The dog, now lying at his feet, began to whine. His grandfather bent down, and rumpled its ears, and soon enough the dog was squeaking with pleasure. He looked back up at Ned. "This here's Augustus. That's Nero, and over there is Julius."

"Roman emperors," Ned said.

"Yes," he said. "Why don't you come down? Join me in a drink." He gestured at the bottles set up on the table.

Ned found his way down. His grandfather had on khaki trousers, a pink-and-white striped shirt and a Panama hat to keep the sun off his cheeks, which had tangles of delicate burgundy veins showing in them. He looked like something out of a Graham Greene novel, the retired Consul General of Panama. He was tall, solidly built, with a bit of a paunch. Much of the hair on his forearms had gone white, and there were a few wiry white hairs coming out his ears and nostrils, his eyebrows unruly, theatrical in their way.

"Why are your dogs named for Roman emperors?" Ned asked.

"The Romans knew how to run things," he said.

"You prefer the Romans to the Greeks?"

"Vastly," he said. "The Greeks were full of imagination, creativity, erratic, but with a few good ideas. And many bad ones. The Romans cherrypicked the best of those ideas, took all those things, and made them work."

"For me, it's the reverse," Ned said. It was evident from his grandfather's face that he hadn't expected to be contradicted. "The Romans may have conquered the Greeks, stolen their Gods, ripped off and bastardized many of their ideas. But the Greeks, it's their myths we read, their gossipy, faulty gods we hear of. Minerva? Who's she? Athena, now you're talking. Who are the philosophers we care about? Plato, Socrates."

"The Romans gave us roads. The rule of law."

"And the Greeks gave us the theatre, democracy."

The judge chuckled two notes, a little humorless, but thoughtful, as he considered what Ned had said. Neither of them had considered their thoughts, just each was drawn to different things, different aspects of the past.

Cora brought out a tray with some olives, lemon slices and cheesy crackers on it. Ned poured himself a gin-and-tonic and sat next to his mother's father, observing him sip his whisky. Ned couldn't see much of himself in the man. He was a couple of sips into his own drink, when Helena joined them. Cora got her a glass of the same wine she was having. The judge asked after Sophie, but didn't seem much interested in Ned's reply. Helena prompted Ned to speak about the law firm where he worked, and that got his grandfather going.

"They instructed me on a couple of cases," he said. "When I was a barrister." He named the solicitors who'd sent the case his direction, and Ned knew one of them. "He's rather senior now."

"Well, he would be, I guess," he said.

"What shall I call you, sir?" Ned said.

"Oh, that," he said. "Everyone else, all the others, they call me Grandfather. Sometimes, behind my back, they call me His Lordship. You know, what judges get called."

Ned nodded. His grandfather spoke in some detail of one case he'd handled for the firm, defending a doctor accused of malpractice. Although it must have been some years past, he could still recall the facts, the key arguments he put to the court, and the outcome.

"Your mother," he said. "She could have been a brilliant barrister. At breakfast, I'd tell her about my cases, ask her what her instincts were. Which of the facts I'd mentioned felt pertinent. Her instincts were strong."

He told them of a classmate of hers who'd gone on to become a barrister in Grey's Inn.

"Yes," Helena said. "You always mention her. I can barely recall her, but I thought she was perhaps a little daft. Shows how much I know."

"You'd have done so well at that."

"Well, you know," Helena said. "I've become rather a good teacher. Some of the same skills. I went to the Portrait Gallery on my first full day here, and I saw all those Tudors in the one room. The Holbeins. I taught that period last year to a few of our graduating students. The class, it went well. I think, if I may be a little immodest, I turned this one girl around. She was a bit of party girl, popular to a fault. And her good mind was going to seed.

And now she's gone off to university, and is studying, is reading history this year. She credits me for her choice of subjects."

Ned was surprised to hear his mother speaking in praise of herself. It was something she hardly ever did. He realized it was the Baby Driver, Marina, she was describing. Her father didn't appear much interested in what she had to say, looking at his watch as she spoke. He got up, directing them to a rolling rack with heavy mallets and balls of different colors on it. "You know how to play, I assume. It's not expected that a colonial will. Are there even lawns in those wilds?"

"I've played some," Ned said. After they'd each taken a mallet and ball, Cora wheeled the rack away.

Ned and his Grandfather both passed through the first wicket and moved on to the second, while Helena and Cora both missed, Helena passing the wicket by, Cora positioning herself just in front of it, readying herself to go through on the next turn.

"She's always so damn cautious. And Ned, not too bad sailing right through it. Beginner's luck, maybe."

On his second turn, Ned hit his ball at his grandfather's, which was sitting squarely in front of the second wicket. He was some distance away, but his ball nicked the other, and he proceeded to put the balls together, hit the back one in such way as to set his ball up in front of the hoop, and position his grandfather's just past it. He then went through it, and hit his grandfather's ball again, sending them both towards the third wicket.

"You see how he treats the aged?" the judge said. When the time came to take his next shot, he didn't hit it so as to go back to the second wicket, through which he still needed to pass, but took aim at Ned's ball, just narrowly missing it.

"Never mind, you'll get yours."

"Will I, Your Lordship?"

Soon enough Ned had whacked his ball into the post, winning the game, with his grandfather three wickets behind him.

"It's almost the same s-s-set we had," Ned said, inspecting his mallet, as he put it away. "The same company—Jaques without a 'c'—just not quite the same vintage." Soon after the boys reached school age, Helena had ordered the set, and the cost of shipping the heavy mallets, hoops and balls over to Canada had almost been more than the cost of the set itself. She remembered, with a wince of retrospective feeling, how Henry had once walloped Ned over the head with one of these mallets, the wound requiring two stitches to close it. They were worried about a concussion, and Oliver and she alternated, sitting up the whole night with the boy.

Cora poured them all another drink, which they sipped at, sitting on the chairs near the table.

"Damned cheek this son of yours has, Helena. Coming to my lawn, and whipping me on it. Comes by it honestly. Your mother always had a lot of cheek to her, too." He took a big sip of his whiskey. "She was a fine little rider. I was cleaning the whips once, near our barn, when she came upon me. I didn't notice her, and was cracking the dust off the bullwhip hard. I don't know if you've ever heard it, but it makes a sound like a gun going off. Her horse spooked. Was it Micawber? That horse we boarded for a bit."

Helena nodded yes.

"Her horse took off, with her on it. She was terrified, you could see that. A slip of a thing she was. But she held on, even when the horse jumped a fence. That was where I lost sight of them. The next thing I knew she was trotting him back here, proud as punch, posting up and down, as if nothing had happened. I could only applaud. I got her all new riding gear to reward her."

"That was not how it happened," Helena said. All looked at her expectantly, but she did not elaborate.

Cora had cooked a nice roast of beef for them. The old man cross-examined Ned further about his friend and former instructing counsel at the firm, but Ned had little to offer. He described his work, but as it was assisting in firming up the paperwork for complicated international deals, not farming out litigation, it didn't matter much to his grandfather. Helena asked after some old neighbors, and spoke admiringly of the house's condition.

"Yes, it needs constant attention," the judge said. He enumerated some of his recent projects. "It was on its last legs when we—when your mother and I took it over from her parents."

"Hardly," Helena said.

"What do you know? You weren't even alive. They needed someone who could afford to give it what it needed."

"It wasn't some sort of charity case," Helena said. "It's a lovely house. And you were lucky to marry a woman who had it."

After dinner, Cora brought out some port, and the old man picked up the wrapped birthday present Helena had brought for him for his 80th, and shook it. "I wonder what it could be." Of course, he could tell, anyone would be able to tell that it had the shape and weight of a hardcover book. "We were hoping you'd make it for the party, but if you can't, you can't."

"Yes, I'm sorry, just the autumn's a bad time, what with the teaching. Miles mentioned it. I didn't hear from you about it, directly. And so I didn't know it was going to be really a big thing."

"Oh, yes, a marquee, a brass band, the whole thing. Still, if you can't make it, you can't. Your teaching career must come first."

Ned didn't like the accent he put on the word "career". She *was* a good teacher, and that was an important thing to be.

The old man began to pull off the wrapping paper, revealing a popular history of the Hudson's Bay Company. He surveyed the book skeptically.

"I thought you might be interested," Helena said, "in the early years of the Company especially, when so many intrepid young men were trekking across the Canadian wilderness." He'd often spoken of his desire to "bushwhack" through the wilds of Canada, but had never followed up by arranging for an actual visit. Maybe it was just as well, Helena thought. When he imagined Canada, it wasn't the manicured lawns of Oakville he had in mind.

Helena spoke to Ned, "Father always loved that poem of Robert Service's set in the Arctic, 'The Cremation of Sam McGee.'"

Ned quoted the first couple of lines: "'There are strange things done in the midnight sun, by the men who moil for gold.' I love that word, 'moil.'"

The old man put the book down. "Yes, moil. Thank you for the book. I'm not much of a reader these days. Once I get done with the *Spectator* and the *Telegraph,* that's me done. But thank you."

He asked Ned which paper he took, and Ned said he divided his attention between the *Times* and *The Guardian.*

"The *Times*, fine, a bit of a bore, but fine. I've had a letter or two in there. *The Guardian*, now that's worrisome. Do you know, why don't you come down, Ned?" he said. "For my gala. Bring a girl, make a weekend of it."

"Thank you for the invitation," Ned said. "I'd love to come, but I'm not much of a one for br-br-bringing girls." The old man looked searchingly at Ned, then at Helena, and she couldn't stop herself from coloring.

A long pause descended on the table, and the old man was the first to regroup. “If you came, it would give me a chance to get my revenge at croquet. I could tell you what's what about the Greeks and Romans. And you could tell me the same.”

As they all made noises about retiring, he asked Helena if she'd join him for a drink in the study. Cora looked at the old man, and he nodded to say she was not wanted, that this was to be a conference between a father and his daughter.

They got settled in the leather armchairs in the book-lined room, him with a port and a pipe, her with some sherry.

He spoke of his will, informing her that the house would go to Cora, for the duration of her life, and then to Helena's brother Miles, that there'd be some money coming to her. “Not much, mind you. The house is more of a burden than a benefit.”

“I had no expectations of you,” Helena said.

“You should go around, put stickers on the back of anything you particularly want.”

“No,” Helena said. “I won't do that. If you want to give me something, then you must do so. You will do, I hope, what seems just with it all.” He wanted her to get upset, and she would not give him that. “Between mother's bequest to me, and Oliver's and my work, we are well set up. And Oliver's mother is generous with us, so that helps. She is helping to foot the bill for Henry's pricey education.”

“I was worried about you,” he said. “When you told me you were marrying a colonial. A scholarship boy.”

“You were mad at me,” she said.

"But when they arrived, that woman in all her finery," he said. "Her husband that rare thing, a gentleman. He could keep quiet as he fished. Anyway, after I saw her all decked out, case after case coming in the door, then I was less worried."

"But not less angry."

"No, not less angry. You were abandoning me," he said. "I'd lost her—and then you. There was, there *is*, no one like her."

"You had a funny way of showing that."

"The others," he said, "They've made their peace with that, with Cora."

"They didn't see what I saw," Helena said. She'd come across her father and Cora kissing on a picnic blanket in that secret little meadow in the woods. Her mother was not dead, then, but desperately ill.

"Well, well, well," he said. "It all comes out. I've always had a strong sense of my own needs."

This was the first time on this visit, Helena felt, that he actually looked at her, that he risked saying something hard and true. He waited, but she didn't give him any response. What could she say?

"Enough of this," he said. "Either you can let bygones be bygones, or you can't. It sounds you've built a good life for yourself."

"Yes," she said. "Do you know, I have, we have. And I did love those breakfasts, you presenting the facts of the case, some of the applicable legal principles, walking us through the precedents. It is a regret, that I didn't do that. But Ned came. Then Henry. And they needed a mother. I could balance it, barely, with teaching. And others have done it with the practice, but it seemed, too hard. Anyway, I do wish you'd not harp on it. It's a tender spot for me."

"Yes, I know. It's just, I imagined us, you and I, perhaps on opposite sides of a case, matching wits. I thought you'd be a part of my life. But, you aren't. It's extraordinary how much the boy looks like Mathilda. When he looked out that window, I almost keeled over. I do hope he comes down, for my party. He can bring whatever, whomever he wants."

"Luca," Helena said. "He'd probably bring Luca. Who is charming. Who would be an asset to any party. He seems to be some sort of Italian marquess. A *marchese*. Or set to become one when his father dies."

She would never usually have mentioned such a thing, and she felt embarrassed that she'd done so.

"What does one call a *marchese*?" he said.

"Luca. You call him Luca. I suppose Don Luca if you're feeling formal."

Her father was a terrible snob, and so it would matter to him. In this time, she was going to take her victories where she found them.

...

When Helena went down early the next morning, Ned was stretched out on a window seat inside a French window off the drawing room, leafing through old copies of *Punch.* "I couldn't sleep," he said.

"Here we are again, the first up. Breakfast won't be for hours. Cora was never an early riser."

Helena took an old album of photos down from a bookshelf. She sat down on a sofa and patted the place next to her. "Come, look at these with me."

There were some shots of family groups in the Lake District, on climbing vacations in the Alps. "There's Aunt Cordelia."

"She never looks at the camera," Ned said.

"No, no she doesn't."

There was a photo of Mathilda in front of the Royal Albert Hall, with her cello case.

"Mother. After her recital," Helena said.

"Is that Cora?" Clever boy.

Yes, Cora, with her flute case. He persisted: "They knew each other, Cora and my grandmother?"

"They were at the Royal College together. They were the best of friends. Two girls up from the provinces. The very best of friends. Father was deviling under some Q.C. at the Temple Bar. They both wanted him. But Mother got Father. Well, sort of."

Ned looked over at her. "I see."

"Cora, Aunt Cora, was always… around when we were growing up."

"That's why you can't say her name," Ned said. "You're wanting to call her Aunt Cora, but that doesn't work now. Why didn't you tell me this, any of this?"

"He was your grandfather," Helena said. "He is. You just don't do that. Speak to children of such things."

"I am not a child any longer."

"And here we are, speaking of it."

She paged to some photos of Helena and Oliver's wedding. “Look how handsome your father was. And Chief looking so absurdly… chuffed. Yes, that's how he looks, chuffed. Fritzie looks—”

“Angry.”

“Yes. Dressed to the utter nines. In her full battle armor.”

Helena leafed through pointing out her school-friends, her chums from Cambridge, Aunt Cordelia with her errant husband George. Ned paid special attention to him. Could you tell from the photo? Was the Mark of Cain on him? No, it wasn't.

She invited him to join her on a walk about the property. She showed him the punting pond with its water lilies, and the goose Horace honked as he sailed about it. She told him, how, as a special treat, they all used to swim here in the nude, under the moon and stars. She showed him the gazebo. “My brother, sister and I and our friends performed *A Midsummer Night's Dream* here once.”

Helena took her son to what had once been the kitchen garden, but was now filled with flowers. “This was where the German Prisoners of War worked, Ludwig and Werner... Mother and Father treated them well, the two of them. We were not to mock their accents, not to make them feel even more like strangers in a strange land. One of them married our cook, Ethel, took her back to Bavaria after the war. How I wish I still had an Ethel, handling our kitchen!”

They walked through a small wood. “Here was where we used to play 'Saxon or Celt'.” She explained the rules as they walked through the wood. There was a sunlit patch of grass in its middle, the likes of which he'd seen in his *Illustrated Kings and Queens of England*, a king pierced through with arrows, murdered by a rival. “The secret meadow,” she said.

On the other side of the wood was a larger meadow, unbounded by trees, a barn on a rise at the far end of it. She showed Ned the tiny, one-stall stable annexed to the barn. "This was where my father was cleaning his whips, waiting for me to come back from my ride. From my regular ride. Everyone knew Micawber was a skittish horse. That was why we got to have him for a pittance."

Ned's mouth formed a circle.

"Yes, O. He didn't want any of us to grow up wet. And he tested each of us."

How she'd hated him then. But there was a part of her that respected that impulse to test her mettle and that felt pride at passing the test. This country had been great, she thought, precisely because everyone agreed to push themselves, not to be wet. Once, we were warriors. What were we now?

But, almost at once, she corrected the thought. These were some strange inherited beliefs, still swimming around inside her. Some of it was maybe out of Gibbon, the historian who, by one, simple reading, blamed the decline and fall of the Roman Empire on decadence. Maybe that idea explained part of her balking at Ned's homosexuality. Things fall apart if everyone follows their baser instincts.

But, no, she didn't trust any of that. She'd read history at Cambridge. Some of her profs had been critics of it all, with the books and research to back up their critiques. She knew some of the toll that building and maintaining empires took. *Pax Romana, Pax Britannica,* such bosh. Peace for whom exactly?

But that wasn't quite right either. She'd never taught any of this. She'd like to try to do so. Her mind wrestled with how to think of this all, in broad terms, as she walked with her son back to the house in which she'd been born.

"Those clouds," she pointed upwards. "Are they rain clouds?"

"No," Ned said. "I don't think they are."

"Good. I want this to be a glorious day."

They entered to the smells of the nice fry-up Cora had done for them. "Your father's got a touch of the gout," she said. "He won't be down for breakfast."

"Well, there you go," Helena said. "And we have to take off shortly to get to Heathrow in time for my flight. Such a pity. I know how the gout torments him."

Helena asked Cora if she might borrow a small spade and drove with Ned to the parish church. The hens and chicks she'd planted around her mother's grave needed some reining in, some weeds needed pulling. Some cows were wandering in a field adjoining the graveyard, and there were small hills around them. Ned thought it a pretty place to be buried, if you had to be buried anywhere.

After she'd set the grave to rights, she and Ned went into the church. It was nearly 800 years old, she told Ned. "Pevsner has lots to say about it. He loved it, except, of course, for the Victorian improvements. The place was packed for her service. They were out the door. Down from London, her friends from the Royal College. The last mustering of our far-flung clan. Our Scottish cousins, the ones who had been in India. The Parisian cousins who'd married into the French nobility. Cordelia was a rock. Even Cousin Fiona who happened to be here from South Africa. And the letters they sent! I have them somewhere. They were practically all I took with me. My mother touched many people."

He thought of her leaving here, leaving all this, with just some letters from her dead mother. The lyric from the Bronski beat song came back into him: "You leave in the morning with everything you own in a little black case." That was what we all did, in a way, he thought.

"When you came something opened up in me," she said. "And then when you spoke to us, in the car, last fall, I could feel it closing. I'd been losing you for some time. I knew that. Part of growing up. But then you were speaking to us in that car, about having no hands, and there was that same falling feeling I had when my mother was dying. Falling, and where was the bottom?"

"Funny, I felt like I was falling, too." There was a coldness, a distance to his voice, but Helena carried on.

"After my mother died, I felt so alone. Even Oliver, your father, though he was so good to me, I still felt alone. A motherless child. Anyway, we are all of us alone. But I felt less alone with you about, this little chattering boy, a dead ringer for her, saying such strange and often perceptive things. Never shutting up, it is true, but even so, good company. Sometimes you gave voice to the same fugitive thoughts I had, ones I'd never voiced aloud. And so, to lose that, to lose you. I didn't, I don't want that."

She gestured at the old pipe organ. "Music was the chief passion of her life. Or the chief requited passion anyway. At her funeral, an ancient husband and wife from the village were the singers. Their version of 'He Who Would Valiant Be' was particularly off-key, reedy, and the organist didn't help. I was furious that this was to be her send-off, but I knew, even at the time, that the *dreadful* music-making would have greatly amused Mother." Helena became unmoored; her eyes and soul went a-wandering, her heart beat at a faster pace than usual. "Cordelia said Mother would be here, but she isn't. She's gone."

She could feel Ned's hand on her elbow. He steered her to a pew, and she knelt down to pray.

In her whispering, she accented one part of the Paternoster. "Forgive us our trespasses" she whispered, but voiced its corollary with difficulty, "As we forgive those who trespass against us." Did she need to forgive her father before she could be forgiven by her son? No. That was too elementary, arithmetic where morality is more of a quantum field.

The hymn, her mother's exit hymn, came back to Helena, not in the feeble version that had been rendered at the funeral, but instead, the many strong voices of the King's College Cambridge choir singing it lustily, from a recording she treasured:

He who would valiant be 'gainst all disaster,
Let him in constancy follow the Master.
There's no discouragement,
Shall make him once relent
His first avowed intent
To be a pilgrim.

All of them were pilgrims searching for answers in this dark, puzzling world. The conscience was not always a reliable guide, that inner voice was not always right, but what else did we have?

Her eyes searched the space, tracking the light streaming in. She felt something ministering to her soul, some soothing balm being applied to it somehow. Maybe her mother wasn't here, but something else was, some ancient spirit in this place that minded about her.

...

They returned to the house and packed up their things. They loaded up the car, and Ned took the wheel. Cora waved them off. Helena looked back and could see her father up in his window, watching them leave. She was sure he wondered if she'd ever be back. She did, too. She patted her purse. She'd executed a theft of her own, taking the photo album.

"I suppose that's how I sometimes respond to gifts, too," Helena said. "Like my father did."

"The thought *had* crossed my mind," Ned said with a chuckle. "But you're not like him, not much like him."

"I am a bit," Helena said. "More than I want to be."

"And you'd come from here, from seeing your father, from this complicated place, when I decided to come out to you right after a car accident?"

"Yes," Helena said.

"What a thing."

"There was never going to be a good time. As you've said. But that, that was the worst of all times possible."

"I am sorry. You know, I found someone, a doctor, a counsellor. A shrink. Not the one Miles recommended. I appreciated him doing so, but we had no chemistry. But another one. It's not because I think it's wrong, what I am. But just, to help me… adjust to this life." To stay in it, he thought.

"I hope you won't stop seeing him, your doctor, if I say that sounds a very good idea. That gives me some comfort, that you have someone… to help you out."

"I wanted someone smart. And kind. And she, yes, it's a woman, she seems to be both."

Helena didn't want to delve too deeply into this subject. Probably they spent entire sessions demolishing her parenting. She didn't like that it was a woman he was seeing.

So, she moved the conversation away from this. "That's what I look for in my friends, too," Helena said. "Smart, kind, and good-looking. I admit, I like attractive. I'm an immensely shallow woman."

They laughed and then went silent for a bit, as the car took them through the West Country.

"I worry," he said. "I like Luca too much."

"Yes," she said. "One person always likes the other more. If it's good, that shifts, it goes back and forth. But yes, that is hard. But, from this distance, it seems he is extremely fond of you, too."

"It was that way with you and Dad, the shift back and forth?"

"Yes," she said. "It was. It is."

They fell again into a companionable silence, and this time it was she who broke it. "I loved it when you beat Father, utterly demolished him at croquet! How furious he was."

"It was terrible guest behavior. If you must beat the host, you do it barely. But I found I couldn't help myself. Who prefers the Romans to the Greeks? And him repeatedly calling us, me colonials."

They came over a rise, and the hedgerows had been shaved low, so they could see a great distance from the hilltop into a deep valley, divided into many fields, some cultivated, some lying fallow. There was a steeple poking out of a village below.

"Do you ever miss this?" Ned said.

"Not often. I find I have become Canadian. It's given me so much, Canada. But yes, I suppose this I miss, the English countryside. Yes." Ned shifted down a gear to allow the car to slow itself as they went down the incline.

"It's not fair, you know," Helena said. "That we should have had so much freedom from want, while want was the birthright of so many. Our history is recorded, our heroes and villains populate our National Gallery. So many others are forgotten. Henry's roommate, the New Yorker, his family came from Poland. Their whole village, gone, most of its inhabitants gassed. It's all not fair."

They came over another hill and looked over another green and pleasant valley.

Ned asked Helena what the fields of yellow flowers were.

“It's rape,” she said.

“Rape,” he said. “What an unfortunate name for something so very beautiful.”

Chapter 10:
The Playboy Of The Western World

Ned didn't meet Tim for a few weeks after his return. “He's swamped with work,” Luca said. Ned and Luca no longer spent nights at Luca's place, at Luca' and Tim's place, but only at Ned's.

At last, it was proposed that Ned come to a dinner party at the flat above the market. Luca suggested Ned arrive a half-hour before the other guests. It was Tim who answered the door. He was slender with a prominent nose and an elongated face, a few inches taller than Ned. He reminded Ned of the sculptures of greyhounds at King's College Chapel in Cambridge. He had prematurely grey hair, and prominent eyebrows. There was something at once solemn and humorous about his face.

“Oh, hello,” he said, and looked at his watch. “We're just in the final stages. You're just a little early.”

“Oh,” Ned said. “Didn't Luca tell you? He asked me to come a little early. So we could meet.”

“Oh, did he?” Tim said. “Well, do come up.”

Together they walked up the staircase where Luca practiced his singing.

“He's doing Russian food tonight,” Tim said. This was something Ned knew, since Luca had talked through the meal, as they shopped for its makings together.

“You are American,” Tim said.

“Canadian,” Ned said.

"Well North American. Though I suppose you don't like to be lumped into the same bucket."

Ned came into the kitchen and hugged Luca.

"Shall I set him up in the living room?" Tim said.

"Yes, why don't you both go out there."

"No," Tim said. "I'll come back to help."

Tim set Ned up with a drink in the living room, but didn't linger, just leaving him there. "The others will soon be here."

Ned looked with dismay at the table, which was set for fourteen. He felt inside him the same question he had asked his mother about their Christmas parties. Why invite so many? Six was a good number for a canoe trip; six was a good number for a dinner party. He'd try that argument out on Luca the next time they were on their own together.

The philosopher Ned met and liked was there, as was the Nigerian pop singer, this time without the Canadian heiress. There was an ad firm's copywriter, some of Tim's fellow travelers in journalism and a woman with pink hair whose job fascinated Ned—she reworked English novels for the American market and vice versa. He blurted out some of the many differences between North American and English usage, and she smiled at him indulgently. "Those are mainly the nouns. The verbs also vary." Ned was hoping to dig into this over dinner, but he found he wasn't seated near her. She was in the middle, while he was at the opposite end of the table from Luca and Tim, between two journalists, one an editor at the *Guardian*, the other a reporter at the Church of England's paper, named Lucy, his mother's middle name, a name Ned fantasized he'd give to a daughter of his. But how would that work? The journalists knew each other well and talked over him most of the meal, gossiping about editor and writer friends they had in common. Between courses, the pair of them snuck off to the washroom, the toilet, and came back with brighter eyes. "I suppose we should have offered," one said to Ned. "Did you want a bump?"

Ned looked blank. One of them clarified in a whisper, "Of coke. Cocaine."

It had just two syllables now, not the three Cordelia gave it. Luca appeared behind Ned. "No, he doesn't want any of that. Come, join me." Ned was happy Luca had been watching over him. Luca wedged a chair in next to him at the other end. "They're such terrible bores, those two."

He was now across from Tim, and somehow Ned and Tim got into an argument over whether David Hare was a great playwright (Ned's view) or the purveyor of agit-prop, a politician in a playwright's garb (Tim's take). Ned felt Tim was wrong, he knew it, but he couldn't quite find the words to prove it.

After the meal, Tim proposed they play Botticelli. Everyone wrote down the names of famous people on chits, put them in hats, and then they paired up. While everyone watched, one of them pulled out chits, describing the person named rapid-fire to their partner, trying to get as many as they could until the time ran out.

"Twins. Gangsters. East Enders."

"The Brothers Kray."

"Tennis player. New Yorker. Superbrat."

"McEnroe." The rival of Ned's beloved Björn Borg. He'd put that clue in.

The names that others had put into the hat impressed Ned: Lucrezia Borgia, Johannes Kepler, Escoffier, Haile Selassi, Daedalus and Balenciaga were among them. He had to pass (for a time penalty) more than most people. "We have different people in North America."

“What, like Madonna?” Tim said.

“No, like, say, Jackson P-p-pollock or Eleanor Roosevelt. Like T-t-tecumseh, Flannery O'Connor and John Muir.”

Ned looked about him. The ashtrays were spilling onto the makeshift tablecloth, a rubber shower curtain covered in traffic signs. Most of the water glasses were untouched, but the wine glasses were all empty, many with lipstick stains. The chits from the game lay in piles on the table.

He picked a chit up: “Savonarola”. He knew who that was, alas. The severe fire-and-brimstone cleric, the book-burner, an actual Puritan. It sent a shiver through him.

The last of the other remaining guests, a trio of Tim's Oxford friends, were pulling themselves together. They had pushed together all the different dishes that Luca placed on their dinner plates, and Ned had watched him wince as they did so. The cab to take them to another party in Clapham had arrived at the door. “South of the River, how adventurous!” Tim said, as he accompanied them to the stairs down to the street. The acoustics of the stairs were as good as Luca claimed: Ned could hear some whispering among them, his name mentioned a couple of times, but he couldn't quite make out the rest of the exchange.

One of Tim's friends, the woman who translated between American and English idioms, came back into the main room to grab a scarf she'd forgotten. Was it Ned's imagination or did she cast a poisonous look in his direction?

“Well, goodbye again,” Ned said. “Nice to have met you. I love your job. I want your job.” She rushed out, ignoring his farewell.

“Silly cow,” Luca said.

Tim returned.

Tim began to clear plates and glasses on a tray. In a few moments, they could hear the crockery clattering onto the counter in the kitchen and the sink's water running.

“O, to have a dishwasher,” Luca said, with a sigh, and got up to go to the kitchen, loading up. Ned followed his example, bringing some dirty dishes with him.

“Just put those down there,” Tim said to Ned. “There's no need for you to help with the washing up. You're a guest. Guests don't wash up after my dinners, after our dinners.”

“Nonsense,” Ned said. “Let me help out, maybe dry, or put things away.”

“You wouldn't know where things went,” Tim said.

Dishtowel in hand, Luca rolled his eyes comically. Ned poured himself some more red wine and took a seat at the '50s-style Formica kitchen table. Tim turned to Luca, “Would you go put something on, something calm, not too frenetic?” Luca went to the main room where the stereo was.

“I so enjoyed speaking with Lucy, during dinner,” Ned said. “I guess she was saying you met early on in your degree.” There was a whole way of speaking about academic matters that he couldn't quite master. You went “up” to Oxford. You weren't thrown out of university, but rusticated. Was it “in” your degree that you met someone?

“Yes, we met on my first day in rooms.” In rooms.

“I guess she's become a journalist at the Church of England newspaper? It's supposed to be a surprisingly good paper.” Tim gave no reply, but Ned soldiered on: “Anyway, I thought she was lovely.”

“She is,” Tim said. “Lovely.”

"Yes, she, that name it's one… "

"I'm not going to chat about my friends with you, Ned."

"I wish you would turn around. It's so hard to talk, to really talk with your back to me. I don't mean you any harm." Ned blushed. What a naive thing to say. Actions were actions and had consequences.

Tim did, at last, turn and dry his hands. Ned had never seen such a look of hostility blazing out at him. He brought all his goodwill into his eyes. It was something his mother always did when the going got rough.

"I thought you might be temporary," Tim said. "Like the others. You flirt, you go to the *Fallen Angel.* The rooftop. You take him home a couple of times."

"Listen I know you, you're fighting this… illness. I'm not going to take him away. He'll be here. I know you have so much on your plate." Ned cringed at the use of this cliché. "Please, Tim, hear me out. I don't have much, I don't have any experience in love."

"Love. Do you think it's that?"

"This is my first… relationship."

"What a choice you've made then."

"Perhaps I ought to have read between the lines of what Luca was saying, but when Luca told me… what he told me. I believed it. And then I f-f-f-ell… But if you t-t-tell me, that's not…"

"F-f-finish a fucking sentence, would you? I'm telling you now. You can find someone else. You have the luxury of time. I don't. And as for what I have on my plate, I have death on my plate."

"Do you have parents?"

"You mean is there someone else who can look after me?"

Ned repeated himself. "Do you have parents? A family?"

"My parents," Tim said and sighed. "They let me go. When I came out. It was like I was some seasonal employee, brought on board to help with the Christmas rush. He said it with regret, my father, 'We're letting you go.'"

This was when it broke for Ned, when this idea that it could all work out shattered.

Some piano music came wafting through from the main room, and Luca bounced back into the bright kitchen.

"Chopin," Luca said, and they realized they all knew about Luca's grandmother.

"Luca," Ned said, "I'd better go."

"Not yet. Stay for a nightcap. We need to discuss." This was one of Luca's passions. The detailed debrief on a party's guests, the food and drink, the outfits, the insults and witticisms exchanged, who might be on the way to bedding whom.

"No, it's high time I went," Ned said. Ned looked at the height of the counter and thought of Luca's joke that they'd make love somehow on it, or against it.

Tim didn't turn around to say goodbye as Ned moved to exit the kitchen.

Luca looked from one of them to the other. "What?" he said angrily to Tim's back. "What did you say?"

"I said little," Tim said, turning again. "Compared to what I could say."

Luca came down the stairs with Ned and walked silently beside him on the street. It was raining, so Ned unfurled his carefully wrapped, expensive umbrella. There was only space for one beneath it. The water stood out in light-catching drops on Luca's shiny chocolate leather jacket. "Doesn't he know if he forces me to choose that I'll choose you?"

"No, you wouldn't," Ned said. "And why should you? I just thought, I thought he wasn't a part of the calculation any longer, at least romantically—that he was a friend you loved and supported. I didn't think there was a choice involved."

Luca reached for Ned's hand, but Ned pulled it away.

"I'll walk the rest of the way home solo, thanks. Clear my head."

A black-and-white spaniel ran by seeming to know exactly where it was headed, and some uproarious laughter came out of the door of a pub they'd sometimes gone to. They embraced, but Ned wouldn't kiss Luca.

...

Luca came to Ned in a dream that night. He was naked except for an apron, and was making tea in their family cottage. The house was not in its actual spot, but sitting exposed, precarious atop a high cliff next to the St. Lawrence. Fog kept drifting in from the river through an open window, and there were foghorns sounding in the distance. It was his mother's teapot that Luca was using, in a Wedgwood wild-strawberry pattern, the Cheshire Cat cozy lying nearby. Luca poured out three cups, one for himself, one for Ned, one for Tim. Then he reached over to Ned and clutched his arm, his eyes suddenly bugging, his cheeks flushing, sweat swimming across his deeply lined forehead. His voice was filled with terror, and Tim entered the room. Luca spoke softly so as not to be overheard: "I want to live."

...

One of Cordelia's daughters called Ned to say she'd gone into the hospital with an aneurysm. "She was so vigorous, you know, slowing down a bit, but... these can strike anyone," she said. "Still, she's stable, she has a good doctor. She's on the right medications. In good spirits." Ned asked if he could visit, and she said her mother would like that. Ned and Luca went to see her the next day, and at the ward desk, a nurse told him she'd gone the night before.

"Checked out?" Ned asked.

"Gone. In her sleep. She didn't even know she was... going. She had no pain."

Helena asked Ned to represent her at the funeral. It was held at the same country church Ned had just visited with his mother. He read parts of her friend Eliot's Prufrock there: "Let us go then you and I, while the evening is stretched out against the sky like a patient etherized on a table." He came to the lament at the end, without stuttering once: "I have heard the mermaids singing, each to each. I do not think they will sing to me." Ned looked up from the poem, and improvised something: "The mermaids, if they sing to anyone, they sang to Aunt Cordelia." Afterwards, he tossed a clod of earth on her casket in a grave next to his grandmother's. Some cows looked on from over the fence, chewing their cuds.

There was a reception his grandfather held at his house. He spared no expense to give his former sister-in-law a good send-off, hiring a string quartet from London. He put out his best wines, bringing in a cook from a nearby manor home. Cora had tracked down some of Cordelia's remaining writer and editor friends, and her former companions in the nuclear-disarmament movement. There were not so many of them left, and they didn't look like much, but in conversation, with Ned, some of them sparked up. The stories they told him were ones he wrote down in his journal that evening.

Ned supposed it was a good way to go, in your sleep, and she'd had a long life, a fruitful one. Still, he was sad. He told one of her daughters how grateful he was for her introduction to London. He wanted to say more, but by then his stutter had come back, and her daughter lost patience with it.

When Ned called his mother to report on the events of the day, his mother said, "She was the best of us," and he could hear her gulping air on the other end.

...

Daniel came to London for a couple of weeks. He'd landed a job at a New York law firm for the summer after his first year at Yale law school, and they needed a team to do due diligence on a U.K. company that one of their clients wanted to take over. The firm where Ned worked was peripherally involved, too. Everyone had a piece of that deal. Daniel was staying with the team at a swish hotel in Hyde Park, and mainly worked around the clock, but he made himself free on one evening, for an early evening dinner party Luca and Ned organized, at Ned's place.

The weather that August day was perfect, so they moved a long table outside, and appended a couple of other smaller tables to it, draping miscellaneous cloths over all of them. The tables sat at different levels and glasses of wine toppled over all evening. A radio reporter was to capture the meal for a piece on Luca's latest culinary enthusiasm, the reconstruction of authentic Roman meals from classical texts. The dinner featured more low wattage folks than the meals at Luca's and Tim's. Cousin Sophie was there, and Ned was glad that she'd get to meet Daniel. There were also a couple of her arty St. Martin's friends. Ned invited some people he knew from his office, a couple of the articled clerks who'd taken him and Luca to join them in a rented house on the Cornish coast.

Luca was trying quails stuffed with rotted-fish compote and gooseberries.

“How do you like it?” he eagerly asked Sophie. “I know the ingredients sound a bit dodgy. It was a favorite with centurions.” The radio reporter directed her microphone towards her.

“It’s not what it is, the ingredients. Those don't bother me,” Sophie said. “It’s how it tastes.” Ned spat out his wine in amusement before he’d seen Luca’s face fall.

“The elderberry custard will be fantastic,” Luca said. He was buoyant, that word Fritzie had used about Chief. How quickly, after being ducked underwater, he rose to the surface.

“What’s the story,” Daniel said, “did the Romans actually vomit up their first courses to make room for the later ones? Did they have vomitoriums, er, vomitoria to throw up in?”

“They did sometimes vomit between courses at a feast, but there was no special room for it,” Luca said.

Daniel looked dubious, and Ned decided to dispute Luca's claim. “I don't think that's right,” Ned said.

“A vomitorium is actually an exit from an amphitheater or stadium,” Luca said, “where the people are belched out after they've had their fill of watching the spectacle.”

“No,” Ned said. “They had them next to their banquet halls. You saw them in Pompeii.”

“Have you been to Pompeii?” Luca said.

“No, but we studied it.”

Luca humored Ned then, but after everyone else left he attacked. “Theater design and ancient Rome are two of my special areas. Here they overlap. You might consider that before challenging me. And the way you did it! In fact, the whole time you were undermining me, making fun of me, having a laugh with Sophie. It wasn't nice. Not appreciated at all. And now it'll all be on the radio. I'll be humiliated. I mean you'll be the ass, because you're wrong about vomitoriums, but it won't look good on me either. To have such ignorant friends."

Luca had been pressuring Ned to think about finding a place together. Ned had thought about it, and everything about the proposal made him feel queasy. He couldn't stomach beginning his romantic career this way.

"Get out," Ned said. "I'm tired. Stop washing the dishes: Get out!"

"What, you're throwing me out? After I cook for all your second-rate friends."

"No, Luca, it's just, it's all too much for me. I'm done."

It wasn't clear to Ned, until he said those words, how final they sounded. He would call Luca the next day, to try to reconcile, but Tim picked up and told him Luca didn't want to speak to him. A fax arrived at Ned's office in livid Latin: "You threw me out. No one treats me that way. No one!" Luca had finished with it, with Ned, too.

It was so sudden, their ending. Though he had initiated it, he hadn't given much thought to what it would mean.

This body in his arms, this person bicycling, walking, sleeping, breathing near him, his smell all around him—that was all gone. All of these conversations they'd been having were interrupted mid-stream. They would not go to Paris, they would never make a pilgrimage to visit the ashes of Wilde and Robbie Ross in Père Lachaise. It had been such an abrupt and mean ending, all the tenderness between them disappearing in an exchange of harsh words.

The summer went balmy, the grass in the parks died, and his depression came back. With the help of his new therapist, he handled it as best he could. In their shared neighborhood, he kept seeing Luca, or rather people he thought were Luca, but who materialized into some worthless and ugly person, someone who was not him. How dare they circulate around looking so like Luca?

The Voice reentered: *You are such an idiot. Anyone but an idiot could have seen that break-up coming. Only an ass would have started that affair in the first place.*

Affair, yes, that was the right word for it, Ned thought, not relationship, the one he'd used in the kitchen with Timothy.

As The Voice became stronger, Ned's stutter became pronounced again, as if there were only a certain set amount of articulacy in his system, and The Voice took most of it. At work, he accomplished the tasks expected of him, but he stopped going above and beyond the call. Once he got through his day's list of tasks, he scuttled out of the office and biked straight home. Often, he forgot about cars driving on the left-hand side of the road, and narrowly escaped getting hit. At home, he took full refuge in the books and music he'd been thinking of on his ride.

But sometimes they didn't suffice to protect him from The Voice.

Luca did tell you right away how it was.

“He said they weren't sleeping together anymore,” Ned thought in rebuttal.

That is clear enough. You're not a stupid boy. Don't pretend to be one. And then, when there was really no room left for any doubt whatsoever, even then, you were selfish enough to keep it going.

“Only for a couple of weeks.”

There had been a battle in Ned between his sense of himself as a person of honor and his desire to love and be loved by Luca. Too late, he'd realized his duty to Timothy. Neither side had won in that inner battle. He could tell himself he'd chosen the honorable exit. Looking back, sometimes, he would tell himself that. But it was not true. He had been unable to figure out what to do, and a burst of anger coming out of his confusion had settled the matter for him.

...

A few days after the end of the affair, Cordelia's concierge friend called. He'd just heard about her death, and was sorry for it. He also said, as a gift to mark his aunt's passing, he wanted to treat Ned to inexpensive tickets for a production of *The Playboy of the Western World* on at an old West-End theater.

Ned had read the Irish play, and seen it once with his mother's friend Georgia at a summer stock festival at the head of Lake Ontario. And so he knew the money lines in the Final Act were coming, as he sat up in the gods, with Sophie next to him. Even so, they hit him hard. “I’ve lost him,” the barmaid Pegeen says at the end. “I’ve lost the only playboy of the Western World.”

He hadn't cried at all after his break-up with Luca, just gone blank, every so often some anger with himself or Luca flashing in him. He walked around mad, madder than a hatter.

But here, on hearing these lines, the actress keening them out, some belated grief flooded him. Sophie held Ned's hand as he wept relatively noiselessly, lamenting the end of the affair with Luca, sad at Cordelia's death, still upset at how changed his relationship with his mother was. Why did he always cry too late?

Below, the audience clapped and cheered, as the cast came back out.

Ned had some reason to clap and cheer, too, even if he didn't yet feel it. He'd been admitted to his parents' *alma mater*, to Cambridge, to continue his study of literature.

Towards the end of August, Sophie and Ned and their roommate Alistair packed up their household. Ned stored his stuff in the basement of Sophie's parents' house in Somerset, while he went on a visit back to Canada. At the door, as Sophie left, they did a pair of dance moves at each other. Ned thought his life and hers would be intertwined, that they'd always find ways to see each other. But the truth was, this was their time. Both had dance moves that originated from the other, ones they'd perform on other floors with other people. But they would not have another time that was theirs. They would not forget it, but nor would either of them ever wish to relive this year.

On his last day at work, his pals there took him to a wine-bar, and said they'd look him up, when they came up to Cambridge. One or two of them would, but that, otherwise, would be that. He'd enjoyed working there, the terms he'd learned, the Japanese businessmen he'd walked through their closings. Though he'd been admitted to a couple of the law schools he'd also applied to, he realized he preferred to study literature. He would never again have need of this knowledge he'd gained, the inner workings of these complicated legal agreements.

The next day was his last one in the house, and he was alone there. He missed the smell of Alistair's many soaps in the bathroom, but the back garden was fragrant anyway. The roses had thrived with the manure they'd spread around them. He took his violin to play a final time in the empty Victorian factories behind them, bringing with him a Vivaldi violin concerto he'd been working at. But he didn't play that day because he heard some plaintive mewing. He followed it, to find, in a pool of sunlight, the cat they'd called Orlando, the one who had greeted Ned so warmly, so soon after The Slash. He, or she, as it turned out, was giving birth. Ned knew to keep his distance in this vulnerable time, and, soon enough, three little kittens came out, one white, one ginger like its mother, and one black. He fell for the little black one immediately.

He knocked on his neighbors' doors until he found Orlando's true owner. Turned out, Orlando's actual name was Beth. He shuttled the mother cat and kittens back to the house in a box and asked if they would mind if he kept the black one, returning for him in a few weeks. They agreed. Robbie, he'd name him, for his relation Robert Ross.

Chapter 11:
Brideshead, Revisited

After completing his master's at Cambridge, Ned applied for and was admitted to the doctoral program in literature at University of Toronto. He'd had other options, but this was the one he chose. While he studied, he worked as an English don at his old college, Trinity. At Cambridge, he'd focused on Evelyn Waugh and his contemporaries, especially his great friend and rival Nancy Mitford. Here, it was proposed that he narrow his focus to Waugh alone. "The more serious writer," was the verdict of the prof who had been assigned to advise him.

Ned had a bigger, better room than he'd occupied as an undergrad, with a sitting room where students could come to seek his feedback on their essays and otherwise get his advice. The cat he'd adopted in London became something of a mascot in the College. He was registered as belonging to the Provost, since, officially, there were no pets allowed in rooms. A montage of shots of him made its way into the yearbook—Robbie on landings, lapping milk on windowsills, up in seemingly perilous positions on the roof. But apart from the cat, three good suits and a few good editions of his favorite books, Ned had taken, it seemed, little from his year in London. He'd gone into neither publishing nor the practice of law, so those placements didn't help him secure any others.

On certain days, in his room, it seemed he'd never left. He still went to the same chapel to pray, to try to regain some connection to the God he'd worshipped as a boy. He still sometimes joined his grandmother for lunch at the Royal Ontario Museum Members' Lounge, so she could show him off to her friends. He still ate most of his other meals in the tall, wood-paneled dining hall, named for his ancestor's teacher and then rival, Bishop John Strachan.

Here, in Toronto, he could never quite get away from his family, both the living and the dead. When he bought food in provisions for a friend's dinner party at the St. Lawrence Market, and passed the lobster tank, he had his mother in his head, telling the story of a French poet who'd kept one as a pet, in part, because it knew the secrets of the deep. When he jogged up the Baldwin steps, past the site of the old family home, he sometimes heard his father saying to him and Henry: "And so, go away, do what you need to do... But come back. You have people here. Your dead are buried here."

In his waking hours, he didn't think often of London, but his dreams sometimes revisited a walk he'd done early on, getting lost near Covent Garden, ending up at the Seven Dials monument. The old and curious column, with the sundials on top had puzzled him. He'd felt alone there, but not lonesome, a quiet hubbub without and within. Roads stretched out in many directions from it, the cobblestoned circle around it. Which way would he go?

One way, the one he'd taken, led back home.

But there were other ways he might have gone. He might have made his life in London, perhaps with Luca, perhaps not. Of the professional lives he'd seen, it was, ironically, Tim's he'd most wanted. And so he imagined London Ned, this alternate self, working as a literary journalist, perhaps as a film or book critic. Often, especially as he read through the early English literature he had to master for his comprehensive exams, he suspected his London self was having a better time.

...

After Henry finished his degree at Dartmouth, he landed a job with the Peace Corps, joining its program for its first year in Hungary. His study of Russian and his consequent interest in Eastern Europe helped him land a spot. He came back to Canada before heading over, driving in on his own from Oakville to have dinner with Ned. They'd never spent much time alone together, and Ned was nervous it wouldn't go well. It was early in the term, and the Dean of Men had invited Ned to join him at the High Table, placed at one end of the hall, on a platform up a step from the dining room proper. Ned asked if he could add Henry to the mix, and the Dean agreed. Ned was pleased that Henry brought back the Benjamina, the weeping fig he'd given Henry to take with him to Dartmouth. "I couldn't bring it along to Hungary, and it's still going strong."

"What a nice thing to have back," Ned said. "The white tree. While it lives, Gondor shall not fall."

After the meal was served, and Ned had introduced Henry around, they were able to focus on each other some, and Ned asked Henry about what, exactly, he'd be doing in Hungary. Before he could get an answer, a group of rowdies hallooed their way in. They laid their hands on a first-year student who was the gentle son of a federal cabinet minister who had already come to see Ned for advice on an essay.

"Here we go again," Ned said to the Dean, who chuckled.

As was the tradition, the targeted boy threw himself on the table, gripping its opposite edge, and three of his fellow frosh jumped up to defend him. His champions proved no match for the more numerous, beefy marauders in the tussle, and the boy was carried out of the hall.

The rowdies manhandled the boy through the swinging doors at the end of the hall, and the remaining students rose as one. The other occupants of the high table also rose. Ned did, too, but a few beats later and with more reluctance. Henry, however, remained seated. The students, meanwhile, banged the rough-hewn tables with their knives and forks in hand, and bellowed the Trinity chant: "Who are we? We are the salt of the earth, so give ear to us! No new ideas shall ever come near to us. Orthodox! Crammed with divinity! Damn the dissenters! Hurrah for old Trinity!" Ned mouthed along to the words, but without any enthusiasm. The cheer was intended both to mock the founder's staunch beliefs and to celebrate them. He didn't know why he thought of his English grandfather then, but he was certain the man would have loved it.

After the meal, the faculty, deans and dons left the High Table and filed through a door behind them. It went by a short passage into the Senior Common Room, which was also lined with wood panels, but was lower and cozier than the dining hall. There were built-in shelves with a motley crew of books on them, clubby leather couches and wingback armchairs set up in groups around the room. A server took around a tray with glasses of port in crystal goblets and one professor lit up a pipe. Ned and Henry both took a glass and found some armchairs, positioned for conversation.

Henry lowered his voice. "That was really weird in there, like some sort of scene from an Anglican *Triumph of the Will*. I kept looking around to see if Leni Riefenstahl was filming."

"It was a little weird, wasn't it? It was so much a part of my undergrad, that I'd not really considered it."

"Do you remember, you saying you wondered what the conscience of our race would look like?" Henry asked. "That old New Yorker cartoon."

"Yes, and I remember you saying, it was probably pretty ugly."

"And after seeing that, I thought of it."

Ned explained the tradition of Pooring Out, and how it was used to punish outliers. "It's supposed to be a way that upper-years discipline first-years, teach them what is (and is not) acceptable, removing those whose behavior strays from the norm." As an undergrad, Ned had never been singled out for this treatment, but he had obsessed about it at the time. He'd tried to do absolutely nothing that was unusual ritual when he first arrived. As he described it to his brother, he grew more ashamed of it.

"There was that weird cheer that came after it, damning the Catholics, non-believers?"

"The *Salterrae* it's called," Ned said, adding, "Salt of the Earth. Latin."

"I would say very few of those boys could be called Salt of the Earth. Those sons of New and Old Money. I don't think so very many have done an honest day's work in their lives. Unless you count tree-planting for a summer."

Ned laughed.

"And when we all stood up," Ned said. "You didn't think it was just good manners to join us?"

"Not really," Henry said. "I don't go in for those sorts of good manners."

"There will be questions asked about my guest," Ned said.

"Well, you'll have to give them my answer then: That was some rank sorta bullshit," Henry said.

"I'll try that with the Dean of Men. I'm sure that'll go down well."

"I guess the rule is stay in line, keep within the pack."

Ned thought his brother often showed more courage than he did. He didn't mind being the lone wolf, the only one sitting down. Then again, Henry often had less to lose.

They spoke of what they'd say about their people, the culture and conscience of them.

"It's about superiority," Henry said. "Every move with Fritzie, every piece of clothing, it's all about setting herself apart, demonstrating her superiority." Ned remembered her telling him that hard times gave you a chance to show others your mettle.

"I think of this thing Mum told me of, about not being 'wet.'"

Ned told Henry about the bullwhip and their mother clinging to her horse as it bolted across the English countryside, returning in triumph when she'd calmed the beast down.

"Anyway, what was that guy's crime?" Henry said, "The one they threw out of the hall."

"I don't know. I think it was his practicing his violin with his window to the quad open. He's no Jascha Heifetz, that's for sure."

"Awful," Henry said, and he began to riff on the instances of racism and anti-Semitism he'd seen in Oakville growing up. At Dartmouth, Henry had fallen in, for a time, with one of the activists pushing the old college to divest from businesses operating in South Africa. Harmony, the girl who called herself Harm, had evidently left her mark on him.

Ned broke in on his enumeration of the manifold sins and wickednesses of his people, as the prayer book had it. "You're always so harsh," Ned said. "The way you went at those poor Bonnycastles."

"I was defending you!" Henry said. "Anyway, harshness in a good cause is no vice."

"That's almost a quote," Ned said. Henry looked blank. "Barry Goldwater saying 'Extremism in the defense of liberty is no vice.'"

"But it's not quite a quote, is it," Henry said. "I did my own thing with it."

"You mean you got it wrong," Ned said. "I've had this thought about our quoting. It's odd. I feel like we're the other People of the Book. Only our sacred texts are literary ones. And when we quote them we're doing what the Catholics do with their rosaries."

"You see," Henry said. "I have another theory. We're all of us unsure what the hell we're doing, and so we grab at whatever straws there are. And these straws are within our reach. Or, within yours anyway. I can't even get Barry Goldwater right!"

After his last sip of port, Henry said to Ned: "You know, as I think about it, the question doesn't really interest me that much. It's other people, people who aren't us, who interest me more. Everyone has heard more than enough about us, from us. The other thing that interests me: what we need to do to make up for what we've done, from generation to generation. To compensate for the sins of our fathers."

They both thought of their father, his years of work at a clinic in a rough part of Toronto, and of Fritzie's longtime effort to get him to find a more prestigious post.

With his brother soon to head off to distant parts for a couple of years, Ned thought he'd ask him something more personal. "Tell me. Do you still hate me as much as you ever did? You remember you said that on the pier, that Christmas?"

"Did I?" Henry said. "I didn't really hate you. I just had to get out from under your shadow. Growing up, your life seemed always more vivid than mine, even to me. At prize day, you never sat down. Whereas, I never got up."

"You did, once. The history prize," Ned said. "And now that you've done that, come out of my shadow?"

"I hate you less than I did," Henry said, with a chuckle. "Marginally. I mean there's still some residual hatred there. Sort of like army-reservist hatred, ready to be called up on a moment's notice."

This was, alas, probably true enough. But at least they could speak of it, play with it, find where they could make common cause with each other, and where they still remained too different, too far apart. Theirs was not a relationship of choice, so they both had to make the best of it. But still, there were opportunities in the relationship to see at close quarters how differently someone else took things in.

As he lay in bed, Ned thought about what Henry had said. What were his obligations? His natural instinct was to try to understand, to describe in his head, using the right words, the world as it was. Not to change it. But all of them, even those who lived small lives, impacted the world at large, via the immediate people and places around them.

What should he do, who should he be, to help improve things? Or, at least not make them worse? He tried to live by his father's professional oath: first, do no harm. But he often caused harm.

And anyway, as he lay in his narrow bed, avoidance of harm seemed a singularly minimal goal. But it was prefaced with "first". It was just the foundation of what one ought to do.

His brother was a swashbuckler. Henry meant to cut a big swath through life. Ned did not. The words of an old jazz standard came to him: "I don't want to set the world on fire." He drifted off.

…

One of the students Ned had to advise as English don was Tish, the redheaded daughter of his mother's great friend Georgia. Though, it was not that she needed much help with her studies. In her three years in Toronto, she had grown into a beauty, as he'd suspected she would. But it was nice somehow that she still thought of herself as a sickly, feeble little girl. She hadn't yet accepted, as only right and fitting, that doors would open in front of her for much of her adult life.

In August of Ned's first year back, they decided they'd go to the Canadian National Exhibition, the annual fair near the lakefront on grounds just west of the downtown core. It was something they'd done together as kids, so this was something of a sentimental journey. Ned hit the bull's eye four times at a concession stand, and won a stuffed pig, which he offered up to her.

"Don't say I never gave you anything."

"Better than the clap," Tish said, and kissed the pig on its plush snout.

Alas, the pig flew out of her hands when they rode a rickety old rollercoaster. They tried to find the pig when they got down, hoping someone might have held onto it for them, but no such luck.

"It was a good time with the pig, if not a long time," she said.

Ned thought of Luca but did not speak of him. He tried not to let his tongue soil those memories by speaking of them, as he'd done a long time ago with his memories of Cameron.

They got hot-dogs, found a bench, and made up stories about the people who passed.

Ned asked after her mother, how she liked her new job running an old age home.

"She's met someone, someone nice. A French-Canadian. A pilot for Air Canada. He's funny, though sometimes you're the butt of his jokes. He uses them as weapons. Usually to protect her. He's a big fan of hers, which I'm not sure, in the final analysis, my father ever was. Or the affection had gone far, far away, by the time I came around. You should go see her."

Ned intended always to visit his old ally, Georgia, his frequent date for movies and plays, but somehow, he seldom did. When he telephoned her, there was this shocking awkwardness: who was this stranger on the other end of the line? He found it hard to push through that.

"And her work?" Ned said.

"It's okay, Ned," Tish said. "But you know, I'm determined not to be in her boat at her age. My Dad—she relied on him totally, and he, he screwed her. Here she is nearing retirement age, still working, likely to be working for a long time still. Not that she complains. Ever."

She took a break from speaking of her mother's predicament by saying unflattering things about her stepmother Siobhan.

Then they talked about Tish's intention to apply to law-school, the route she planned to take to avoid her mother's fate. "You'll be old money bags."

"I intend to be young money bags," she said. "Not old money bags."

"You should talk to Daniel," he said. After Yale, Daniel had clerked at an appellate court, not with one of the Supreme Court Justices, as he'd hoped, but at a good court, with a respected judge. He was now living in Manhattan.

As they passed out of the fairground's eastern end, through some big gates, Ned looked up at the angel atop it. During his childhood, this angel had seemed to possess a mystical beauty. It was the Lord's stern, graceful messenger. "I bring you glad tidings of great joy, which shall be to all the people." He'd seen so many angels on statues in Europe, and he expected to find this one, a being he'd so admired in his childhood, diminished in comparison. But it wasn't. He looked at it, and imagined its lips moving, it giving voice to the pre-communion prayer: "The gifts of God for the people of God."

On the way back from their day at the fair, Ned and Tish stopped at a bookstore not far from the campus. There was a book on a display near the counter that had the sort of cover they put on gay novels then, a nude male torso shot from the rear, a candle underneath a spoon full of drugs, an eye at a glory-hole. Ned picked it up and began to thumb through it. The book was set in London, and Ned felt there were some familiar elements in the brief description of its plot. When he looked at the author photo, he realized why. It was the novel Tim had been working on in New York, and it was more than a little bit autobiographical. The plot description had fictionalized versions of things Luca had told Ned about Tim's life.

Tish came up to him to show him a book she was hoping to buy. “What,” she said. “You look like you've seen a ghost.”

“Only a friend,” Ned said. “Or really, a friend of a friend. He's come out with a novel.”

“And you're terribly jealous,” Tish said.

“Something like that.”

Ned bought a copy and took it back to his room. Tim's book was dedicated to several friends, one of whom was Luca. It was literate and funny, by turns raunchy and moving. A nice little fillip from a section describing the narrator’s adolescence: “We all go through periods where we take the lyrics of pop songs seriously.” Ned realized he'd gone through that phase in London, in Cambridge. Come to think of it, he was still in that phase, seeing them often as signs, as oracular pronouncements to be interpreted and applied. He was not discriminating, or at least not compared to the other students in his doctoral program. The texts that interested him came from both of the two solitudes, of high and low culture.

Ned tore through the remainder of the book, waiting for his turn as the young, callow villain who tries (but fails) to steal the narrator’s man. He didn’t make the cut. It was as if he never had been there.

After his initial disappointment, Ned found he was relieved not to have his worst moments to date recorded. When Tim told Ned that his parents had let him go, Ned's feelings for the man had shifted. The book cemented his liking and respect for Tim, not that Tim would have cared for that. Would the virus allow Tim time to write another book?

...

After his day with Tish, Ned added a note to his to-do list about calling Daniel to set up at least a phone-call between him and Tish. But, as if the thought had conjured him up, when Ned picked up the phone a few days later, it was Daniel on the line.

"I'm coming to town," he said. "I have a Christening to go to. And I have to tell my parents about Susan."

He was living with a short, blonde girl originally from Kansas, whom he'd met at Yale. While he clerked, she was working as an associate at an old white-shoe firm on Wall Street. The firm Ned had worked at in London had frequent dealings with her firm.

"How will they take it, your parents?"

"Not well." Susan was far from Armenian.

"I had this idea," he said. "That I could take you out to that restaurant we went to. Have a do-over of our Last Supper. At the same restaurant, only this time, my treat."

Ned agreed, and met his friend there, at a table not too far from the one that he, Cameron and Daniel had once eaten at. Daniel had on a proper suit this time.

After they hugged, Ned said, "I m-m-miss the old suit, the velveteen number."

"Me, too. I can't fit into it now!"

Ned put his hand in his leather messenger bag, and Ned brought out two boutonnieres encased in plastic, pinning one on Daniel, and letting Daniel pin one on him.

When they sat down, Daniel said, “You called that guy, Luca, that crazy Roman meal, you called him your Rosenkavalier.”

“Good memory. Yes, he was wearing something a little like this when I met him, at this S&M party.”

Ned described it briefly to an unimpressed Daniel.

“Do you ever hear from him?” Daniel asked.

“No, no I don't. I don't want that. It would be too strange. Not that I've found anything else.”

Men fell for Ned sometimes, and sometimes he fell for them. But he didn't seem to be able to sustain a relationship. Their fling would last a month or so, and they'd sense his doubts, his absence and exit. Or, if they persisted, he'd have to sit them down for a dinner they seldom finished.

“And how about Cameron, the Cro-Magnon? Do you guys hang out?”

“Never. You were right. He just wanted that job. And he has it, and is doing well there. My uncle loves him. More than he'd have loved me, if I'd joined it. I see him sometimes. And we're friendly, as you'd expect. But not friends.”

Ned found he still didn't want to speak about Cameron too much, to soil his memories by approximating them in words. They placed their orders.

“Do you remember how we obsessed over what we'd choose from the menu?” Daniel said. “And I didn't really even give it much thought this time.”

“Nor I,” Ned said. “Ingrates, we are ingrates, to our good fortune.”

"I liked those younger men better," Daniel said. "They valued things more."

When their appetizers came, Daniel asked Ned, "I wondered, I sort of wondered. Why you didn't stay in London? It was a crazy scene you were in. Lots of cool people in it. Or people who looked plenty cool to little old me."

Law school had only accentuated Daniel's instinct to dig into the meat of things, to find out what the real issues in any case were. "I guess," Ned said, "it was a species of vertigo. I developed a fear of heights. I think I was, I am ultimately more of a small-town boy. Or, I guess, Toronto's a big city. I guess I'm just, you have to find your level."

"There's no shame in that."

"Only, I came away thinking maybe I was, maybe I am a coward. First sign of trouble and I bolt."

Daniel let that sit on the table for a while, and Ned was glad he did so. It was something Ned struggled with, about himself, and a too-quick dismissal of it would have belittled this internal tussle.

"Well, you came out," Daniel said. "That took some guts."

Ned laughed. "I kept whimpering as I did it, but yes, I got there. 'This is the way the world ends, not with a bang but a whimper.'"

Ned knew that Daniel knew the quote was from Eliot, and also that Ned had used the quote to prevent any further probing of that still sore spot.

Ned remembered Cameron laughing with faint appreciation at Daniel quoting Wilde, not knowing, Ned suspected, that the witticism was not Daniel's own. For a number of reasons, Daniel was a better fit as a friend than Cameron had ever been. Ned firmed up a coffee date between Daniel and Tish, so Daniel could brief her on the American law schools. Tish had also worked hard and done well at Trinity, so she'd have some of the same options open to her that Daniel had. They spoke about how much more diverse Trinity had become in even a few years, how many other non-WASPy names had joined Daniel's on the hero board.

"It still needs a bit of a shake-up," Daniel said. "I mean I loved it, but when I look back on some of the shit I took. Shit I took gladly, not knowing I didn't have to."

"You were the king," Ned said.

"I had to play the jester a long time before I became king. And during my reign, too. I was always there on sufferance."

When the desserts came, Ned reached into his messenger bag again, pulling out a copy of Toronto's gay biweekly, *Xtra*. He opened it up and showed Daniel its regular feature, "Proud Lives". It contained small obituaries marking the passing of gay guys. Daniel counted them out. There were twenty six. He read little snippets: "Here's a guy who left behind him a pet ferret named Sheldon... and this guy's friend writes, 'I told him to meet me in the coat-check line of the Great Club up there, where we always met down here.' So sentimental. So sad." Daniel looked up: "What a fucking tragedy. Thank you for showing me this. I'd like to keep this if that's okay."

Outside the restaurant, they waited for Daniel's cab.

"The thing is, this is not maybe the right moment, but, if we get married, Susan and me, you'll come to the wedding? Even if it is in Kansas."

"Of course," Ned said. "I m-m-mean have you asked her?"

"I guess I have," Daniel said.

"You buried the lead this whole dinner."

"It doesn't, until I get my parents on-side," Daniel said. "It doesn't feel real."

"You've got your own coming out to manage," Ned said.

"I'll try not to whimper, but I might do some of that," he said. "And you'll be one of my men, you'll stand up for me?"

"I'd be honored," Ned said. "You always stood up for me."

It was true. Daniel had ferreted out Ned's secret, and, having done so, stood up for the man who might, one day, own that secret.

Ned lit up a smoke, offering one to Daniel. "I quit," he said. "Hard as hell, but Susan insisted. You gotta ditch that habit, Ned."

"Oh, piss off, Daniel," Ned said, and they both laughed.

Daniel's cab pulled up. "I have one more question," he said. He jutted out a leg, pulled up the trouser of his black suit some. "Didn't you fancy me just a little bit?"

"Would you get a hold of yourself?" Ned said. "Not for a second did I fancy you."

"You could do worse."

And you probably will. The Voice didn't pipe up all the time these days, but when it did, it still had plenty to say.

He smiled at his friend, they hugged and Daniel was gone. Daniel had found his Susan, and Ned, Ned had not. On his way home, on Philosopher's Walk, he whistled the tune of the old jazz standard, *Lover Man, O Where can you be?*

...

He was, at least, meeting eligible men. And that came courtesy of another childhood friend, Marina, the girl who'd dressed Goth as a protest against their Christmas party and all it entailed. The reunion with Marina was not arranged by either of them, or by their parents.

In his first year back, a friend of Ned's from his undergrad invited Ned to a Pride Party. Like Ned, this friend from his undergrad came out after finishing his degree, and he now lived in one of the round, phallic high-rises near the Gay Village, known to locals as Vaseline Towers. Late in the evening, this woman with crazy big hair and sunglasses on grabbed him by the arm. "Ned Baldwin! Is it really you?" She lowered her shades. It was Marina, the raspy-voiced daughter of his mother's friend Babe Mortimer, Oakville's top realtor. There were luridly colored, micro-bikini bottoms hanging out of her purse. "I went to a friend's pool party two days ago, and well, I just stayed out."

Her perm had maybe been stylish at some point, but it wasn't then. Her mascara had clumped into black clots around her eyes. She was either drunk or high or both. She flung her arms around him: "Happy Pride, bitch! I just knew you were a homo. I knew it! Listen up everyone, a toast, to Ned Baldwin, Practicing Homosexual!"

Glasses were clinked all round.

"Charlotte Peele said you were gay."

"Just because I decided not to kiss her," Ned said. "That didn't make me gay. There were lots of reasons not to kiss Charlotte Peele."

Marina laughed, and started to slur out something scandalous about Charlotte, but someone near the window started screaming, "Call 9-1-1! Somebody Call 9-1-1!"

Marina put her arms in the air. "WOOOOOOOOOO! O my God, I fucking love this song!" She sang along to the recording in her head, the song she thought was playing. "'Help, help, my pussy's on fire. Somebody call 9-1-1'."

As it turned out, the people near the window had just seen a man fall to his death from the tower across the way. They read later that the man had forgotten his keys, and was climbing from a neighbor's balcony onto his own, when he lost his grip.

"God, I feel just terrible," Marina said, sucking down a cigarette, shaking, as she looked down from the party host's balcony at the ambulance lights flashing. The sirens were screaming. "I just thought it was that song, you know. 'My pussy's on fire.'"

"Understandable," Ned said. It *was* one of the year's big songs.

"Listen, I need a favor. I left enough kibble out for the dog, but he won't have been out. Could you come with me, go see him? Give him a walk. I, well, you might have noticed I need some assistance with keeping vertical. You know, that walking thing?"

Ned remembered that off-kilter smile from when she was a little girl. Ned was not the first man persuaded to do her bidding by that crooked smile. It was no doubt the one she turned on his father, when she'd not only convinced Oliver to help her extricate her parents' car from the snowdrift, but persuaded him not to inform on her.

Marina and Ned left the traumatized dregs of the party and taxied to her mid-rise apartment overlooking Mount Pleasant Cemetery, the place where his grandfather was buried, and where Fritzie would join him. While Marina passed out on a couch, Ned cleaned up her frantic Jack Russell's shit. He then took the dog out for a long walk in the Ravines. It was the same set of paths where he'd walked Fritzie's Rhodesian ridgeback and he wondered if he'd run into her. The rising sun lit up a picturesquely situated Japanese Maple tree that he remembered from years back. He had few un-layered experiences in Toronto. Something had always happened there before. He was learning that he didn't mind that, largely preferring a thick experience, to the thin ones he had had in London.

When he got back, Marina was up. “Tell me something,” Ned said. “Why, with the life you seem to lead, do you even have a dog?”

“Don't,” she said. “I already feel like shit. I know, I should be better to him.” She had the dog in her arms, and he seemed perfectly happy there. “I've had him for a while. From a time when I lived a different life. I couldn't let my ex have him.”

Ned stayed silent, and he brewed them both some coffee, while she laid out her post-Oakville story.

“I scraped my way through undergrad,” she began. “History. Your mother's influence. I mainly majored in Montreal, and I had this gorgeous Quebecois boyfriend from Rimouski. And so, I learned French. Or, as much as I needed. We never could quite communicate with each other, but we got on. If you know what I mean.”

“Oh, I do,” Ned said. “Do you see Tish at all?”

“God no,” Marina said, exhaling smoke. “She's become so boring.”

“We went to the Ex. Last summer. She's going to go to law school, here.” Tish had settled on the University of Toronto's law faculty for the next year, which sat just across Philosopher's Walk from Trinity, just next to the museum. Although Daniel had encouraged her to go to one of the US schools, she'd decided to stay put.

“You see! So boring! My mother, Babe keeps *mentioning* her. I think the idea is that Tish's example will make me want to try harder, will keep me from going right to rock bottom. I haven't broken it to Babe yet: the strategy isn't going to work.” She let out a broad, meaty laugh.

After McGill, Marina had landed a job at an accounting firm and became engaged to a nice-seeming guy, a young lawyer who was working as an associate at a downtown firm, one of the so-called Seven Sisters. "I was *way* on the straight and narrow. But then he tells me, we're on the way to a cottage, he tells me he's made a terrible mistake, had it off with a colleague of his. It won't happen again. It didn't help that she was a woman I mistook for a friend. I said, 'Stop the car.' He said, 'Don't overreact. It won't happen again. I'm sorry.' I said, 'Stop the car.' Middle of fucking nowhere. Moose scat, road kill, some big pile of something on the road, with flies all over it. That's my soul down there. Eventually, eventually I thumb a lift in the back of a pick-up to Webers." The hamburger stand everyone stopped at on the way to and from cottage country. "I get my mother to pick me up there. Threw him out of the place we shared. When he came to pick up his stuff, his underwear was burning on the lawn."

Ned broke out in laughter. "That must have made your neighbors talk."

"Didn't it just? The fire department may have been called. There may have been some minor charges laid. But it didn't matter, because he got to see it, all the expensive boxer briefs that he filled out so poorly. He got to see all of them smoldering away." Another big puff of smoke came out of her. "And then, then I decided why not have a little fun in this life? And who was having more of it than you guys, the gays?"

She'd quit her salaried job, temped until she had some cash, then blew it. Ned's Trinity friend had actually mentioned her before Ned ran into her, Marina, the Queen of the Gay Rave Scene (to give her her proper title), but he had never imagined it was the same Marina, their Baby Driver.

He felt akin to her. They were Oakville's wreckage. No, that was too harsh—to both of them. But they'd grown up in a milieu with perilously high expectations, with a very particular code of behavior. And both of them, in their respective ways, were not going to meet those expectations. Neither would live by that code. He recognized in her that desire he'd felt inside him also: to dissipate, to throw away. And maybe, after that, to start afresh. But maybe not, too. Ned felt guilty because he found it so much easier to spend time with Marina, after they reconnected, than with Tish. Though Tish had grown beautiful, he also, increasingly, found her a bit of a bore.

Marina brought Ned into her scene, taking him the weekend after their reunion, to Byzantium, a swanky cocktail bar recently opened up in the Village.

They got there a half-hour before their dinner reservation, and had dry gin martinis at the long thin bar that took up half the place. The décor ably mingled those ovals, the elongated forms, the mosaic and gold leaf that became so popular when the Roman Empire shifted Eastward, moving its capital to Byzantium. The cocktail menu had a quote attributed to Dorothy Parker: "I like to drink martinis. Two at the most. Three I'm under the table, four I'm under the host."

He was relieved that Marina, though already a little drunk, knew who the American writer was.

"Resumé," he said idly, wondering if she'd know what he meant. Not only did she, but she quoted bits of the poem. "Razors pain you, rivers are damp."

He wasn't sure why he told Marina, of all people, that he'd tried to take his own life, but he did. "I'm sorry," Ned said, blushing. "I didn't mean to lay something so heavy on you."

"No, I'm so sorry, Ned," she said. "How, how did you try?"

He showed her his wrist, and she ran her fingers, with their painted nails, along the ridge.

"I didn't really want to… go all the way," Ned said. "I read about the people who jump off Golden Gate Bridge. Most die, but some, through some miraculously good entry into the water, through some kind tides, find themselves washed up on a beach. Or a passing fishing boat scoops them out of the water. When they're interviewed, these jumpers say they realized on the way down, that they wanted more life. I'm a little like that, too. I had a lucky escape."

"It puts you in good company at least. Every half-decent gay guy, half my friends, they've thought of it at least. And so, for that matter, have I. I was pregnant. With my ex. I was so down. I had the abortion and felt better almost at once."

"I love," Ned said, "that you brought this back to you. So efficient, the way you moved on from my drama into yours!"

She batted her eyes at Ned. "It was impressive, right?"

A glamorous, short Latino drag queen in a leopard-skin-pattern dress sashayed over to give Marina wet smacks on her cheeks.

"Oh, girl, it's been too long."

"It's been like a week," Marina said. "Since Jonathan's."

"What a terrible party. No one was there. I mean except us." She extended a ring-covered hand to Ned, "Carmen." He was going to shake it, but then he realized what was asked of him. He bent down and kissed it. Luca had told him that your lips never touched the hand when you did this. "Now, Marina, where have you been hiding this one?" Carmen drew them into a group with some of her friends, Bitch Diva and Sofonda Cox among them. One of them had just MCed the Best Chest Contest down the street at the cheery bar Woody's, and went into raptures over the winning pecs. "Firm, with just a lovely bit of jiggle. And his ass, o, honey, you just wanted to crawl in there and live in it for a while."

Their table was ready, so Marina and Ned moved to the adjoining room.

"I know her from somewhere. Carmen," Ned said. "Is that possible?"

"From billboards, from the back cover of this month's *Vanity Fair.* She's in an ad for Bailey's Irish Cream. That one about 'true originals'. And she is one, that's for sure. Seriously, though, she's the heart of this scene. You get in with her, you're in. You piss her off, oh, you don't want to do that."

It was through Marina that Ned made his first gay friends. Though he'd sometimes take one of her circle home, it still never firmed up into anything more than a short-term thing. She didn't care what happened, or didn't. She was cool either way. Ned increasingly worried that he did not have what it took for a real relationship. But he was in good company, at least.

At one of the fly-by-night clubs they went to in some soon-to-be-condemned buildings on Yonge Street, Ned danced, with Marina, to a song by the aspiring pop star he'd met through Luca in London. Evidently, he'd since made his way.

So you want... to be free.
To live your life, the way you want to be...

They joined the throng on the floor, just as the chorus Ned loved came on:

Solitary brother, is there still a part of you wants to live?

They mainly wanted to live, but many of the boys on that dance-floor wouldn't see out the next five years.

His second winter back, Ned went with Marina and a few others to Miami. His eyes, after the grey and white palette of the Toronto winter, gloried in the lurid pastels of the Tropical Deco buildings, his ears made joyous by the squawks of the parrots from the palms above. He danced with her on a vast floor set up on South Beach with handsome, shirtless men all around them, as the sun came up over the Atlantic.

But, death was in attendance at all the parties. Even though the circuit of parties around the world for Ned and his kind were intended to spite death.

When he later looked at a photo of their Miami posse, he counted off those who hadn't made it through. Three of the six guys in the photo, poof. One of Ned's friends through Marina told him the news that he'd tested positive for AIDS, at a patisserie in midtown Toronto named Just Desserts. He would die, despite the best efforts of his doctors, of Ned, Marina and the rest of his care circle. It felt terrible but apt, when there was a shooting at the cake place a few years later, and a bystander was killed. Vivi Leimonis. Ned kept her name in him, a stand-in for all the names of the dead boys. Proud lives. It was her name on the file folder, in his mixed-up files, with all the obituaries of the boys he'd known in it.

At the law firm Tish eventually joined, a lawyer was showing off how strong the windows in the office were, bouncing against them, when one broke and he fell, just as the person from the party across the street had. It seemed to Ned that death was stalking his once peaceable city. Somebody call 911, my pussy's on fire.

Ned tried not to get it, AIDS. He practiced safer sex, he played the odds. But even so, there were evenings when he slipped up, and anyway, condoms could break, lovers could lie. But he would be one of the lucky ones. After each of his anonymous tests, the Hassle-Free Clinic had good news for him. It was the good news that sounded like bad news: he was negative. He would live, as his mother sometimes said at the end of an evening, to fight another day.

...

In the meantime, he slogged away at his studies. He got through his comprehensive exams, and moved into the thesis-writing phase of his doctorate, focusing on *Brideshead*'s author Evelyn Waugh. He was ABD: all but dissertation. Ned and his supervisor agreed to a list of books that he needed to read to help him to place Waugh in the context of all his contemporaries, in the stew of ideas then popular, to establish where he stood with respect to the controversies brimming in England and Europe before, during and after World War II. (His supervisor said *Helena* should not be a major focus, agreeing with Ned's mother's verdict that the book was far from Waugh's best.)

Ned worked his way through the research and then the writing, week-by-week, trudging along, submitting chapters as he went. At last, he completed it and submitted it. Then came the oral defense, which, especially since he still had stutter days, worried him. His fellow doctoral candidates shared stories of the examiners failing people for forgetting a character's name. Everyone advised him to maneuver around the egos of the professors involved, treating their pet authors as relevant, demonstrating some knowledge of, and interest in, their areas of expertise in the answers, reading all their most recent publications. The committee assembled in a bland conference room in the neo-Gothic University College, just across the street from Trinity. This was the college, Ned remembered as he walked towards it, without religious affiliation, the house built by Robert Baldwin, his ancestor who'd opposed one established faith. And yet they had gathered to discuss faith, in a way, or at least an author obsessed with it.

One of his examiners was a leading scholar in the burgeoning field of post-colonial literature and asked, by way of opening gambit, that Ned expand on a passage in his thesis comparing Joseph Conrad's *Heart of Darkness* to Waugh's *Handful of Dust.*

Ned stalled for time by framing his answer: both were books focused on the empire, written in different phases, one before WWI, at its seeming height, the other, later. He then brought Kipling into the equation and enumerated some of the common qualities of the literature written when the empire seemed likely to go on and on as opposed to those, like Waugh's books, written as it all fell apart.

Ned took care to emphasize how all these men were writing from positions of privilege, unlike the outsiders in which his questioner specialized. Even when these writers were critical of this man-built behemoth, they were inside it. He saw some looks of doubt, and he thought he knew what was worrying them, and said, "Conrad, a Pole by birth who wrote in a language not his own, he was a more complicated proposition." The furrows left the brows of his examiners.

He then laid out the ways in which these writers and others had spoken of this, the largest empire in the world's history, and the cracks they saw in. As he did so, Ned thought of his grandfather, of the muscular Christianity taught in England's schools, of the test he'd set his mother by spooking her horse. How important to the English it was not to be "wet". He spoke of the relevant adage, that the values on which the empire rested were supposedly taught on the playing fields at Eton.

What interested him, and what he explored in his answer, was how there was a contrapuntal theme to the pro-Empire jingoism, seeded in the literature. He spoke of this critique, and led the examiners back to specific instances in both the Conrad and Waugh books. How far did the critique go? Maybe not far enough.

He'd made a bit of a hash of his answer, but he got the two dueling principles, of celebration of all the pomp and circumstance and critique of same, out there. He'd set up the dialectic in the literature, and pointed to at least parts of the argument constructed in the books. But fiction wasn't argument, or not just argument, was it? It was about the people trapped within the arguments, the social structures of their times, and how they maneuvered with respect to it all.

Next, he was asked to place Waugh's trilogy of World War II novels, *The Sword of Honour,* in reference to other English literature about war. How were these three books in keeping with the tradition, how did they depart? A woolly question, one that had Ned thinking of his mother's reflexive pride in her country's martial history, after Luca quoted Napoleon's gibe about England being a nation of shopkeepers. In his answer, he made sure to pay particular attention to the World War I poets, since another of his examiners was an expert on Wilfred Owen. He traipsed over the speech in *Henry V*, touched on Robert Graves's trench memoir, *Goodbye to All That*, even managed to horn in a reference to Tolkien's fantastical war allegory, *The Lord of the Rings*.

It was too vast a question, but he did the best he could with it, in each instance, finding ways that the older literature made its way into Waugh's fiction, and then, what Waugh did with that, how he took a certain idea further, weaving something more into it, how he rejected another bit of older thinking. "He had, of course, a wholly different kind of war to write of, than the others did. One that ended with the dropping of not one, but two atomic bombs."

Then came a question that was more manageable. His supervisor put it to him: "According to the terms set out within *Brideshead Revisited*, who was lost and who was found?" Every oral examination has a money question, and this, he knew, was it. He would stand or fall on his answer.

He began by explaining the concept of sin as Waugh and his Anglo-Catholic contemporaries would have understood it. His supervisor was a convert to Catholicism himself, a fussy and pedantic man, so Ned took exquisite care in defining his terms, referencing some of the more eloquent of the Catholic essayists. He spoke of Waugh's own conversion and how the author had said, "The Church is the normal state of man from which men have disastrously exiled themselves." And so, he argued, the flamboyant Sebastian Flyte was lost in these terms because he separates himself from the church and its dictates. He thought of Henry and his decision not to attend church with his family.

He lost the thread of what he'd been readying himself to say and tried to find his way again. "Sebastian parts from the person who represents the Catholic principle in the book, his fierce, uncompromising mother. And yet, the life he leads in literal exile from his Anglo-Catholic family, in Morocco, in figurative exile from the church, is somehow noble. In Morocco, he takes care of a repulsive man, a German who shot off his toe to get out of the Foreign Legion. Sebastian's life becomes, in its minor way, a life of service. In modern terms, he's not sold out."

"And so he's lost but then found?" His supervisor sounded doubtful. "Is that by the terms within the book, or is that something you're superimposing on it?" Ned did want to find some redemption for Sebastian. Was he simply trying to append a nice moral, to reduce the complicated novel to a quaint fable?

"The book opens itself to the paradox, to the idea that one can be both lost and found." He quoted some lines to show that the novel itself allowed such a reading. That wasn't hard. He'd read the novel how many times? He put his hand on the copy of the book Daniel had given him, one he'd brought along to the exam for moral support.

"There's a paired story within the novel," he continued. "As you'll recall, the novel's narrator, Charles Ryder and Sebastian have a special relationship in their youth." Here he had to be careful. He knew his supervisor was touchy on this point, resisting any efforts to allow the novel to be co-opted by "gay liberationists", by "activist academics". But it *was* a gay novel.

"It was, there's no way around it, a homosexual friendship—perhaps consummated, perhaps not, it makes no odds. Whatever the, the m-m-mechanics between them, they fall in love with each other. Ryder's love for Sebastian is transmuted. He denies it, he puts it behind him. He puts away childish things, and marries Sebastian's sister, Julia, whose physical resemblance to her brother is made much of. He draws closer to Sebastian's mother, as per the Catholic principle. He succeeds in the eyes of the world. He appears to be saved, at least by the terms set out in the novel."

And yet, Ned went on to argue, Ryder ultimately loses his way, loses his wife and is also exiled from the family he's married into. "He fails to understand how important it is to his wife and her Catholic clan that her father die in the bosom of the One True Church. In the end, Ryder seems to have kept the faith with no one, neither with Sebastian, nor with Sebastian's family. There was one true thing in his life, his time with Sebastian in his youth. He has not stayed true to that, where Sebastian has."

He looked at the interviewing trio. Were they with him? Maybe he'd droned on too long on this point. Best to wrap it up. "Ryder, the man whom we took to be saved is lost. And Sebastian, whom we took for lost, perhaps he is saved? It's a profoundly Christian parable, about the lost and the saved. It's difficult to tell, until all is said and done, until we're at the very gates of Heaven, who is lost and who is, well, not." His supervisor hummed the snatch of "Amazing Grace" that went along with the lyric, "I once was lost, but now am found."

"Quite," Ned said. It was a book about integrity. There was a dignity in living according to your lights, even if you got lost doing so.

"I don't know," one of his examiners said. "Doesn't being saved involve some sacrifice, some submission to the church's authority?"

Ned remembered his mother once saying, "Submission never has come easily to me." And Luca, charming Luca: "Everyone dominates, everyone submits."

As he spoke to his examiners, unfolding his essentially simple take, then complicating it, then simplifying it again, he found himself strangely comfortable, stutter-free, fluent as he'd been as a child. He retained command of the books he'd been asked to read, and many others besides. He was sure he'd made errors in this examination, but he was too passionate about the material to be overly careful. He lacked a true scholar's detachment, but maybe, he hoped, that enthusiasm would ultimately help him to teach the book, and the other books he also loved. For that, he needed a degree, and to excel in this examination. As he breathed out after making his answer to the final question, he hoped his level of engagement with this material was evident, and sufficient.

He got up to head out. His supervisor cast an approving glance his way. Ned might just have pulled it off.

A letter awaited him at the Porter's Lodge, one from his cousin Sophie. It enclosed obituaries on Tim from *The Guardian* and *The Times.* Ned looked at the birth year, and did the math. Timothy had died at 37. He had been granted enough time to write only one novel, but that was better than none. Who could say if, in the end, he'd been lost or saved?

Ned visited the chapel, and prayed. "Why have you forsaken us, O Lord?" He heard nothing back. He expected nothing back. And yet, there was still something akin to faith in him. He did not know how or why, but it still pulsed in him. It was idiotic to believe still, but he did. It was his Reverend, the tall, wounded minister of St. Jude's, who had reached him, even as the choirboy Ned dreamed away. It was the priest who had underlined one of the things that Jesus reportedly said: "In my father's house, there are many mansions; I go to prepare a place for you." 'Mansions' was probably a mistranslation, but for Ned it gave a cosmic feel to it, a heaven of mansions within houses. Wouldn't that be nice, if it were true, if heaven were a bigger place than many here on earth think?

A quick question: If you were among those dying now, would you still believe? No, no, I don't think you would.

The Voice was probably right. Ned found himself irritated with his efforts to make sense of all this with only some child's idea of religion as a tool. He muddled this all out of his head. Anyway, he thought, I've already been to heaven. Heaven is a gay club under Charing Cross station, isn't it? No, a glib evasion was not what was called for.

He pushed himself deeper into prayer.

...

Helena came into the city to go to the opera, and invited Ned to come along. They were Fritzie's seats, so they were near the front, but not too near, and right smack in the middle of the barn-like theater. Few wore furs anymore, but there was plenty of finery on their neighbors. It was one of Luca's favorites, *Turandot*, and Ned remembered his lover's instruction that he was to pronounce the final 'T'. He was disappointed in the show. It felt a bit of a one-trick pony, Ned thought. Sure, "*Nessun dorma,*" let no one sleep, sure, but what of the rest? Afterwards, they went to an Austrian restaurant across the street from the brutalist building that then hosted the Canadian Opera Company's annual productions. The place was named Graf Bobby, and, as they scanned the menus, Ned tried to recall from another of Luca's lessons, where a Graf stood in the aristocratic pecking order. Higher or lower than a Baron, above or below a Palgrave? He found he couldn't remember.

After they ordered, his mother asked him for his thoughts, and he told her he'd been thinking of Luca's lessons, adding, "I liked how much he knew. About acoustics and the sex lives of chimpanzees. About why we find certain things beautiful. How he could talk, 'of shoes and ships, and sealing wax...'"

"'Of cabbages and kings.'" she said, completing. "I did like him, you know."

"Everyone did. I have this terrible feeling that he was it for me," Ned said. "The one, the only."

"Poppycock," she said. "You're so young yet."

"Dad said to us, to Henry and me, that our family, we only fall in love once. That awful story of our ancestor Robert Baldwin wanting to get a cut made in his body after he died."

"Don't," she said. "That story gives me the willies. And you know, falling in love just once, maybe on his side of things that's the case. But not mine. As you've seen with my father, remarrying Cora before my mother's corpse was even cold. And, you know, I don't want to belittle your connection with him, with Luca, but you reach a certain age, and like a fish rising to the surface, you are ready to bite. You only hope that the juicy bug bobbing along above you, that there's not a hook attached to it."

Was there a hook with Luca? Ned supposed there was. But he didn't like her metaphor much. "Was that case with you and your poet? Was he just a juicy bug who happened to bob along on the surface near you."

"Yes, you know, I think it was. As magical as he was. He was there. I was in need of comfort. I could have done worse. Far, far worse. He was funny and wise. Wiser than me anyway. But not wise enough to resist my advances!"

They spoke of the opera. She, too, had not been impressed. They discussed the food, and then, when they came to the coffees, Helena turned serious.

"I wasn't great," she said. "It's just you were trying to be someone for a while, and I wanted so much to believe in it."

Ned gulped at his coffee, worried about what she had left to say.

"I knew it was a lie," she said. "But I still invested so much in it. I'd ignored how you were with Cameron. How you hung on his every word. And then, of course, after you told us, with Luca, when I met him, you and him together, if I'd ever had any doubts, it was clear by then what was true."

It wasn't enough for Ned, this new attempt at what—an explanation, an apology? Even so, what his mother said was something.

"I'm glad you met him," Ned said. But then some anger flared up in him. "You know, you hurt me. I am not what I could have been." He wanted to forgive her, to have a clean slate between them, but he didn't know how to do that. Her God would have to do that for her.

She exhaled. "The world as constructed hurt you. It will go on hurting you. That is what it does. To all of us, but especially those… like you. And, yes, I hurt you, too. Certainly, I said some things. But then I waited a bit. Your father's good advice, that I let it be. I think so much of life is waiting things out," she said. "I've always liked this instruction in the cookbooks. I know, I know, I'm lousy at it, cookery, but I'm coming on, don't you think? There's this nice instruction in some of them. Some of the receipts, the recipes. You're to braise the meat, so you bung some oil in the pan, turn on the burner, and then you have to wait, wait, wait, until it shimmers. I feel it's sometimes that way in life. You wait, you despair sometimes in the waiting, but then, lo and behold, there it is, shimmering all around you."

And Ned thought of his friend, his Luca, biking by the Serpentine, his long scarf dancing in the wind, his hands gesticulating, one going down to the handlebars every so often to correct course. Yes, the long pond next to them had shimmered that day.

He would wait. There would again come a time for him, he hoped, a time when it all would make just a little more sense. He was someone, at least, who knew how to appreciate it, when it shimmered, when, for a little while, the light from on high illuminated everything around. In the books he'd studied, there weren't many good endings for characters like him. But things were changing. Maybe he could find his way.

...

Every so often, Ned returned to London. For Sophie's wedding. For academic conferences. To see some theatre. Just because. It was the best and the worst of places for him.

He once walked by Luca's flat and nodded hello to the hawkers in the vegetable market he remembered. But when he risked a glance upwards, at the building where Luca and Tim had lived, there were strangers in the window. Although it was wintertime, no amaryllis bloomed on the sill there.

As the turning of the Millennium neared, Ned's then boyfriend proposed that they ring it in in London. Ned agreed, though he wasn't sure it was wise to visit that city together. They took the massive Ferris wheel on the South Bank built for the occasion, the London Eye, up to survey the city where Ned's adult life began, where it almost ended. "To be tired of London is to be tired of life." There were new high-rises in the Docklands where that warehouse party had been. No longer was the skyscraper, the Centre Point, near his former publishing firm, one of the only exclamation points in sprawling paragraphs punctuated only by commas and periods.

He had a wooden box full of playbills and other souvenirs of his year in London to prove his presence, there. But the city had no memory of him. A faithless lover, it had changed, it had forgotten. "Do I know you?" Ned thought of the words that came to him when he finished Tim's book, and they were correct.

It was as if he never had been there.

ACKNOWLEDGEMENTS

Moving this book from start to finish has been, ahem, something of a long haul. These, in chronological order, are some of the people who helped most.

My heartfelt thanks to the leader of an early workshop at Stanford, Nancy Packer. Long before we met, she'd won just about every teaching award that school had to offer. She didn't have to spend her later years running workshops for the mixed bag of writers she did.

In her classes, I met some writers who have helped move me along, while becoming friends: Denise Chen, Andrea Donderi, and Ksenija Lakovic. In Tom Parker's workshop at Berkeley, I was wowed by Ebony Haight's work, happy to get to go back and forth with her after the workshop ended – in a small group with another strong writer, reader and friend, Lisa Hills. A college pal and writer Karen Goettsche Lubell was a great, sensitive ally of the book's early on – as was another Dartmouth pal, the late, much lamented Jamie Kershaw.

One of the many great gifts that my time at *Toronto Life* gave me, Olivia Stren supplied intelligent cheerleading throughout ("keep going, dog"), as did my roommate Brydie Bethell, who, when we lived together, somehow tolerated my chaos, befriending this mess machine. Two other former *Toronto Life* colleagues, Mark Pupo and Sasha Chapman, gave early versions a good read – and solid, clear counsel.

I am grateful for the time at Bread Loaf – and the advice I got there from Chang-Rae Lee and, especially, Patricia Engel. There I was lucky enough to find more of my people – it was a welcome respite from the isolation. At Banff, I was particularly happy to fall in with Larissa Douglass, who laughed loudly, at the right moments, during my reading.

And Allison Moir-Smith and Gordy Slack helped me bring this draft home – thank you so much.

I also want to nod at these people for helping, in various ways over the course of this long haul:

Tim Cahill, Dawn Calleja, Novella Carpenter, Irene Edwards, Martin Friedland, Sarah Fulford, Angie Gardos, David Gluck, Twilight Greenaway, Susan Harris, Joan Hilborn, Lauren Ladoceour, Michael Lowenthal, John Macfarlane, Stephen Marche, Marie-Hélène Mayer, Janet Miller, Lisa Morehouse, Ted Mumford, Samin Nosrat, Katie O'Reilly, Kelly Pullen, Judith Pereira, Mary Roach, Larkin Tom and Deb Wandell.

My thanks to my editor Michael Occhionero for his stewardship of this work, and to Ace of Swords.

With gratitude for my remarkable, sympathetic siblings, Tom (Alix), Will (Stephan) and Kate (Malcolm).

And above all, to my husband David Bruckmann, dear to many and especially to me.

AUTHOR BIO

Alec Scott is a Canadian writer living in Oakland, California. A former barrister, he has worked as an editor and columnist at *Toronto Life* magazine and a producer at the Canadian Broadcasting Corporation. Since moving to the Bay Area, his work has featured in the *Guardian, Los Angeles Times, San Francisco Chronicle* and magazines including *Sunset, Sierra, Report on Business* and *The Smithsonian.* His pieces have been nominated for 13 Canadian National Magazine Awards, winning three. An avid traveler, he has gone all over on assignment, and some of these resulting stories have won awards – a Lowell Thomas gold, a North American Travel Journalists' Association gold and an Eureka.

He has studied literature at Dartmouth College (A.B.) and Trinity College, Dublin (M.Phil.) and law at the University of Toronto (J.D.). This is his first novel. He has a history book coming out in 2023, *Oldest San Francisco,* from Reedy Press. *www.alecscott.com*